Dancing
the
Labyrinth

Dancing *the* Labyrinth

KAREN MARTIN

DANCING THE LABYRINTH

First published in Australia in 2021 by
KazJoyPress (Australia)
www.kazjoypress.com

Cover and page design by WorkingType Studio

ISBN: 978-0-6451922-0-9 (paperback)
ISBN: 978-0-6451922-1-6 (ebook)
BISAC: Fiction/Historical/Ancient
FIC01410

National Library of Australia

 A catalogue record for this
work is available from the
National Library of Australia

Essential to the task of finding out for oneself is the willingness to engage or be engaged by a process of reflection and fabrication — of seeing and making ...The woman who can bend enough to go from reflecting to fabricating will be the one who can make up for something that is missing in the world. She is the one who can give shape to things lying beneath the surface.

Nor Hall
The Moon and the Virgin

CHAPTER ONE

C ressida hugged her book. She had studied the Australian
classic *My Brother Jack* by George Johnston last year in
her literature class at college. It had been transformational
— nothing less than her passport to a new life — for it had
revealed a precious secret: you could choose to go and live
on a Greek island. It was an epiphany, she decided. She sat
smug with the knowledge that she was escaping her drab
neighbourhood of monotone houses with rigid doors that
remained closed against the sunshine. The grid of confor-
mity had finally lost its hold.

She re-checked her safety belt. The reassuring band
held her tight against her window seat. She replaced her
book with an in-flight magazine. Idyllic beach scenes lazed
across the page. Crete was renowned for its turquoise seas
and white sands. *And pink,* she grinned, the thought offering a maverick sense of joy. She fumbled in her pocket and
retrieved a small container. She slipped a pill into her mouth
and swallowed. One could never be too sure.

Crete had been an easy choice. Get away, the sirens had
sung, and lured by an array of aiding and abetting cheap
flights, her usual struggle in making decisions went on
hiatus. It made sense to run away to the birthplace of the

1

Gods; as a child, she devoured Greek mythology, never fairy tales. She had read everything about the goddesses of old: Artemis, Athena, Hera, Demeter and Persephone. Time had been her co-conspirator as she immersed in their fantastical tales — eons away from her desolate reality.

Sitting compliant in her seat, she counted the minutes to take-off. Countdown to forever. Forever would take a bit over four hours to reach from England, and as she gazed up, distracted by its possibilities, a crack opened just wide enough to let an image of her mother slip in.

What the fuck?

Mother had no forever, not now. Cressida shifted in her seat. The man next to her had taken up all the armrest. She examined her mother's image cautiously. Mother who, despite years of physical beat ups and emotional teardowns, never left the man she loved. Cressida turned the page of the magazine. She coughed and rubbed her nose.

As the plane began to taxi, she pushed her head firmly against the headrest. It wouldn't be long now. Her hands lay clasped in her lap, her elbows in tight — a lifelong lesson of constraint. Body memory shuddered as he swaggered in, uninvited, trespassing her mind. She tried to block him but it was too late. She could at least avoid his face by focusing on the damage to his car. Side-swiped by a young learner driver. The car was a write off. Both cars were. The young driver had survived. Cressida felt glad about that. One less victim.

Her mother had stayed with her father in the hospital, sitting bedside for the two days of his coma and then mourned at his graveside, before succumbing to the eternal embrace of grief. Cressida had thought, had hoped, she was free of them.

The island airport greeted her with nonchalant hospitality and casual security checks. The bus into town maintained an aura of effortless welcome. Sipping her coffee, Cressida marvelled at the Venetian port. She never knew such beauty existed. She bought an English-Greek language book and set about organising a few day trips to learn more about the paradise she had inadvertently chosen. It seemed impossible that she was breathing in mythological air and walking down ancient paths.

Delight coloured her discovery of an older civilisation than the familiar pantheon of Greek gods. These Minoans worshipped a Snake Goddess. This Goddess was not any Adam and Eve fly-by-night snake, but a full-on Earth Mother, Divinity Goddess of Everything. The Minoans had been the most advanced European civilisation in the Bronze Age around 2000 BCE, and the island bore testament to many ruins of their cities, temples, and palaces. It was unbelievable to think this history had not been in the curriculum.

'Perhaps it was taught on a day I wasn't at school,' Cressida thought, instinctively touching the slither of a barely visible scar on her forehead.

Brilliant sunlight streaming through the open window of her small flat in the picturesque village on the south coast woke her. Waking was never easy. Had she slept, or been hit? Possibly worse, was she waking from a panic attack? Immediate signs were noted: her pants were dry, there was no blood in her mouth or taste of vomit. She blinked rapidly to help recover memory and take in her surroundings. It took a moment to register where she was, and then her smile matched the sun's. She had done it. She had a new home, a new job, a new life. She still couldn't believe that she had been living here for several weeks. She had found the perfect village, where you could either walk in on trails or take the ferry. There were no cars, only pedestrian traffic. It was a destination, not a thoroughfare.

She had not dared to hope. She had learnt that for such a small word, it weighed heavy with expectations. Hope came with no instructions, only tears. She had come to Crete looking for escape; hope held no place in her dreams. Escape had been achieved.

Opening the door, Cressida welcomed the day. The crisp morning air kissed her skin. She struggled down the sand-bank, her pink feet still tender against the particles of rock and stone, and was rewarded with a quick swim to the buoy and back, in pristine water.

It was a short stroll to the taverna where she worked; one of many, lining the shoreline with umbrellas and beach beds. The steady pace of service and laid-back attitude of her island's hosts made work a pleasure. By late afternoon, the horn from the departing ferry was her prompt to collect the empty glasses, plastic frappe cups and overspilling ashtrays.

Cleaning up was already agreeably routine, and her thoughts wandered freely into stories, myths, or songs. She was accountable to no one, mindless work allowing for traversing trails of daydreams. Such was the power of the island that she could not help but be inspired. Tables cleared; she retrieved the mop from the back cupboard behind the bar.

"Where is my Greek broom?" she joked with the manager, searching out the hose. What he called the 'elastic' did a fine job, and she took pride in the glistening marble floor. Once done, all was ready for the next shift of patrons who would arrive any time after 10 pm for dinner and drinking.

It was when the day's work was done, the current book read, and time was her own that Cressida struggled. Settling in was more difficult than she anticipated. She was not hungry, but her stomach complained. It felt empty, like something was gnawing away, creating a hole, a gap — some sort of nothingness. Keeping busy meant walking, swimming, drinking. And drinking. And drinking. She revelled late into the midnight hours with her new friends, Tequila and Margarita, and danced with Dionysus in uninhibited glory.

Waking up became more difficult for different reasons. Her head hurt. Over the weeks, strong Greek coffee became a morning ritual. It was a relief when the nothingness in her stomach began to feel full. She blamed the fluttering on the copious amounts of raki shots and beer she consumed. It was, however, persistent.

Unbelievable. You idiot.

She lifted her head from the toilet bowl, before having even peed on the stick. Her self-criticism was familiar.

Bet it will be blue — just my luck — blue for positive, blue for a boy. Fuck.

Mother would have called her tardy.

More 'negligent', I reckon.

"*Kalimera*. Umm..."

Her Greek had not progressed very far.

"Umm, I want *ah, na thelo* oh, you speak English? Great."

She booked into the city hospital for a thorough check up, slightly more invasive than the urine strip.

Anxiety hitched a ride to the hospital. Her clammy palms reminded her to take deep breaths. The ferry was on time, gliding effortlessly into port over an oil-slick sea. Choosing a seat upstairs in the morning sun, Cressida adjusted her sunglasses before turning the page of her book. There was irony in considering terminating the residue of a random night of passion while immersed in a paperback romance. The ferry snaked its way past sheer rock cliffs standing sentry.

With the cold jellied tip of the ultrasound pressed to her

tanned belly, she stared at a blob outlined on the screen. In the background, she heard the nurse proudly exclaim that she may be right, perhaps it was a boy, although admittedly it was too early to tell. Contempt seethed. A boy — not bad enough she was pregnant — but a boy?

"I don't want a boy. Actually, I don't want a baby, but especially not a boy."

The nurse discretely left the room, avoiding the dark tone of Cressida's outburst. Cressida poked her belly.

'Whoa, now what would he say about this?' she asked. She had not thought about her father for such a long time. She swallowed and tried to laugh it off. It sounded hollow and empty.

"Hey, you there, do you think..."

Tears started to fall. She ignored them.

"Do you think..." sniff, "you can come..." another sniff, "... come into my world." She swallowed. "And... and... just change everything? Demand everything... just cos, just cos you're a boy. Like your dick makes a difference? Do you?"

Memories as a daughter contaminated any possible maternal instinct. Accusations scratched at her throat.

"Are you gonna be a...?" she whispered hoarsely. "A fucker like him? Are you? Comes with the territory, you know. It's in your DNA. Oh, he would like that."

Tears prickled their downward path. The thin thread of emotion binding her to her father was a baited hook and leaked pain. Jagged breath splintered her lungs. Faded bruises and unseen scars rose to the surface of her skin. She sweated loathing.

What would he have said about this? The ache in her heart diluted her wrath. Incessant thoughts and questions started to crowd out her thinking and she could not find any clear space to sort it out. She bundled up her belongings and fled the women's clinic with its scent of responsibility.

Outside, a glint of light flickered, catching her attention. "What the...?"

She looked up. The sky was blue. It was an enormous wide blue sky. The brilliance of light shone through its blueness. It was so absolute and certain. She had never noticed before. The blueness of the sky held everything, and yet nothing, in all its vastness. It stretched into infinity. She breathed in the pause. Breathe out, breathe in. Relax.

OK.

The lapse was short-lived. An incoming tidal wave of released emotion crashed through her mind, tumbling thoughts in its wake: *Fuckfuckfuck. What have I done, what should I do, how could this happen, why, what should I do, what can I do, it's not fair.*

His words rode her tears as she dribbled angst into the world.

"You were right Daddy, I am dirty, I'm nothing, I deserve this. It's my fault, it's all my fault. I'm a dirty, dirty slut. You said so. You were right. I am so sorry, so sorry. Daddy?"

Disgust reached down into all her dark hidden places. She cramped in response and moaned. It ripped through her gut as disdain flexed its muscle. Wiping her streaked face, Cressida sneered at her pitiful state; no backbone, no grace. Woeful.

Numbness crept up, offering respite, but Cressida shook it

away. She deserved to feel this bad, to be punished. It felt like home. Her thoughts scrambled through a maze of dead ends. She could not find any answers, consolation, or resolution. Her head spun. She stood up.

"Get out!" she pleaded aloud. "Enough. Enough now."

Determination entered her game plan and speaking into the world outside her mind helped regain some control. Revulsion retreated and her thoughts receded to background clamour. This, Cressida could work with. She resigned to being pregnant for a few days longer, until she could clear her head of the white noise that had turned red.

Feeling like she had somewhat corralled the unrelenting chaos, Cressida boarded a bus to return to the port. She sat down the back where it was empty of passengers. When the bus stopped again, at some indistinct part of the main road, a large woman in a colourful scarf climbed aboard with her equally large and colourful bags and packages and array of children of varying sizes. She carried a baby strapped across her very ample bosom and a small, skinny child clung tightly to her one free hand. The woman was followed by a young boy holding the hand of a smaller version of himself. They trudged down to the back of the bus and sat opposite and next to Cressida, filling all the spaces and places of her desired solitude.

The woman heaved her large form onto the seat with a grateful sigh and the assorted children appropriated the remaining space around her as if neatly arranging a life-sized jigsaw puzzle. Well, not quite neatly. There were overflowing bags, bra straps flopping down dimpled arms, shoelaces flapping and was that, oh yes, thick yellow snot riding the inhale and exhale of the toddler's breath through one nostril. Cressida shifted in her seat to minimise any hint of body language that might be confused as an invitation for interaction. Her attempt to blend into her seat failed dismally. Her blond cropped hair did nothing to help.

"Hello dear, *yassas*." The woman addressed her in accented English. Cressida smiled weakly; there was no escape except point-blank rudeness. Before she could answer, her attention diverted to the young boy. She watched as he pulled a tissue from his pocket and wiped the toddler's nose. Just like that. Everything in that moment seemed to change. Cressida felt a wave of gratitude. Nope, that was nausea. The woman turned and thanked the boy, "*Efharisto, kalo agóri mou.*"

She returned her gaze to Cressida. "This one is like his father, sees the smallest things and makes good," she explained, and ruffled his hair with a hand that miraculously seemed to be free of child, bags strap and burdens of retail. She laughed easily. "We raise our sons to be good people, yes? That is our job. Well, at least we try."

The bus lurched and the family scene shifted abruptly with the jolt. Cressida now saw a fat perspiring woman burdened with a sleeping baby at her breast, with a hardening trail of vomit and milk dribbled on to her dress. A child clung to her hand with a plastic nappy smelling oh so unpleasant in the afternoon heat. The two boys were squabbling over some minute plastic gadget banned in any self-respecting first-world country, which, having dropped onto the floor, was rolling down to the front of the bus, sending both these brats chasing forward in howls of protest. It was a sweaty, smelly, loud, dirty example of domesticity, and, overcome with this stench of humanity, Cressida gagged.

"Stop the bus!" she blurted, "err … *stasi, na stamatisei*"

Standing on shaky legs, she pulled the cord to make good her escape. Fortunately, it was a short walk to the port and relief rode on a fresh afternoon sea breeze. The ferry waited patiently at the dock for her to board. It was thankfully an uneventful return trip, save for a buffeting wind and a bigger swell than usual. After disembarking, Cressida walked along the shoreline of black sand. Waves tumbled awry, splashing her calves, then sucked at her ankles as they returned to the depths.

She sat on the warm sand and watched as the waves took it in turn to crash onto the shore. She wished the day would sort itself out.

Cressida woke disorientated, suspended in the faint smudge of a dream. She wriggled her fingers; pins and needles prickling her hands. Had she screamed? She looked around. The beach was strangely deserted. Stiffly she rolled over and sat up. She looked out to the ocean. The waves seemed bigger than usual.

She could not remember falling asleep, but she could remember the dream. The sole gift of a recurring dream is in knowing the outcome. She shook her head hoping to shake out the dregs, but the images remained. Caught between wakefulness and sleep, she could still see a younger black-haired version of herself rowing a small boat. The craft was laden with woven baskets filled with animals. A previous dream stocktake had revealed a rooster, several hens, a urine-soaked billy goat, two does accompanied by knowledge one was pregnant, two sheep and a ram. They weighed the boat down. Although the ocean was calm, Cressida knew a storm would come.

She also knew that the boat would land safely in a small harbour. Yet her fear remained in the creases of time, for when the storm broke, with the rising crescendo of waves and rain lashing her face, it was impossible to see the cove from the water. Moreover, the young dark-haired Cressida was only a child and she had to carry the heavy responsibility of keeping the entire livestock safe, a weight just as solid as the massive oars held in her weakened arms. Cressida would wake screaming and drenched, soaked from either the waves of her dream or the sweat of her fear.

The mayhem in her mind realised she was awake and raised its volume. Her thoughts lobbed back into overdrive. Dozing off had only provided a temporary reprieve. Swallow, focus, deep breaths, plan of action — her doctor's instructions echoed. Meditation might help, medication definitely would.

She looked for her pills — were they in her bag? She had not needed them since arriving in Crete. Was that four, maybe five weeks ago? Time here seemed to move at a different pace. Time was different; everything was different. If only she had not ruined it.

CHAPTER TWO

C ressida stood up and shook the loose sand from her legs. She lost interest in her half-hearted effort to assess the swell of the sea. Her thoughts splattered; an internal Jackson Pollock painting redefining the pictorial spaces of her mind; her visit to the hospital, choices she had made and choices yet to make — all colluded to create an abstract dog's breakfast. It was a far cry from what she had hoped for in starting a new life.

The wind blew off the water. She squinted. Her fingers were now relaxed with blood flow. She shaded her eyes. Her busy mind took in the hugeness of the sea but failed to advise of the changing weather conditions. She did not see how heavy the clouds were becoming. Clouds, which had started out as mere wisps, gathered together sulking behind the cliffs. Lightning struck further inland, behind her and hidden from view.

Maybe I should go for a walk?

A flippant thought had somehow manoeuvred through the overbearing chatter in her mind. Cressida nodded, vaguely agreeing.

A walk to clear my head. Yes. That might help.

The conditions suggested otherwise. Had she been aware,

she would have, should have, returned to her flat. She wore her ignorance like a red bandana as she entered the arena of a bullish storm.

Habit navigated Cressida towards the gorge, the routine providing comfort. The gorge was a huge crack in the island spanning heart to coast. Following the river's pebbled path, the track bore traces of myriad journeys over centuries of villagers, tourists, goats and sheep. The cool air at the entrance of the gorge tingled. It would get warmer further in towards the old village, which was an entanglement of stone buildings, animal pens and ruins of indiscriminate age. On this route, she sometimes passed an older Greek woman who was very beautiful in that classic long dark hair, high cheekbones, big nose and lush lips way. She wore a whisper of sadness that, despite their age difference, Cressida felt was somewhat familiar. They would nod and acknowledge each other; *Yas sas*, hello, or *Kalispera sas*, good afternoon — always grammatically formal.

It didn't take long to reach the mouth of the gorge. She looked up the dry riverbed into its shadows, taking in where the river had patiently weaved through rock — splitting and opening the earth to return to the sea. It was magnificent and easily seduced her into its fold. The clunk of goat bells announced her arrival and she looked up to see several goats clamber over scree. *Ugh.* She shuddered. Scree pretended to look like a beautiful cascade of pebbles, rocks and stone, but she knew better. Two years ago, on a holiday weekend, in what Cressida now classified as a fit of mountaineering madness, she had followed her then boyfriend on a guided hike. Hah, more like some special forces training program for stupid, stupid people, and while crossing the tumbled pathway of the rockslide, on what appeared to be no more than some dumb goat path, she had rolled her ankle. Over time, the persistent ache became a nagging reminder of what physical activity could do. It hurt now just thinking about it.

The goats however were nimble, agile with abandon. They scoured the rockslide for some fresh young bud of edible herb or shrub, ignoring the oleander and wild thyme. The overbearing smell of urine-soaked buck filled her senses. She grimaced and this time, for the first time, she gagged at the stench. Her hand rose to her belly. She stopped mid-movement before picking up her stride, as if to run away from the implication.

The goat-bells tracked their movement. It never occurred to Cressida that this was the only sound she heard; that the soundscape around her was mute. There were no cooing doves. There were no singing cicadas. She had learned that cicadas, protected by the Muses to attain knowledge, shed their skin and lived underground to be reborn as souls — or so the myth went. Usually, they burst through the afternoon's heat in chorused symphony.

Cressida walked deeper into the gorge along the packed gravel path oblivious to the unnatural hush, mocking her ignorance. She negotiated places where rutting goats on overhead ledges had sent large rocks to the gorge floor and where, in the past, large tremors and quakes had dislodged massive boulders to create amazing aesthetic installations. She focused on the task of picking her way carefully over rocks strategically placed to enable crossing the stream at various intersections of path and water.

She walked past the old village, following the riverbed further and further into the narrowing chasm. The deepening shade of the gorge camouflaged the congregation above her. No longer content with passive amassing, clouds now jousted for position. An enormous clap of thunder augured the beginning onslaught. Cressida jumped, startled. *Rain?*

Another distant growl rolled through the sky, closer and closer, until exploding above her. *Dynata* — loud, yes like dynamite. She covered her ears, cowering. A few drops fell. Large, forceful, smacking drops.

It took another loud rumble for Cressida to realise her peril. Having strayed far from the confines of home, she was alone, in a gorge, with a storm approaching. Her eyes widened. It was not approaching but had in fact arrived. With force.

She looked around. Oh God, she had made it so far into the gorge. Really, this far? On the one hand, she was impressed. She had walked oblivious to the invasion of competing thoughts. She had achieved mindfulness, finally. A short-lived glimmer of smugness celebrated her meditative capabilities before she realised she may be facing imminent danger. Who knew how long the storm had been releasing its anger upstream? Cressida had heard the story of a group of hikers in this very gorge caught by surprise from the deluge of an up-river storm and swept to their deaths.

Another raindrop smacked her face. It felt like a tennis ball flung from the sky. *Ouch!* She stood rooted to the spot. Flight or fight? She could not decide. The menace of the storm struck again. Then again. It was not going to stop.

Owww! OK. Higher ground. Away from the river.

Survival screamed, took control, and spurred her into action. To her right was sheer rock face, gorgeously etched with ripples of earth's experience throughout the ages, bearing testament to shifts, shudders, fires, quakes, volcanoes, and ice. But not a rescue option to scale without the means of rope, picks and all those fiddly bits and pieces and things rock climbers have in their bag of accessories. Nope.

The rain now succumbed to full-on bastard downpour.

Well at least there is no wind.

Her moment of thought was cut short as a screaming, howling banshee twisted around the contours of the cliff and slammed into her, bowling her over.

"Owww. Fuck you!" she screamed back.

OK, this had now become serious. Granted it was serious before, but now Cressida was short of options. The cliff was out, and the scree was definitely out.

Wherewherewhere? Up a tree? Oh, for God's sake. There must be something.

Spurred on, Cressida ran head down into the horizontal rain. Well okay, not quite running, given she was on a path of slippery, uneven rocks but her mind said she was running; every cell screamed she was running. As she rounded the bend and crossed the stream that was now swelling into a near-raging torrent, a shadow high to the left caught her eye.

Yes, perhaps.

She willed it to be a ledge and, stumbling across rocks, she leapt up the crumbling slope. Again, there was disparity between reality and her mind's eye. For Cressida, it was a mighty leap, but to anyone watching, she barely managed to haul herself up and over a huge rock. She grabbed at a plant to pull herself up further, only to have it come loose in her hand. She threw the dangling, useless plant and roots aside and lunged at another jutting rock.

She could hardly see. Mascara stung her eyes. Thunder continued to bellow through the unrelenting, pounding rain. Even the river's exhilaration at its new-found strength added to the cacophony. The whole world seemed to have raised its volume.

Barrage, a fricken barrage.

She clung tightly to the rock and earth and kept scrambling, not quite knowing where or how, driven on by her loudest thought.

Up. Gotta get up. Get high. Higher.

Her recently French polished manicured hands, now with broken nails and full of dirt and possibly even goat shit, gripped onto a horizontal section of the cliff. It was a ledge. She had seen truly. *Yes!* Adrenaline shot straight as a yellow arrow through her dreary, grey veins, bringing a burst of energy disguised as optimism and fuelled her attempt to drag her sodden, aching mass onto the ledge. Celebration remained subdued as she lay, exhausted, on the ledge. Erratic gasps to fill her lungs punctuated her panting. Tears of relief mingled with the water streaming down her face, washing out the remaining bits of mascara from her eyes.

It was a narrow ledge, but it had a sort of rock overhang. Perhaps she could even get some shelter out of the rain. She wriggled closer to the cliff face. Ouch, knee on sharp rock. Or leg. Down there, somewhere below her face. She had lost sense of her body, existing in the present moment as a spongy, water-sodden blob without form or definition. She had soaked up too much storm to know where she stopped and where the world began. It hurt, regardless.

Pain gave way to elation. *Yes, yes, yes!* Not only was there a rock overhang that offered some shelter but the ledge sort of dipped at a slight angle which meant she could edge her body closer alongside the cliff, under the overhang and out of the direct slap of rain. Once there, she managed to shuffle herself into what seemed to be a small cavern-like mouth opening. She could not roll her body, not that she wanted to, but she could worm-like wiggle deeper into this space. Once wriggled into the safety of the crevice, shock tenderly held her, and Cressida surrendered a trembling sob. Its release invited another and another.

CHAPTER THREE

C ressida opened her eyes. She blinked rapidly as was her custom upon waking. Grit stuck to her lips. She sniffed at an unfamiliar smell. A cave, she was in a cave. It smelt somewhat musty, but there was nothing suggesting death or decay. Or goat. Lucky — grit, she could handle, now remembering to spit it out — but not goat shit. Don't disturb goat shit in a cave, she was told. As if she ever would. *Yiati?* Why? There might be scorpions.

She wriggled her toes and slowly, ever so slowly brought her knees up to her chest, then rolled over to sit. She moved cautiously just in case there was any pain. Managing this she assessed there was nothing broken, although her bleeding knees complained of being scraped.

Taking in a deep lungful of air, she relaxed on exhalation. It was okay. Hey, she was grateful. There was air, which was a good thing. Her heart drummed loudly. She willed her eyes to become accustomed to the darkness. There was no rain coming in from the angled gap that she remembered wriggling through. It was higher up from where she now sat — higher than she expected. Not that she had expected anything, but she could not remember falling. Perhaps she had rolled to where she was. She tried to organise her thoughts. She remembered pulling herself up onto a ledge and then wriggling her way to this ... hole? Who was she, Alice?

And the difference between a cave, cavern or chamber, is?

Her question remained unanswered. A slither of outside brightness penetrated the dark space from the mouth of the cave. It was about a body length up with a gentle slope, which presumably, she must have rolled down to her present location on the floor of this — cave, she confirmed.

Despite becoming accustomed to its shade of dark, the gradual deepening of darkness further away from the crack, made it difficult for Cressida to ascertain the actual size of the cave. She was able, however, to check out her immediate surroundings. It was big — in fact, it was a massivly high cave. She squinted at the blackened roof, dappled in shadows. The rock walls were tinged slightly greenish. Moving her head quickly side to side, she caught bits of glitter reflecting the light. Pebbles and stones lay strewn on the ground, and there were larger boulders also embedded with the dancing glitter. The earth was damp and firm. Coolness drenched the space. She shivered. She was not cold, but wet, soaking wet.

There was no sound of the outside storm, but Cressida guessed it was still raging. She figured to stay put and wait it out. While outside was manic, inside offered a deeply ingrained stillness.

"Cooee, cooee." There was no answer, no echo. Stillness was quiet.

Wishing she were better prepared; like having torch, towel and dry clothes, or not being in the cave at all, she cursed her situation.

If I had some rope, I could take a bit of a look.

She snorted at this idea. She had never ticked 'adventure seeker' on any magazine quiz listing personality traits. For some reason now, it seemed perfectly reasonable. She did not want to get lost in a possible maze of tunnels. Even if it were a labyrinth, with one way in and out, she wanted reassurance.

And no Minotaur. This thought made her laugh. Was she really going to look around the cave? When had she decided this? This island was definitely changing her. In less than a month, she had been in two caves — albeit in different circumstances, but two more than she had ever been in her whole life.

She had visited the other cave a few days after arriving in Crete. Informed by a Travel App of a cave sacred to Artemis, Cressida had trekked down a hill following the footsteps of pilgrims. In a state of mid-morning sleepiness, she wavered, fearful of what she might encounter but encouraged by curiosity. Inside the cave she found the Virgin Huntress in the form of a she-bear stalagmite, worshipped thousands of years ago. Cressida had tried to feel what sacredness might feel like. She had also tried to ignore the screaming children of French tourists, running around shrilling with delight at the shadows thrown by their torches. Both her attempts failed. The solitude she sought eluded her and any wish for some sort of mystical connection waned. Defeat crowned victory. Perhaps the pagan power had died, its flame snuffed out and supplanted by a newer legend: one of those 'once upon a time' stories.

For once upon a time, a bear lived in the cave and drank the water that dripped into a hollow in the rock. The monks, who had recently moved into the neighbourhood, were thirsty and wanted the water. So, they prayed to Virgin Mary to help them. The Virgin heard their prayers and turned the bear into stone.

Surely, the Virgin could have produced water from another rock where the monks could have sated their thirst.

Cressida scowled, this version of the story finding no favour. Why wasn't Artemis still patron of the cave? The Virgin Mary, in all due respect, had not lived there. Cressida did not think so, anyway.

'If this cave has a patron,' she thought looking around, 'it must be Gaea. It befits the great mother of all creation.'

Cressida contemplated her next move. Unlike Theseus, she had no golden thread spun by Ariadne to help her. She turned to the next best thing. Her mobile phone had a torch. Emboldened, Cressida turned away from the entrance of the cave and opened her tiny beam of light to illuminate the darkness in front of her.

She made careful progress, discovering as she went, that parts of the ground comprised slippery rock of a black, streaky marble variety. Large boulders winked at her. The sound of water tinkling somewhere beyond the light beckoned and the normally scaredy-cat Cressida started to probe further. The generosity of the cave provided some comfort, for she could stand and walk freely, and when she spied a passage — or was it a tunnel — leading off to the right, intrigue fed her courage. Peering into its deeper darkness, she could see the passage was large enough to walk through. This was important; there was no way she would crawl or squeeze through any small spaces. After all, this was merely a distraction from her situation, not an exploration. She looked around and bent to collect and stack some small rocks. Her cairn was more symbolic than functional. She doubted it would indicate the way to any future cavers, and the bright crack shining from the outside world would guide her back to the entrance.

She paused to rest her hands on the cool, smooth rock wall. Crete was an island carved from rock. It was solid and ancient, instilling in her a sense of acceptance. She was yet to fully explore its landscape etched with memory; from Minoan ruins to the more recent headstones honouring the fight against invasion, occupation and oppression. Contemporary stone cairns chorused silent tributes as well as way-marking its many trails. It was a strong, vibrant and passionate land demanding honour, courage and love to unravel its mysteries held sacred within its stone.

The deep solidness of the rock was calming. She lingered over its comforting stability, an anchor to the mess of her situation. Nothing had gone to plan, and now, here she was, pregnant and stuck in a cave. Could things get any worse?

She entered the passage. As it curved gently to the right, she was ensconced in semi-darkness. Her torch light ushered her onward. The passage was not long, or at least did not seem so in her cautious journey. There were several small chambers to her left. Yes, chambers, she decided, for they were smaller, and, if her torch shone truly, were self-contained without further passages concealed in shadowed corners. Here and there, bits of outside light penetrated from the rocks above her and further beyond, assuring her that the outside world was not too far away.

Maybe the passage will lead out through another entrance?

She stopped at a large boulder blocking her path and tried to see what was beyond it. She could make out shapes around the walls of the cavern. They looked somewhat different from the black and greenish boulders she had become accustomed to. A choice confronted her: squeeze through the gap, which she reckoned was possible, or turn back. Why did everything require a decision?

Cressida squeezed in her tummy, lifted her arms up over her head and, breathing in, manoeuvred her body though the space between boulder and rock wall. It was not that hard; the thought had been far more difficult to navigate than the actual deed. Cressida felt elated by her conquest. She rested on the silky-smooth boulder in triumph, her light illuminating the roof of the cavern. She gasped into the space.

She closed her mouth. What she had assumed to be smoke patterns of bygone fires, lit by the hippies who frequented caves, were paintings of some sort. She shone her torch into the cavity and froze from the enormity of what she saw. In front of her was an exquisite display of rich, colourful drawings against a deep red ochre background. She stepped into the space and slowly turning full circle, pointed her torch above and around her on the walls and ceiling. Animals, bulls and what looked to be goats, birds, fish, swirls, and an array of weird patterns decorated the whole cavern. There were figures of women everywhere. She felt small, overwhelmed by its immensity.

Cressida walked toward a section to her left. On close inspection, it seemed different to most of the drawings. Shapes were similar but it was as if this section detailed every minute line, outlined every shape. Parts of it seemed almost carved, like a wall relief — a story created for perpetuity. It was beautiful.

In comparison, the rest of the paintings covering the larger area seemed less crafted, perhaps rushed, or done by an artist with less skill than the first.

"Yeah," scoffed Cressida out aloud, "cos I am an expert on this."

She turned on her phone video and panned slowly to capture every detail. Not confident about the lighting, she started taking photographs, sending out a brilliant flash with each press of the button. Flash mob photography at its finest. Images flickered creating a montage comprising: waves on the ocean, fields of crops, spirals, big horned bulls, penises, axes, birds and breasts. There were many, many women with huge voluptuous breasts.

The flash lighting took on a life of its own. The cavern became alight with images. Visuals flavoured with sensuality, brutality, dancing, fire, and explosions, flew out at her. Too fast. Confusion spiralled around her; she could not see straight. The space grew smaller. The flickering faster. Cressida tried to swallow. A wave of nausea rushed up. A great hole appeared in her thoughts, drowning, choking, frantic for air, for space. A familiar growing numbness spread throughout her body. A premonition — something terrible was coming. She felt in her pockets, struggling vainly to find her pills.

Oh no... ohnononooo.

Fear sneered from the shadows. Closer and closer it crept upon her, stalking her. Tears welled and she swallowed again. The lump in her throat remained obstinate. Waves pounded. Her palms were clammy. She struggled for breath. Terrifying familiar sensations took over. Hold on. Too late, too late. Her pulse surged into her temples forging a jarring song, reverberating through her veins. She vomited.

Cressida dropped her phone and followed it immediately to the ground, onto her knees, in a feeble attempt to grip something solid, desperate to hold onto something stable. Fear swam around her. Was it inside? From her? Outside? Seeping from the walls? She tried to focus but could not see anything but a fuzzy spinning dot of light. Everything seemed so far away. Everything kept moving, spinning. She heard a wail, a deep guttural cry of anguish. Was that an echo?

Cressida curled up into herself, holding her knees tight into her chest. Everything streamed; eyes, nose, mouth dribbling out liquid woe. She heaved against the dampness as a deep aloneness pervaded every pore of her trembling, shaking body.

There was grit in her mouth. Again. Not goat shit. Vaguely she remembered this was good. Staring into darkness told her nothing about where she was. It smelt musty. It was cool, damp. It was still, very still. Only her breathing convinced her she was not dead.

Her breathing faltered slightly, then slowly slipped into a feeble rhythm. She clung to it. She was not inclined to sit up. She was not sure she could. She did a slow internal scan. Mouth, yuck. She spat. She realised she was not panting. This was another good thing. Her heart felt like it was still racing but it was in her chest where it should be, not in her throat. That was also good. She cleared her throat to make sure. Okay, she was alive in a dark room, no, a cave, she was in a cave. She acknowledged this with a sleepy nod. Memory returned somewhat sheepishly. She had survived the attack when at the height of it she thought she was going to die. She closed her eyes.

Eyes open. It was still dark; she was still in a cave. Her mobile was on; she observed its beam shining up. It cast shadows. The shadows played games with her mind, for she swore she could see the outline of a woman. She slowly turned her head to look properly. In the shadows sat a woman. There was a woman sitting on a rock watching her. A solitary tear traced Cressida's temple before it dripped on the ground.

The woman seemed powerful but not menacing or threatening. An image of her mother crying on her knees came to mind. Cressida could not register any connection. This woman sat with dignity. She was composed. The woman looked at her, holding eye contact. The woman's gaze was strong and confident. Cressida blinked and wished she could roll over and bury her head in her pillow and go back to sleep — to wake in the morning as far away from this nightmare as possible. She could not look away. The woman saw everything.

What does she see?

Another silent tear followed the first.

Their shared look created a space, which filled as the woman spoke; her voice reminiscent of a mountain stream flowing over river rocks: smooth, clear and pure. It came from far away and imbued the cavern with a delicate, yet strong sense of presence.

My story is your story is our story.

Her voice laid a blissful gossamer quilt over Cressida's weariness.

In times to come the spirit of the Great Mother will be discovered when She is least expected. One who clings to faith shall lose it and one who loses her faith for the sake of truth and adventure shall find it.

Cressida felt a deep surge of — she paused — of something. Words were too tired, or too lazy to aid her. With every breath, she inhaled sensations akin to peace and comfort and she lay embraced in this refuge of serenity. She felt the woman's voice meander over her and soaked in the pleasure of sound rather than what she was saying. There was no need for her to do anything, be anywhere or respond in any way. As the woman gently began to weave her tale, Cressida was not even sure she heard any spoken words. The woman's story emerged in images with hues and texture, poetry and song. Cressida sank into an intimacy of grace as the woman began.

We share our journey to sustain the Mother's seed, protected from the darkness. He, who has polluted Her rites and rituals, has brought destruction on a scale unimaginable. Our ancestors rejected his seed and sought a future of a blood-line blessed. Her sun has set into a dark night of disharmony, polarising before balance. Hold strong your belief in the light. For when the Great Mother returns, awakened from Her sleep, She will be within us all as one.

Shake loose the notion things happen to us and we must respond. It is we who happen to life. Open your heart to the cooling rain or warming sun, the movements of the seasons that, in following their own nature, remind us how to follow ourselves.

The woman paused and looked to the side. Cressida followed the direction of her gaze and saw another woman standing tall and graceful, facing the paintings on the wall of the cave. *Pythia.* Her name slipped into Cressida's mind and she understood these images were her story — the vibrant colours inscribed into the surface proclaimed her truth. These images bespoke a journey back to another place, though simultaneously of this place. There was no 'once upon a time,' for the story was of now, as it was of then. There was no beginning and the thought of whether there was an end, fluttered briefly as Cressida drifted in and out of the wanderings of a long-ago tale. Pythia turned. A golden glow infused gentleness filtered Cressida's vision. Pythia turned back and as she traced the outline of the images with her long slender fingers, her story unfolded.

CHAPTER FOUR

Pythia's Story

The womb of the Earth clamoured for sustenance. Pythia braced herself as the ground heaved, sending a series of shudders rippling to the surface. She nodded gently. Attuned to the spirits of trees, birds and insects, she knew of the oncoming upheaval. The sentient ground she walked upon, slept on and worshipped, had spoken loudly. There were no secrets. Life was always full of danger and uncertainty, defenceless against the maelstrom of the Great Mother's mysterious ways. Pythia knew the Mother sought nourishment. *She would reclaim what She had birthed.* Despite her training in becoming a Pythia — the High Priestess for the village, she hoped the Mother would honour Vrados and claim his sacrifice. She stiffened slightly. He who was Consort, the Anointed One, had become an aggressive adversary. Yet the Great Mother had chosen him. As Pythia tucked a strand of her long black hair behind her ear, her hand softly brushed against her scarred cheek.

A state of disharmony had lingered too long. Pythia hoped she had prepared sufficiently for her task. It would not be long now. Pythia stood tall and composed and addressed the women gathered at the table. There was an air of trepidation and anticipation. The Earth had been groaning in Her labours from the moon's first quarter through to waxing crescent.

"There are two Mothers," Pythia said, "One of the Earth and one in your heart. When the Great Mother wearies and the world darkens, the Mother inside us blazes more strongly. Prepare yourselves. At moonrise we leave."

Pythia left the Temple for what she knew would be her last walk around the village. She strode through the narrow, paved paths that wove in and out like an intricate spider web. Central was the platia. There, in the large open area was Vrados' shrine to the Great Mother. To her right were the administrative buildings for counsel and meetings, as well as storage and distribution halls, a threshing circle for grain and finally, further afield, piles of cut rock stacked ready for the construction of more compounds.

Pythia walked past many single- and two-storey stone dwellings; the area to her left had new compounds containing small courtyards. She passed the large water cisterns, erected to minimise the need for labouring at the wells. Finally, she turned northward, walking around the outside of the stone walls of the village, some now tumbled and in disarray from recent tremors. The path led her back to the Temple and women's compound. After her slight detour through the village, she headed up through terraced rows of olive trees to a cave, high above the village.

The walk uphill was steep. The many switchbacks carved into the cliff face drew a glistening line of sweat. There were steps to the mouth of the cave as well as a stone wall that created a front facade. It could be secured to prevent wild goats getting in.

She reached the cave and sat to draw breath. Closing her eyes to the stunning panorama in front of her, she opened her heart. She felt a wave of giddiness as if standing on a caïque in a high swell. Swirling and swaying sensations washed over her. Surrendering to these feelings, she focused inwardly on her dissolving flesh and blood and bone joining with the particles of earth, merging with air and wind, floating on currents within an ocean of the unborn. Complete surrender, melting and melding, giving up all form, merging with the Great Mother.

After awakening from her meditation, she sat quietly, allowing time for her form to return to shape and become solid on the earth. The familiar sounds of hustle and bustle of village life drifted upwards to the cave. Some were of the present while others slipped in from past memories. The loudest were always the goats, their constant bleating and clanging of bronze bells accompanying their perpetual motion. Then there were the roosters who crowed regardless of the time of day, sounding as if death were constantly upon them. Hens celebrating the laying of each egg joined them, ad hoc. Other sounds wafted up to compete; those of manual labour, building, paving, washing, the shouts from the harbour, the ringing of bells.

The most endearing were those of the townsfolk; daily chatter, worthless gossip, hidden tears and sorrow, complaints, laughter of children, grunting and bickering, aimless meanderings of thoughts, opinions and considerations. These noises, heard from her vantage point provided Pythia intimate knowledge of how best she could serve.

In the early evening heat, a slight breeze danced its way up through oleander-laden hills. The Mother seemed at rest after her last violent shaking. Pythia felt the magic of this place and was grateful. Her stillness became a target, and memories, like children, clambered over her, demanding attention. They were persistent, pressing for release, too insistent to ignore. Pythia knew the importance of stories and succumbed, albeit hesitantly.

Slowly, slowly.

'Boundary to the self is arbitrary,' she thought. 'Our experience is the experience of the whole.'

She hummed a gentle tune, seeking calmness, aware of the discomfort hidden amongst the shadows. Her melody brought with it an image, a face, tranquil and rosy-cheeked. Daphnis. An identical face also appeared before her. One could not think of Daphnis without Kleodora. They were twins. Identical. Inseparable.

The villagers were wary of the two strange slender women, who rarely spoke and never sat with them in the shade of the cypress to while away hot afternoons with banter. People would avert their eyes at any mention of them, their images bringing an unfamiliar, aloof energy. Daphnis had the gift of song. Her exquisite voice sang in harmony and joy, but also contained a hint of something dark, a power and strength that unnerved people. Kleodora, on the other hand, possessed the gift of hearing. A gift so sensitive she could hear any trespass against the Mother, be it a ship approaching the shore or a hunter's strike against Sacred Boar. Today had been monumental for the sisters.

Pythia's thoughts rested on the two women. She had seen they would eventually travel with Ashtar to the navel of the world, to be ensconced in a mountain settlement north from the coast of Phocis. It would be called Delphi. There, they would attend Ashtar as Pythias in a new sanctuary for the Great Mother. This would be some time off in the future. Pythia smiled. Any thought of Ashtar always brought pleasure. She loved the child as if she were her own.

Pythia paused and as it extended through time, Cressida, riding the rhythm of her story felt suspended in a void of dark, cool, tranquil space. She lay content, waiting for her to begin again. The woman sitting on the rock exuded deep respect as she explained, "Pythia was a great Oracle." She looked around the cave. "Her time is inscribed in antiquity. So too is Ashtar's."

Ashtar? The name whispered into Cressida's heart. Cressida sunk deep into the bosom of an abiding peace.

Pythia released her breath with a long exhale. Having calmed her heart, she stopped humming, needing to reflect on events of this last day in the village. It had been pre-dawn, hours before she was due to attend the Act of Relinquish, when she returned to the Temple from the harbour. She had finished loading a caïque with supplies in readiness for their forthcoming departure. The sky's gentle complexion surrendered to bright clarity erupting from the east. Light bounced off the cliffs turning pale softness into brilliant hues of yellow and gold that heralded a clear day with a hint of promise: the Mother in all Her grandeur.

The last touch of night air remained crisp on her skin, salt from the ocean spotted around the hairs on her arms. From the shadows, an owl beckoned its mate. This was a good omen. She had followed the Great Mother's counsel and hope lightened her heart. It was finally time to leave behind the pain and sorrow, her teachers of resilience and fortitude. She had a destiny to fulfil. Gathering her robes so as not to trip, Pythia walked slowly, her breath laboured as she made her way along the stony path from the port to the Temple. She knew every step, every incline and descent as well as she knew the lines on her palm. Soon she would exchange this familiarity for new paths. Each step she counted as one woman on the journey. Twenty-eight steps from the bend to the old olive tree. Twenty-eight women selected to follow the Mother, to share the load and cultivate the future. Her preparations had taken their toll. While she was no longer a maiden of the Mother, she was not yet a Crone. The physical demands of her task were arduous and had measured up her emotional and physical endurance.

At the Temple, she stripped off her cloak and dressed quietly in ceremonial robes. With the Mother's recent turbulence, Vrados had decreed a sacrificial offering of a Sacred Bull. He had also sought the blood of a youth. Pythia had no respect for this new rite of mingling blood. She believed the chosen youth was someone Vrados viewed as a potential competitor to Consort. She remembered earlier in the week an older woman of the village had sought her out.

"My son has been selected," the woman had proudly proclaimed. "Tonight, he bathes in oil."

Pythia had nodded, continuing to gather fallen pinecones and load them into the sack she had slung across her back.

"Will you do a lamentation?" The older woman paused. "Will you officiate?"

Pythia stood and stretched out the muscles of her back. The weight she bore had little to do with her sack. She looked at the woman kindly.

"This is the Consort's Rite of Relinquish. It is for the Consort to lead. He seeks to placate the Great Mother," she gently reminded the woman. A passing cloud shadowed the sun and hid a fleeting look of resignation that had skimmed like a flat stone across her eyes.

"The sacrifice of your youth is at the Consort's behest. Yet dear mother, your son's blood shall still nourish the Earth regardless of who officiates at this new rite. His blood will provide nourishment. The Great Mother shall take back her progeny. She will dissolve him and become fruitful," she reassured the woman.

"But will she remain angry?"

Pythia heard the woman's apprehension. Vrados had introduced the Act of Relinquish at the last planting when the Great Mother had held back the rain. For this ritual, men now dressed in robes as Select. These had become confusing times.

Pythia sought to alleviate the woman's anxiety. "As you know, the strengthening of life comes from sacrificial death. The Consort may claim your youth's blood, but ultimately it belongs to the land. The shedding of blood is always a Sacred Act. The Great Mother will not be denied."

The old woman, somewhat comforted by Pythia's assurance, whispered she would claim her son's phallus and make her own offering to the Great Mother.

"Things are changing." She shook her head sadly before confiding, "Too quickly for me."

For the Rite, Pythia dressed in sacred garments consisting of a woven flounced skirt, girdle adorned with pearls and precious stones linked with beaten gold threading and a vibrant, purple-dyed, woven vest that exaggerated her breasts in honour of the Mother. Her role was to attend as an honoured observer.

Joined by the Temple women, she made her way to the ceremony, stopping only at the gates of the Shrine to let Vrados and his entourage of men pass. Neither Pythia nor Consort acknowledged each other, but while passing, Vrados' younger brother Kastos arrogantly pushed past her. Pythia did not flinch, nor did she acknowledge he had touched her body. Her disdain and aloofness angered the young man and he stopped to face her. As his eyes sought hers, he brutally pinched her nipple. Pythia slapped his hand off her breast as she would an irritating fly, and he responded without thought, punching her in the face, knocking her backwards. As she stepped back to maintain her balance, a deathly silence descended, bringing with it, a vacuum of stilled time.

Men and women froze, staring in disbelief, horrified by this transgression and sacrilege. Their shock was palpable. The hush stilled all movement. Creatures of the earth paused in unison at this act of treason against the Mother. In this disquiet, an ominous apprehension emerged. And then, ever so gently, softly, barely discernible, came the sweetest sound, soft as lace, floating through the cypress trees, drifting down from the Temple. The sound was like a gliding euphoric vibration, comprised of clear summer breezes from mountains high, the deep earthy breath of the desert and the powerful whisper of oceans. It snaked its way, washing over the entranced crowd, towards Kastos. It was a glorious sound, a luxury of golden honey harmony, a silken rhythm drawing everyone into its embrace. The crowd swayed in unison, fuelling the vibration with the energy of their bodies. All except Kastos. He stood transfixed, unaware of the significance of the swirling around him but with a growing fearful unknowing knot expanding and sticking to the sides of his throat. He swallowed.

The sounding entered his body through his orifices; cool, enticing, somewhat smooth, before transforming into an insidious manifestation of the ugliness and malice he bore in his heart. Sudden perforation of his eardrums produced pitched and frenzied screams spun with terror and panic. The reverberation raised its decibels like a cobra ready to strike. Kastos desperately tried to block it, holding his hands to his ears. Blood dripped through his fingers and he vomited. He fell to the ground, screeching, screaming, begging for mercy. The sounding held no pity for the writhing, tormented man. Blood poured from his mouth, nose and ears, and his vomit mingled with the stench of his expulsions. Then, quite abruptly, everything stopped. The sounding, his screams, the swaying crowd, all became still. The only movement was the wind, carrying a faint residue of celestial punishment in the telling. Vrados, freed from the timelessness of the moment, raced to his brother.

Pythia and the Temple women walked past as Vrados knelt and gently cradled the limp body. He glared after Pythia, his body taut with rage, his hate fuelled by her complicity in his brother's death. She heard his muttered curse swearing for revenge.

Upon her return to the Temple, Pythia discovered Daphnis and Kleodora entwined and asleep. Their exhaustion lay upon them like a blanket. She would let them sleep until the final moments of departure. She did not need prophesy to know that the time had arrived. She would not survive Vrados' revenge. Pythia had been waiting for a sign. This was it. She was ready, she had prepared well. She had been preparing since Vrados returned after their first Sacred Union.

From her vantage point in her cave, Pythia looked out over the shadow of land to the sea. The Mother groaned suddenly, rumbling uncomfortably and shaking Pythia from her reverie. Retrieving her thoughts from the day's events, she looked up into the dusky early evening sky.

'Soon,' she assessed, 'not long now.'

41

The village sat beside a river which, having laboriously snaked its way through rock, now flowed through undulating hillsides and flat lands to its destination, via a natural harbour. To look up its path was to glimpse into the very crevasse of the Mother. The cliffs along Her fissure contained many caves providing sacred space to return form and matter from whence it came. It always reminded Pythia of the gorgeous outline of the Mother's legs flayed open giving birth. The curve of Her legs reminiscent of the horns of the Sacred Bull.

The harbour was unnaturally empty, the Mother's recent movements having ceased all enterprise. Usually in the trade season, it was a hive of activity. Full with caïques from other lands bringing gold, silver and copper to trade for weaving, oils, honey and perfumes. In the cooler seasons when the seas refused to allow voyage or entry, all manner of food from Her clear ocean waters sustained the village. Earthen pithio vessels were filled with bounty, harvested from both land and sea.

Abundance had created opportunities to develop crafts, hone skills in fine weaving and decorative pottery. It had also provided time to gather, discuss and debate the wonder of all around them. Teachings were well respected and contributed to the wellbeing of the whole community in myriad ways. Such was the business, joy, and celebration of life that, as a young Select, Pythia had been unaware of a menacing dark shadow. Season after season, it slipped unimpeded into the village psyche through many strange stories shared from foreign tongues. It grew stronger with each trading season. Pythia became aware of the first inkling of change after Vrados, her childhood friend, returned from a voyage excited with the newness of the lives he had witnessed and the stories he had heard. The differences resonated with his odd thoughts.

Pythia swallowed, the taste in her mouth turning sour from thoughts of Vrados. They had grown up together in the village — a long time before she became Select. Together they explored the gorge, climbed cliffs, swam and played in the ocean. He had been cheeky, daring but a thoughtful boy. He could cry easily and laugh hard. She recalled that fateful day she shared her news with him.

"Vrados, Vrados," she had cried out breathlessly. She took a flying jump landing on him and pinning him to the ground. She sat astride him, bursting with the energy good news brings. Taken by surprise the young boy had not fought back. He lay looking up at her. Her face was flustered, her long black wavy hair mattered with sticks and dirt and sand. She was sweating from her run to his compound and consumed by excitement.

"Vrados, you will never guess what!" she cried, her eyes alight. She threw her head back and laughed with a freedom she was never to experience again. "No, no, you never will. I... I," she gasped for breath, "I have been selected! Yes. It's true."

Vrados' smile slipped as he stared blankly comprehending her news. He finally moved when the words found weight in his heart. He rolled her off and got up. Sitting on the ground, stunned, she watched him go. Her joy and excitement leaving with him.

Since then, she had watched him leave many times, each time hurting a bit less. Long ago she reasoned that Vrados had felt abandoned, rejected by her because she had been selected by the Great Mother. It had saddened her that he had never celebrated her honour or acknowledged her destiny. She should not have been surprised. She knew he was different. He once said in earnest, "You do not know the Great Mother wants to force me to do wrong. She forces me to think abominations to experience Her Grace."

At the time, Pythia had not understood what he meant.

She recalled how he wore his oddness in small ways easily missed if you were distracted. It was hard to grasp, to hold firm in your hand, but he saw things differently, in ways he could never truly explain. The words he needed did not exist.

"I will decide. It is my choice," he had once said. His choice? What did this mean? There had been many times when they could not share a single mind. His oddness seemed to skew things. His growing propensity for destruction, his tendency to kill things, like insects or birds when there was no reason, no need, concerned her. Where had his gentleness gone? The smell of difference seemed to hang around his neck like a heavy gold medallion. From across this growing gulf, she saw he was often ostracised by other boys his age.

After he returned from his first trade mission, his strangeness seemed more pronounced. She had talked with him, trying desperately to understand his strange thoughts.

"What is *married*?" she had asked, her tongue fumbling around this new word.

"It is when a man takes a woman and couples only with her,

and she only with him. From this union, the child belongs to the man," he answered.

"Preposterous," she said. "Children are gifted from the Great Mother to the woman."

"Select," he paused, using her new name like a chastisement, "I learned many things from foreign shores. Our Mother is strong and we run brave. She invites us to connect deeply with the timeless Self. She is country and place. Elsewhere, traders worship different deities, not just one Mother. Do you know that there are places where people bow before both Mother Divine and her Consort Son?"

Vrados became animated. "There are many Gods. Our Great Mother is just one. She has many names. In some places She is revered for Her fertility, for seasons, soil, harvest and plants, but in matters of the compound, or oceans, or skies, even animals, things are different. These villages thrive, regardless of their different customs, some of which do not require a Consort sacrifice. Or any sacrifice, for that matter."

His talk had baffled her, and over time had been forgotten or tucked away under the fold of her religious duties at the Temple.

The Great Mother had woven an intricate fate for Vrados, full of contradictions, knots and holes. His was a great burden to carry and sometimes, she thought, he fought against it, struggling needlessly against the Will of Divine. His was a transitioning energy — always the hardest to carry. She sighed. She remembered their argument at the Rites of Renewal. It was many seasons ago, but it had set fire to the fuse of change. Its imprint witnessed in the scars she bore.

Vrados

Vrados' older brother Eyristhenis had been the chosen Consort, anointed by the Great Mother. He had led with great compassion and goodness, in all matters politics and business alongside Crone Pythia. His Sacred Union with the Great Mother had produced healthy live twin daughters. The lands had flourished, the crops provided a bountiful yield in his honour with a surplus harvest, and the rains had been quenching. There had been much to celebrate and rejoice. Eyristhenis was in preparation for his ritual sacrifice at the Rites of Renewal, his blood and flesh and bones to be spread across the fields. What honour, what joy. It was a triumph of his leadership. A triumph felt by all except Vrados.

Vrados had neither celebrated nor rejoiced in his brother's destiny. On the day of the Rites of Renewal, prior to Eyristhenis' bloodletting, Vrados had argued bitterly with his older brother. He sat now, having cried out his tears and wrung dry his shattered heart. He sat alone quietly, while celebration of the Rites progressed. A sad longing kept him company. In the background, drumming filled the empty space of grief. His tanned face caked with salty tracks, his eyes swollen and red.

'Too soon,' thought Vrados, 'too young, too soon.'

The Mother had acknowledged her Consort and shaken violently for the last two days. Her movements had created great gapes inland past the lake region. News had come of several villages swallowed completely. Soon She would claim his brother. Vrados frowned, comprehension unpalatable. Passion distorted his sight. Blurred and cloudy, his mind struggling to find clarity. The Great Mother ignored him and he battled to hold tight his devotion to Her.

He dared not speak aloud this poison. He had tried to wash it away with Okri and ritual cleansing, but nothing worked. He had dutifully attended Negation at the Temple with the purpose of releasing his seed, thereby cleansing his troubles. The Select had taken up his transgressions, interceding on his behalf to purify him. To no avail. He agonised over his failure to attain peace. His distance to the Great Mother grew rather than diminished.

The last two days before the bloodletting celebrated with many Bull dances. Usually, Vrados loved watching the young men and women performing acrobatic stunts with the large Bulls. The way they would grasp the Bull's horns, and as the Bull violently jerked its neck upwards, use the momentum for all sorts of somersaults and aerial twists. The Bulls were magnificent creatures, possessed of athletic bodies with strongly expressed neck and shoulder musculature. The acrobats performed their tricks and stunts with intense energy, full of respect and bravado.

Music filled the air while dancing coloured the paths and platia with movement and devotion. People streamed in and out of the Temple, many participating in Negation rituals as well as sacrifices and offerings to the Mother. The whole village thrummed with excitement and growing anticipation during the festivities. It was a time of good will and harmony. Especially this year. Already stories sung of Eyristhenis' prowess and the Mother's satisfaction. It seemed everyone would celebrate his bloodletting, his final sacrifice and honour.

Once again Vrados felt ostracised from his community. Riding solo on an offshore breeze, waves of confusion washed over him. Seeing a break between the waves, Vrados would raise his head in search of understanding, only to be dumped from behind by a larger, more powerful wave comprised of frustration, anger and obligation. This was not of his choosing. His fate seemed woven with threads of agitation and distraction.

Vrados held his head in his hands. Things he had previously understood he saw differently, now. He shook his head. His thinking had become strange, incongruent. Decisions and choices seemed contradictory and his ideas antagonistic. Even his feelings were coloured a different hue and intensity. Thinking without emotion was becoming his modus operandi. He shook his head again as if to shake it clear. Yes, he had changed; the way he thought, the way he saw and calculated things. Although Vrados could not make sense of these changes, he realised that this new way of thinking distanced him from the vibrations of the Earth. But it seemed to clarify things in ways he had been unable to before.

'Before what?' he tried to analyse.

From his time on the trade boats, travelling to and from the rising sun, he had witnessed many strange traditions and practises. He carefully observed the difference of other cultures. Some traders had slaves. Other cultures had weapons of death, not for sacrifice to the Great Mother but for reasons of control and power. Crones and Kings ruled side by side, as if men were of equal standing. Women's capacity and emulation of the Great Mother in matters of birth, death, destruction and creativity were not always revered. One tradition from the north assigned children from Sacred Union to the man. He had liked this. It felt solid, and showed men's strength. In those communities, there was no sacrificial bloodletting or Rites of Renewal.

Vrados looked up, listening to the drumming. It was not long now. Slowly his thoughts shifted from sacrifice and surrender to power and control. Through the children? He snickered. The foreign thought tasted bitter so he took another swig of Okri. He remembered last year, when these rituals were performed for his cousin Damos. He had celebrated his sacrifice as much as everyone else had. It was when his brother Eyristhenis was anointed by the Great Mother as the Chosen One that things seemed to have changed. How could this happen in just one year? What was the difference that made Damos' sacrifice acceptable but not Eyristhenis? What had changed?

He recalled the sacrifice of Damos. Drawn by curiosity, he had slipped into the Temple. It had three chambers and an annex that lead into each of them. Each Chamber had different functions, purified accordingly for various celebrations, rituals and ceremonies. One Chamber stored clay Pithio, used to hold bodies for re-burial once the flesh had dissolved. These were usually for those who had crossed over through sickness or age, rather than returning to, and feeding the land.

The East Chamber contained a stone altar on the south side of the room used for offerings of milk, honey, grains and pulses. Frescoes decorated these walls in vibrant colours with many small clay and brass representations of the Divine Mother positioned against them. Larger clay statues were smooth, worn through constant kissing and caressing during ceremonies.

The Central chamber had a large altar made from hewn rock from the hillside. Beside the altar, overlooking the raised platform stood a life-size wooden carved image of the Mother with clay feet, large breasts and belly. She too was shiny, worn by many kisses and caresses of worship. Beside her was the Sacred Stone. Sourced locally, it was carved with elaborate and intricate sacred designs. At the base of the altar was a trough.

Vrados did not see Damos kiss the stone in devotion to the Divine Mother, for by the time his eyes had become accustomed to the darkened chamber, he saw Damos trussed up with his heels tied to the back of his thighs and his arms stretched back, forcing him to lie on the raised platform. The Crone Pythia, clothed in a golden thread skirted robe with live snakes entwined around her arms, had already severed his skin and pierced his heart with a bronze dagger. Vrados could see it sticking out, the blade as long as his thigh. He could make out the carved images of the Sacred Boar. Blood flowed out of the wound, pouring steadily into the trough below. The Crone Pythia took a bronze cup and scooped up some of the warm liquid. She poured libations over the stone and smeared some over her breasts before drinking from the cup.

The drumming had now reached a pitched crescendo. Boom Boom Boom. Vrados stood up, pacing and snarling, then threw his jug of Okri across the room. It smashed into the stone-wall, splattering its red contents. He sat and watched as the fluid dripped unceremoniously down the wall forming a puddle on the ground.

Even though Pythia felt Vrados had avoided her since she wore the robes of Select, he was still her dearest friend. She sought him out on the day of Eyristhenis' bloodletting. She had observed his reluctance to participate in the celebrations, but she wanted to congratulate him. During the morning festivities of the Rites of Renewal, the Crone Pythia, in honour of Eyristhenis had bestowed the next cycle's leadership and anointed Vrados. Brothers united in fate, and surrendered to the Great Mother.

She sat awkwardly next to him. He did not seem happy to see her. She could see he was pained, his anguish worn loosely around his shoulders.

He cleared his throat.

"I have a premonition of changes to come. My part in this

is predestined. My brother is now slain, bled and reborn through Her. Succumbing to Her in death and devoured. But I cannot deny my feelings reveal a separation I do not understand."

Pythia watched him grapple with his thoughts, confusion furrowing his brow. His words did not come easily and many times he stuttered out a few renegade words only to withdraw them from their path of explanation and shake his head.

She could witness his struggle, but she could not help. She did not understand what he was trying to explain. His role was that of the storm and impending doom. These were new sensations he was trying to voice and all she could do was sit in wonder how one could survive without connection to the Mother. There was an air of foreboding when Vrados spoke of mortality, impotence and isolation.

'He is dangerous,' she thought, and as she rose to leave, Vrados grabbed her arm, pulling her back beside him.

"This will be the last time," he said.

His muscles twitched involuntarily, before he managed to regain control. She watched the softness retreat from his eyes, blinked away forcefully, replaced with a steely, impenetrable gaze. A shiver of misgiving shuddered through her.

"The Mother gives you this opportunity," she answered. "Reflect on what it is you crave so much it hurts you, and for those things you dread losing. Contemplate the difference between the desires of mind and those of heart. When you know what you want, with heart and soul, the fleeting desires of the mind may lose their shine and your true needs will take precedence. Only then can you take meaningful action in Her light and take your journey aligned with Mother's Sacred Source."

Vrados released her arm.

"I am the Anointed One, Her Consort. I am to be leader, but I will not be slain. I proclaim now, to you, there will be a new Rite. I..."

He thought quickly for an alternative. "I will fight the one chosen to replace me and whoever shall win this battle will win the right to life by the Mother's side. I shall be victorious. I shall be Consort for a new year, and for the year following. This is my proclamation; this is my decree."

Silence divided them. Moments passed before Pythia comprehended the words he spoke. She stood up, more to compose herself than to leave. She faced him squarely.

"Legitimacy for your position is taken at the Mother's lap. It is She who anoints you, bestowing Her favour and leadership on you. You do not decide this. She will select another when your time of bloodletting is upon you."

She did not wait for an answer, her outrage rising above any confusion.

"Who are you to challenge this? Leadership is instituted through these rites, though the Rite of Sacred Union. The power you seek comes through Union with the Mother. Without the Divine Mother, you have no flesh, blood or bones. You, you are nothing but creature of the Creator. She comes before creature, prime giver of life, not inferred from the creature."

Shaking her head in disbelief, she softened her tone.

"Succumb to Her in death and be devoured. You are what comes from Her. You will return to Her. You fear your role? You hide from your destiny? The Great Mother is here, in the heart of surrender."

Pythia clenched her fist and punched her heart. She started to speak but Vrados interrupted.

"No," he said. "Enough."

Vrados paused into this new silence. His voice dropped, relinquishing its intensity as he quietly asked her, "What determines reality?"

Pythia looked at him, baffled. "You are not in the world but of the world. How can you no longer feel this? The divisiveness you follow will drive you to destruction."

"That is not an answer," he argued.

"That was not a question," she replied.

She straightened up and looked at him. "I will greet you at the ceremonies and Great Mother will reveal what is required."

Vrados stood then and left the room without another word. Pythia became aware she was trembling, and felt somewhat soiled by the bitterness of his grief and anger. A new beginning was upon them. She breathed deeply, hoping to rid herself of the sorrow sinking into the pit of her gut.

At the time of their meeting neither had been aware that, in three nights at Sacred Union, she, while not yet a Pythia, would be chosen by the Great Mother to couple with him as the new Consort, the bridegroom god.

CHAPTER SIX

Pythia

Pythia exhaled slowly, hoping to find some ease to the tightness that had wrapped itself around her chest. The past was difficult and she was reluctant to retrieve it. She had once loved him despite all his confusing ways.

Even now, the memories felt too close. Pythia felt she could almost reach out to touch them. She shivered, although not from cold. Pythia squinted, looking for a distraction in the distance. She coughed and shifted her hips.

It was only this morning she understood there would be no future Sacred Union at the village for her. She felt a tug at her heart, knowing once she left, there would be many women without Sacred guidance. She hoped the young woman left in her stead would hold herself with honour and strength. Pythia felt the pull of sadness but shook it off. These times required sacrifice from all.

The breeze had softened and the temptation to return to the Temple was great. Yet, despite her turmoil, she knew it was important to reflect on the ache in her heart. Resolution would come by shining her light into this darkness. If she were to begin anew then she needed to face this issue, not avoid it. See it in the light of day without the illusions of this world deceiving her. Courage and commitment were required. She took a sip of water from her flask, not to quench any thirst but to distract her hesitation. She sat still, scarcely able to breathe, knowing the next thought held a thread of dark anguish.

Sacred Union

Sacred Union provided seed, nourishment, blood, fertility and growth. It honoured the Great Mother, surrendering human flesh to Her arousal and desire. Training in the Temple taught love exults.

"Our bodies are the receptacle for spirit. When we come together, we join our bodies and bring together our spirits in an act of devotion and celebration of Sacred Union," said Crone Pythia.

Her words echoed what everyone instinctively knew. True union existed when trust was present. When there was knowledge of each other and respect for consecrating the combining of life forces. It was a celebration of the most Divine.

"Our Mother teaches us this," Crone Pythia had instructed. "It bestows the ultimate gift of creating life. The act of union is a holy and euphoric gift."

It was tradition for the Crone Pythia to incarnate the Great Mother and couple with the newly anointed Consort, bestowing him a year of honour in Her service. However, this time had been different. Great Mother had chosen Pythia, although still a Select, to couple with the Anointed One.

Pythia stood among many young Select at their first Sacred Union, chanting preliminary prayers in unison. Crone Pythia walked around the Temple sprinkling Holy Water. She let out a blood-curdling cry that seemed to arise from the very Earth herself. She welcomed everyone.

"Whosoever offers with devotion, a leaf, a flower, a seed or pine, water and oil, offering of the pure heart, I accept," she said as she scattered a concoction of pine wood, needles and dried snakes' skins into the fire pits.

The Select, having bathed in the holy spring and caressed oil into their skin, passed around a bowl of sacred figs from the sycamore tree. In consuming its fruit, they ate the flesh of the Mother Divine. Gathered around the largest fire-lit pit, they wafted the rising smoke of the laurel leaves over their shining and gleaming bodies, breathing it in.

A gong sounded and a younger group of initiates started to circle the Select around the pit. As they circled left, the Select started to circle to the right. Devotional chanting continued with low guttural calls from the Crone Pythia. She stood tall, and raised her arms upwards, enabling the live serpents entwined on her arms to rise and sway in unison to the beating of her heart and the stomping of her feet. Immersed in smoke, she began to sway and stamp her feet, beating out a rhythm that accompanied the drumming and hand clapping.

The inner circle of Select, facing to the right, simultaneously made their circles smaller and smaller until each woman circled independent from each other. Standing on one foot, they spun themselves around on the spot. Spinning and spiralling, their feet kicked up dust that mingled with the smoke. The beating and pounding of drums kept raising the energy. One by one, the Select started to shake uncontrollably, and Pythia recalled the familiar sensation of connection to earth under her feet, the rising tingling up her legs and thighs, setting her groin afire. She jumped at the impact of heat, and felt compelled to keep her legs open wide to enable cooler air to ease the fire of her loins.

The gong and drums continued to beat out a strong pulse of rising energy, a wave of intangible force that grew, rousing Pythia's heart to a pounding pace. Sound vibrated through her body. She swayed in harmony. The music in her ears, her heart integrating to its rhythm, everything in the moment striving toward an ecstatic crescendo.

In trance, Pythia surrendered into the immediacy of the moment, every breath in every cell pulsated. She did not consciously respond, but reacted spontaneously with everyone else around her. The women whirled as if synchronised, breathing as one, bonded in unity. Yet within that extraordinary sense of oneness, a separateness of each woman, unknown in her everyday life, remained preserved. The intensity was complete, without inhibition, and with equal freedom in connecting to the utter fullness of the shared moment. Their simple actions and dancing shifted them into an altered state of presence — opening their hearts to the Great Mother.

Pythia's spirit reached out and touched the spirit of those in the circle. Their energy transcended as one, something larger than each and every one of them, and despite the frenzy of whirling and circling, the women remained serene. All dancers connected with the Great Mother through a magical sense, with each woman identifying with one another through tribe and stories.

Unified in breath, they bonded through a deep internal possession that pulled them closer and closer in frenzied motion. They joined hands, laughing, caressing and kissing each other with joyous solidarity. The drumbeat softened and slowed, but the women did not notice, now seemingly detached to their surroundings and only sensing the nearness of bodies. They swayed together, licking the sweat off their bodies while stroking and dancing.

Some Select sang out with a high-pitched trill while others started to talk in a language so fast, so old and forgotten that it was difficult for the Scribes, who were assigned to record and recite back any spoken word, to comprehend. The Scribes, too young to interpret the Mother's words, memorised the spoken content, which the Select and Crone Pythia would later decipher.

The drums maintained a pure, simple beat as the Select emerged from their frenzied state. Still dazed, the young Pythia reeled with a deep longing and passionate throbbing between her legs. Desire spread through her body. It came from a force that flooded out thought, spinning her into a timeless state within an internal abyss as deep and ancient as the Mother Herself.

The Crone Pythia had already chosen a beautiful youth and as she commenced her coupling, the other tranced women and Select followed her example, removing their robes to join in union with their consorts and lovers.

Pythia saw Vrados approach. She wanted to smile. She wanted to hold his hand, kiss his palm. He was erect and ready for Sacred Union. Entranced she sensed him, and she watched him move towards her through the firelight. She smelt his familiarity, breathing deeply his scent. As a child, she had loved him, and even now, despite their recent bitter words, she knew he loved her as well. The trance heightened this feeling and she felt the blessed light tingling inside her skin.

He smelt of Okri and she noted his stagger and that he did not make eye contact. She was unable to tell him of her love, of her desire. The pulsing of her loins from the heat and throb, all belonged to the Great Mother, and called to him through her body. As he neared, she felt an overwhelming sadness seep from her heart, bleeding out a sorrow she did not recognise. She wished she could call out to him, to prevent him from some purpose or deed. She shook her head to try to clear herself from the trance but instead a wave of sheer bliss showered down, as if ocean sparkles were set free from her hair.

His body radiated its wrecked state and path of destruction, and the young Pythia realised that this coupling would herald the beginning of some new direction. She was unable to fathom its meaning or significance. A tiny flicker of identity called to the Mother for guidance and a surge of strength and love fed her courage. Pythia understood that sacrifice must sometimes be borne for the destiny of all things greater. She would endure, though may not wish to.

Vrados grimaced and furiously scratched at his body. His eyes were wild, tormented, the Okri having unleashed a wild inner turmoil. His arms bled from self-inflicted knife wounds of ceremonious stabbing. He stumbled. Truly chosen for Her holy lap?

"Mother I will perform for you the Rites which constitute my life. I will accomplish for You the Divine pattern," he slurred as training took hold.

Pythia responded accordingly, "I shall make for a good destiny; I shall make for him shepherd of the land."

In moments of clarity that indiscriminately filtered through his drunken haze, Vrados recognised he was in some state of possession and should be cautious. But these moments held no strength nor persuasion. Instead, he submitted to the ugly darkness, and watched himself, detached, grab the Divine incarnate. He ordered the Scribe assigned to witness Pythia's words for retrieval at the Speaking, to leave. As tradition required, he linked hands, but instead of laying her down on the flowers laid in the Temple for the Great Union, he led Pythia to the small antechamber behind the alter. Flushed by trance, she followed.

Divine presence overwhelmed Pythia as she succumbed to the sensations of skin, sweat, salt and now touch. In the distance, she heard a melodious paean, expressing triumph and thanksgiving to the Great Mother. She joined in with the poetic lyrics and opened her arms to embrace the Mother's Consort: for Earth, for all that was bountiful, fruitful and abundant. She opened her heart with that of the Divine to welcome the seed of life through Sacred Union. In her state of vulnerability, immersed in trance with lulled senses from the heady incense, burning offerings, the pound of drumming, singing, chanting and her own exhaustive frenzied dancing, she completely misread the moment and only smelt his violence seconds before he pulled her outreached arm, yanking her forcefully onto her feet.

Body and spirit separated from time and place, and she watched detached as he twisted her arm backwards, forcing her to turn around. Pain shot through her dulled senses, screaming into her shoulder. She struggled, trying to turn to face her lover, to look at Vrados, but he held her twisted arm tightly and she could hardly breathe, let alone move. Vrados released a deep guttural primordial growl that startled her. Who was this man? Thoughts scattered through her mind finding no peace.

Vrados tugged at her hair, loosening it from its flowers and pinning. He wrenched hard, pulling her head back as he gathered up a fistful of her hair in his clenched fist, and used it to smash her face down onto the altar's hard rock surface. She stopped struggling, blood spurting from her nose, her cheek-bone shattered on impact. Vrados was too strong, too intent on his own purpose. He lifted her slightly to bend her face-down over the altar. In her dazed state, Pythia saw there were no flowers laid here for their Union. With brute force,

Vrados penetrated her from behind, like a blunt instrument pounding at her soft flesh with animal brutality.

An image flickered. She latched onto it. The sun was shining. A walk. She was walking. Walking along the beach. A walk along the beach where she had first felt the Mother's presence. Strong. Powerful. On the pebbled beach. It was a long walk, when combined with a refreshing swim would easily take up most of a carefree afternoon. At the mouth of a small gorge, the sweet-water from underground springs mixed with seawater to create a palette of differing shades of cold. She could identify the coldest parts where the fresh spring water bubbled itself gently though capillaries under the seabed. It created a distortion in the water. Like a heat haze only wet. And cold.

Pythia succumbed to the clarity of the image. She remembered that day, a hot day following a stream of other hot days, without any breath of wind, her sweat running a river off her body. She had walked to her favourite place. She'd stripped off her robes. Then she had laid them over the stones, scorched hot from the unrelenting sun, to create a pathway to the water's edge. She'd kicked off her sandals and stepped carefully into the inviting ocean. Ahh … she could still feel that first sumptuous kiss on her skin; cool, refreshing, revitalising, washing away the sweat and grime and dust from her day's labours.

She swam, duck dived and floated, luxuriating in the coolness. Slow wide arm strokes, gentle lolling and bobbing around aimlessly in the turquoise clear waters. Her effortless buoyancy in water that was salty and pure, warm in some places, colder in others. She swam to the shore relaxed and spent, and lay down on her path of robes, now a make-shift bed. She could sense the Mother around her. Divinity filled her soul with light, warming her skin with sun and cooling her simultaneously with the water gently lapping at her ankles. She stretched out in a state of total bliss, at one with the heartbeat of land and sea and air.

Her soundtrack of wave-tumbled stones and pebbles was interrupted by a crunch underfoot. She had opened her eyes to see a youth looking down at her and she had felt the Mother's desire. It had surged through her belly and inner legs, a hot surge, wanting, and she stretched out in her naked-ness, welcoming his eye to appraise her body. She felt a throb-bing sensation, new to her then, from between her legs, and she felt for the first time the natural longing for Sacred Union.

She smiled at the youth, and he at her. He too had felt the Mother's connection and was erect at the prospect of fulfill-ing the passion, the power of Her desire. He deferred and waited for an invitation, and as Pythia held her arms open to receive him, he knelt on her robes, kissed her lips and licked her nipples. His tongue set off spasms of ticklish delight. She trembled and arched her back, her skin ignited with plea-sure. She slowly sat up and gently laid him on his back. She kissed and licked him teasing, playfully, before mounting him. Slipping him easily into her. Her delight deepened and their pleasure entwined in a rhythm of thrusting, rocking, clutching and holding. Groans borne from the deep sensa-tion building up through her body emerged from her lips, and they pressed harder together, until both gave way to panting, gasping, hanging tight together, moaning, until finally voicing the deep spasms released from her very core.

She experienced a wave wash over and through her. Her legs relaxed, as a tingling sensation rose from her toes and up her thighs, or perhaps it was down to her toes, and up and over and through her body until she was no longer solid matter but lightness and essence of salt and air and breath and flight. A shudder swept through her body returning its earthly heaviness. He lay, eyes closed smiling, panting, sated from their Union. She kissed him; he opened his eyes and returned her kiss.

She gently lifted herself over him and slipped back into the water. He joined her in the water's cool caress. They hugged in the water and gave thanks to the Great Mother Divine. Then, without speaking, they returned to the beach. He put on his loincloth, she her robe. They kissed again, kissed palms and he continued his way eastward. She felt immersed in the deep love borne from Union.

Sharp piercing pain returned her to the altar room. Pythia flitted between comforting blackness and white searing light. She bit hard on her bloodied lip preferring to draw blood than to scream out. Each thrust ripped her flesh. She closed her eyes and tried to absorb Vrados' cruelty in a distant chamber of her soul, the intense burning existing in some other reality.

She drifted out of body and hovered over their forms, watching with a distant regard as if they were shadow figures from another time. She witnessed his hate, his anger and the violence he used to rid his body of his own venom by ejecting into her. Her? She was unable to distinguish the object of his brutality. There would be no seed in Her womb. This act was not one of surrender but attack. On the Great Mother? Inconceivable. The struggle to make sense dimmed her mind and she felt him expel his liquid, wasted in her body. Her heart melted into the rough stone; his blasphemy tore shreds from her soul. Vrados was lost. He was empty and pitiful, devoid of spirit. He finished with a grunt.

Vrados awakened from his stupor upon ejaculation. He stared at the crumpled bloodied body in front of him. Vomit rose threatening to choke him. He paused before wiping the blood from his phallus, then sprinkled himself with holy water and unconsciously started to chant his mantra of Sacred Union to the Great Mother. He stopped. There were no thanks. No gratitude. No blessing. He awakened to the destructive force of his actions. The urgent need to leave propelled him forward. He picked up his jug of Okri and returned to his compound.

Pythia's Scribe had remained outside the Temple and on seeing Vrados leave, entered the chamber to discover her mistress bleeding and dazed, possibly still in trance. As trained, she memorised everything spoken. It was not her role to judge the violation. She wiped away her tears to listen carefully to the words dribbling from Pythia's swollen lips. When the mumbling ceased, she sought out the elder Crone Pythia.

They returned to the chamber to sprinkle holy water and gently bathed Pythia's broken, battered body. In a state of incomprehension and distress, for the Crone Pythia had never witnessed such violation, she placed her hands over the young woman to ward off the disease of despair and shame. The presence of the Great Mother lingered amongst the blood.

"This one," she whispered, "this one we cherish for her courage, suffering and sacrifice."

The Crone Pythia turned to the Scribe, "Call me when your mistress is ready to interpret."

Two rising suns later the elder woman returned to Pythia's cot and the Scribe repeated the words of Divine. At times, Pythia asked the Scribe to repeat, and at other times to pause, to give her some space for her thoughts to make sense of it. The Crone Pythia sat quietly despite the chilling oracle received.

"What will you do with this information?" she asked Pythia, aware that the young woman was in transition to replace her in Service of the Great Mother.

Pythia shook her head slightly. The older woman looked at her young successor. She took her hands and kissed her palms. She removed her charmed neck beads, gold ring with its sacred seal and silver wrist cuffs. These she placed by the young woman. Pythia gingerly raised herself on her cot and the two women gently embraced.

"You have guided us well, mother," Pythia lisped through swollen lips.

The older woman replied, "I have been honoured by the Great Mother. From the Mother, I am all things alive, all things in form."

She sprinkled more holy water over Pythia, blessing her. "Nurture life. Walk in love and beauty. Trust the knowledge that comes through body, and hesitate not to speak truth. Take only what you need. Practice generosity."

She paused and swallowed. "The oracle of your Sacred Union reveals your destiny. Great Mother will hold you and guide you. Maintain an open heart. The seeds of your destiny will set the path for generations to follow. We are born of infinity and eternity, boundless presence and sacred source. These are challenging times and we all must find new ways to navigate its often-choppy waters. But these are also times of birth and renewal, deep wisdom and insights and life anew. We are never alone, never cast out from Divine source of all things."

'How can one cast out the wind?' Pythia thought.

The Crone took her hands and said, "When you are ready, I will gladly preside over your communion and we shall join together in dance."

Pythia slowly answered, "I extoll your wisdom and honour your connection that has led us in ceremony, maintaining the rhythm of seasons."

She stopped to take a proper breath. She closed her eyes. Talking was difficult and the exertion drained her energy. Finally, Pythia looked up and whispered, "I will dance with delight at the Serpents Festa. I will couple with, and for, and as Great Mother, flesh of Our Mother."

She tried to raise herself but was too weak. Her crushed cheekbone and tilted voice through the one side of her mouth caused her words to sound like a hiss of a snake.

"The Sacred is embodied, and within this body shall Sacred

Authority reside. But together we will listen and guide all in harmony with Mother Divine."

Pythia paused while the Scribe gently took a corner of her tunic and wiped the dribble from her chin.

Addressing the Crone, she repeated her words, "My self is not confined to my body. It extends into all things I have and all things around me. From the Mother, I am all things alive, all things in form."

As the Crone left the room, Pythia looked to her Scribe.

"That last section. Again," she sputtered.

The Scribe closed her eyes and repeated the words Pythia had spoken while in trance.

The new age is born through us, we do not enter it. But I shall destroy all that I have created. My body shall appear once again as ocean. I am that which shall remain, after I have changed myself back into a Serpent.

Vrados remained away for the seasons of Sun and Harvest, returning only when the winds had whipped the waves into a fury and coldness had snuck into the bones of the old people. Olive tree prunings were fuelling fires to warm the hearth. It was nearing dark when he arrived at the harbour, the post-solstice moon restraining itself to a faded glow through clouded drifts.

"Pythia, Pythia" gasped a young Select, her words

scrambling breathlessly from her run up the hill laden with news. "The Consort has returned. The Consort is back. He's back!"

The Crone Pythia and Pythia had chosen not to tell anyone about the night of Sacred Union. Pythia had healed slowly from her ordeal and once she could perform her Temple duties, had taken on her full mantle of responsibilities. Only three women shared the dark secret of his hideous violence. Pythia had anticipated Vrados' return and requested they not refer to the incident. He was still the Great Mother's Consort, after all.

On receiving confirmation of his arrival, Pythia walked with several women from the Temple down to the village to acknowledge his return. By the time Pythia descended the hill, the whole village had turned out to greet Vrados. The cold night air and approaching darkness did not diminish their joy at receiving their prodigal son and Mother's Consort. They left their compounds to line the path from the port and filled the central platia to welcome him.

The procession from boat to town centre was like a carnival. Whilst Vrados had slipped away quietly after the Sacred Union rites, he now returned as if a conquering lord. Arrogance masked any pretence of a humble entry from the harbour. Mules and oxen led the way with carts filled with incense, spices, silks and cloths. Vrados had gained weight and his girth fell over his kilt. A purple cloak adorned with gold lacing draped over his shoulder. He led an entourage that included his younger brother Kastos and other family members. Beside him walked four young petite women, with their heads lowered but who glanced up now and again at the large gathering. The women wore robes of various shades of blue with gold trimming and their coiffure adornment and jewels transmitted a sense of opulence and prosperity. Together, they were a composition of richly dressed and lavishly bejewelled figures.

Vrados strode forward greeting the villagers all and sundry with a loud bellowing voice. "I have returned," he proclaimed.

Pythia, in her role as Chief Administrator of the village stepped forward. She looked him in the eye, sole witness to his slight falter.

"Consort, the Great Mother welcomes your return."

Vrados regained his composure. She could see he was annoyed that he had betrayed his thoughts at the sight of her. She watched him carefully. He returned her gaze, and she felt him searching for some indication, or residue in her demeanour of his violation. His eyes took in her scars and he frowned slightly. He turned to the woman at his side and spat out an introduction.

"I have returned with a wife," he said, "I present to you Shari, Queen for the village."

"You are Consort to the Great Mother, that is not necessary," Pythia replied, "but we welcome all women to Her Temple."

"No," replied Vrados. "She is not of our ways and will not accompany you to the Temple. This woman is mine and will live under my roof and bear my seed to fruition. The children born will be my children."

A buzz of overlapping conversations coloured with confusion

saturated the air. The villagers turned to each other, puzzled by his words. A pervasive darkness swirled around their collective thoughts; what does this bode? Has the Anointed One become foreign from his time away? Is he not the Consort? Perhaps the distance travelled has brought a mind sickness.

Pythia listened to the murmurings search for explanations for his comments. She watched as Vrados wove his words, seeking control to secure his position in the eyes of the people. She barely registered his promise to the villagers.

"As leader and Consort, I undertake the establishment of a Shrine for the Mother Divine, right here in the Platia. It will be built in harmony with the movements of celestial bodies." He raised his arms to the night sky and stars. "It will capture their place tonight, so the forces of the natural world are accessible to all. This Shrine will complement the Temple. Her altar will honour all the spirits of the landscape, to propitiate and appease them and provide access to those powers for visiting pilgrims."

The Oracle's words filled Pythia's head:

The ocean whispers of change riding a high tide. Those with evil and empty words, speak dishonour and contempt. The shift to property of seed, the claiming of commodities, will enshrine paradigms of false economy.

This shift will falter only as the earth warms and old knowledge returns to claim its natural connection. You are to birth a new day. Through your blood, hope will be reborn in a time of balance and equilibrium. Until then, much sorrow will flow.

Pythia turned from Vrados to address the women beside him, "You are welcome to the Temple of the Great Mother."

The women stared at her blankly and moved closer towards each other.

'Not of our tongue, not of our ways', thought Pythia as she watched closely the one he called wife. Pythia saw she was fearful. She was a child in a maiden's form. Pythia smiled warmly and held out her hand in welcome. The other women behind the young woman giggled nervously. Vrados spoke to them in a foreign tongue and the young woman reached out her slim hand to Pythia.

Vrados gathered his robes and leaned in to address Pythia quietly. "Here we sow the seeds of a new way of living, planted in the sacred ground of our being and watered with full awareness. We are no longer bound by desires that keep us running exhausted toward craving. Nor are we beholden to our demand for gratification at every turn. We can unhook from all of that, instead connecting, with the deepest movements of the soul which, until now, were hidden from view."

"The inner journey is vital if we want to recalibrate desire to better reflect our core-essence," Pythia agreed. "A time of insight and understanding to better perceive what motivates the choices we make is needed."

"Pythia," he breathed in as he leaned closer. It felt almost intimate and tinged with familiarity.

She frowned. He abruptly straightened back, upright. She saw he was uncomfortable.

Vrados coughed. "You are not travelled. You do not know how things are in the world. When I left to explore foreign lands, seeking new trade and knowledge," he coughed again. "I gathered wisdom, and learnt far more than what we have previously spoken of."

She thought he looked exposed, but he quickly regained his posture.

"Many things differ from our experience. Now, upon my return I am responsible to introduce changes to sustain our community. We will continue to flourish and prosper. I do this as King of this land not just Great Mother's Consort."

Her reply was a quick retort.

"King?" she snorted. "Of this land? What is this 'king of this land?' The land as you call Her is Mother Divine. You are of the land, correct, but king? Do you, mere mortal male, think, nay believe, you have some sort of an entitlement? That you are more than who you are? Come next rites your blood shall nourish the soil as all Consorts' blood has done. What say you?"

She gave him no time to reply.

"Land, Earth, Mother, all is one. What are you? You are flesh and blood of Her making. She who chose you, anointed you. You who..." Pythia paused. Her anger seared with heat and intensity, but she maintained a low almost inaudible level of volume to accuse him, "You who," she continued, "contaminated Her consummation. Wasted your seed and abused Her chosen vessel."

Vrados admired her courage, her strength. "We both know I am to bring change to the village. A powerful force guides me. Great Mother or perhaps another God."

He let this last statement hang in the air. His words were provocative.

"I no longer seek to block out the dark and confusing pathways of my wandering mind. You always told me to accept my destiny, from which I could not detour. Well, I now acknowledge the wisdom of your words. For, Pythia," his voice lowered, "We are all guided by the Great Mother in one way or another. If we are not mindful, we may feel great resistance to the message, for She places vast responsibilities at our feet, which could feel like blame."

He waited for her nod of acknowledgement before emphasising his point.

"Our destiny in Her hands heeds no mortal judgment."

She could not refute this. The Divinity of the Great Mother was not up for question or debate. He knew this. But what he didn't know was that Pythia had already divined the changes he implied. She had seen a tidal wave of terror and bloodshed across the country and beyond. He was not to know that he was one of many messengers. Her concern was his haste.

"Your reverence for the Mother is undermined by your emphasis on your own power and identity. A sickness has crept upon you. It poisons your sight and thoughts with illusion. Your song is discordant. You are but a fish in the sea demanding to see the ocean," she answered.

"The Mother will be as She always has been, it is the mind of the people that will change," he replied.

Pythia shook her head, as sadness filled her heart. 'He does not see that he is longing for his own destruction.'

"Consort," she said, "I understand your intention, but for the harmony of the community, I beseech a slower journey. Let us ensure all unite in this time of transition and in the direction ordained by the Great Mother. Follow Her Divine path, rather than the illusion you allude to. Walk beside me if you must, but keep the community together in adapting to these changes that you hope will grow and benefit them."

Vrados blinked and stared at her. Pythia knew her apparent acquiescence would surprise him. He would not have expected anything but confrontation. He nodded, but seemed cautious as if walking into a trap and answered bluntly. "The Mother will determine."

He turned and motioned his entourage to keep moving. Pythia watched as he walked through the crowd, shaking hands and kissing palms of those lined to welcome him back. His new wife, the other women, his brother and family members, followed him. Pythia turned to head back up the hill to the Temple.

The villagers stayed in the narrow lanes until his compound gates closed, and then they too returned to their hearths, filled with the gossip of his return to share at the fireside with those too young, too old or too frail to have attended.

CHAPTER SEVEN

Pythia stood up and stretched. These memories had held her captive far too long and she wanted nothing more than to return to the Temple, but she had yet to receive guidance from the Great Mother. She looked down at the village to Vrados' Shrine. Vrados had engaged the most skilful artisans to create this glorious building. Even though it was a true work of art, she thought it lacked heart. Vrados had none to give it substance. Pythia longed for the day his name would not touch her heart. She recalled their last conversation. It was just before the Ritual of Sacred Union. A full cycle ago. How quickly the seasons had moved toward this time of departure.

It was the first Sacred Union she was to ordain as Pythia. Memories from last season had begun to interrupt her sleep, her daydreams and meditations. How was she to face this celebration of the Mother with open heart to couple with the Consort? Would he seek to destroy her? His force, his brutality, his evil? Pythia had been scared for the first time in her life. It was an unfamiliar feeling and she did not like it. Did this mean she was unworthy of the Great Mother? She sought counsel from the Crone Pythia who reassuringly kissed her palm and let the younger woman openly name her fear.

After listening, the Crone Pythia said to her, "Child, I can only advise that you are a vessel of the Mother. It does not serve you to look forward to ascertain what She has for you. Nor be held by the past from what has already gone. But stay, weep out this erosion of your soul, it serves no purpose. Let me massage you. Stay awhile, bathe in Her waters, soak in Her beauty and accede to the Mother, for you will embody our Mother and open for the Mother. You will do as She requires. Your flimsy protestations have no place in the greatness of it all. Turn within and make your peace with the Divine."

Strengthening her resolve, Pythia decided to visit Vrados' compound the day after the Rites of Renewal, two suns before Sacred Union. She sought an audience with the women residing in the compound, hoping to explain the rituals and celebrations of Sacred Union. She did not want to meet with Vrados, nor debate his edicts. Vrados, whilst respectful, refused to cooperate.

"It is a shared domain here in this compound," he informed her, "between Great Mother and their Gods. In all due respect Pythia, the Mother does not guide these women. You have no purpose here."

"I hear your words, Consort, but they do not speak a language I am familiar with," she replied. "These women live on this land, live within the Great Mother's embrace. It is expected they pay homage."

"That may be, but I have learnt lessons bestowed from the

Mother," he reminded her, asserting his authority, "and of course, with your understanding, will be implementing such adjustments as necessary. Some of which we have already seen. These women will retain the worship of their gods."

He sat relaxed on silken cushions, luxuriating in an air of arrogance. Having successfully vanquished a younger rival at the Rites of Renewal, the scent of smugness pervaded the room. Try as she might Pythia could not find any trace of the young boy she used to know. This relieved her.

"We have just witnessed a wondrous change." He paused and looked at the group of men sitting around the room. Pythia having declined his invitation to sit, remained standing in the hope she would not be detained for long and could meet with the women.

"My victory confirms the Great Mother's intentions. Beforehand..." he waved his hand in the air, "the young men selected as Her lovers may have impregnated Her but they were only phallic companions, drones serving the queen bee, killed off once they performed their duty. Consorts were more pet than lover. Before, it was the youthful phallus and its rampant sexuality that was revered. Flower-like boys unable to resist the power of the Mother. For She, full of desire, chose boys of beauty and roused their sexuality — the initiative was never theirs. Moreover, they were always the victim, dying like adored flowers. These youths were weak, living only a ritual existence."

A collective intake of breath harnessed the shock in the room. The Consort's entourage would not look at each other. Ritual was their lifeblood: the bridegroom god dies a sacrificial death, and resurrected three days later at Sacred Union. This cycle brings fertility to the land, renewing it through death and rebirth. Pythia observed their vexation and heard their thinking as if spoken.

Eyristhenis was never a flower-boy.

Vrados speaks a tongue unknown. His words chagrin my ears, perturbs my heart.

He speaks as the youth; he still is foreign in his mind.

Vrados seemed oblivious to their discomfort.

'Or,' thought Pythia, 'ignoring it.'

She interjected, no longer willing to listen to his slander. "She is the Mother of all that has been born and will be born. Your power seems to be influenced from foreign soil," she spat out. "It will not serve you well. You seem driven by distortion. You are isolating your mind in its own sphere, severing your oneness with Mother. Your alienation is to be pitied, not lauded."

She continued, aware of the men watching her.

"There is no integrity in your leadership. The absence of Rites will develop toxins. You disturb the natural progression of our being. Our youth will lack passage into the world and will have trouble facing the demands of life, adapting to community. Without our true Rites, connection will falter and there will be much adversity. Sickness will dominate the soul."

'As it has yours,' she thought.

Her words echoed, filling the room. "Consort, this path

you seek, will be littered with the debris of human affliction. It is corruption you bequeath."

Vrados chortled. The men said nothing, silenced by their own inadequacy. Not one of them found the courage to support Pythia.

"Yes, yes," Vrados answered. "Have I not spoken plainly? Let me explain it to you. I have decreed amendments as the Mother Divine has directed. We have now witnessed the Rites of Renewal replaced with combat. I have fought the claimant and consolidated my position. Had I been defeated, I would then been sacrificed, but I am victorious and my opponent has been honoured. The land has drunk the blood it craves and needs no resurrection."

No one felt it opportune to comment that the claimant, a slender youth selected by the Consort, had appeared at the combat somewhat stunned and seemingly unable to focus on the battle at hand. His death had been quick. His body carried to the altar stone and bled according to tradition, with Pythia carrying out the necessary libations.

"I have been gifted with a vision I need to share with you. With you all." Vrados smirked at his seated companions. "Our sacrifices to the Great Mother, our offering of blood at these Rites, will no longer be human, but an offering of a mighty beast. A Sacred beast."

'He has no intention of having to face a younger and potentially stronger buck every year.' Pythia thought.

Disbelief flooded the room. Mouths dropped open, heads shook and an involuntary gasp registered the impact of Vrados' words. He ignored them all.

"We will honour the Great Mother with Sacred Bulls and Boars and Goats. The blood of men shall no longer flow from her altar. By Her decree, Her Consort shall be enduring."

Pythia remained motionless, her heart seething, but she said nothing. Vrados filled the silent space. "What say you Pythia? The Great Mother has also guided you in the light of these changing times, has She not?"

"I would tell it clearly, but all truths are not good to say," Pythia replied.

Vrados' smile delivered a stab. "And now we have the Ritual of Sacred Union upon us; Consort and Great Mother."

He watched Pythia for signs of vulnerability. She did not flinch. He bared his teeth like a wolf.

"There we sow the seeds of prosperity, planted in the sacred ground of our being. This is a time to connect with the deepest movements of the soul. Is it not?"

Pythia looked at him. She tasted his scorn, his abject contempt.

"You are not separate from the Earth, human or non-human, as object," she replied. "You are flesh of the Earth — a living being, sensing and being sensed. If you shake my hand, your hand both touches and is touched. The two experiences cannot be separated."

Vrados tensed. His eyes flashed, before settling back into the steely gaze that was now familiar to her.

She walked towards the door. She stopped and turned to face him.

"Be that self which you truly are," she said. She returned to the Temple without having spoken with the women.

Sacred Union (Vrados)

It was a stunning night. The heat of the day ambled into balmy, amatory ambience. The pits were alight with offerings, smoke drifting and circling swaying bodies. Heady incense perfumed the air and as the drumming seduced his heart to beat in unison, Vrados stood entranced, every cell absorbing the power and energy around him. Pythia's song of welcome and blessings intoxicated him.

He watched her, arms akimbo, silhouetted from the fire's blaze, standing tall, beautiful. His heart leapt. He swam in his instincts like an animal. He watched her dance as she succumbed to trance and the Great Mother's presence. He could feel the heat and desire of her loins as she turned and looked at him.

Vrados could not avert his eyes. He watched Pythia's features shift before him. Her eyes flickered, rotating forward, fixing upon him as if he were prey. Her gaze penetrated to his core and claimed him. Her long fixed stare transformed into a serpents discerning appraisal. Her hair found form, rising up as a mass of writhing snakes, hissing and spitting. Ready to strike.

Vrados trembled, reduced to nothingness amidst such power. The Mother sneered. A garland of skulls and a skirt of dismembered arms rustled, adorning her darkened form. Transfixed, Vrados became spirit, and in his purest state, witnessed Her truth: She was the changing aspect of nature that brings all things to life or death.

Vrados saw in Her fearsome form his own demise. She was

a fearful destroyer riding on the black night of death. She was Mother Divine, from which all of creation arises and into which all of creation will eventually dissolve.

He lay prostrate before Her.

Pythia called for him.

On soundwaves held tight by air, her voice pulsated deep into his being.

"Come," she compelled him. "Consecrate your devotion. Harmonise your heart and body. Embrace Truth borne from Union. Honour the power of the Divine."

His ears filled with a rhapsody of voices serenading verse and poetry. His blood throbbed, ravished by the euphoria snaking through his veins. Filled with joyous abandon, his flesh tingled, his phallus erect, answering the Divine. He moved towards Her, to co-join and fulfil the sacred yearning that flushed through his body.

Vrados had intended to maintain control to orchestrate this Sacred Union, but all was lost in his exaltation as deity.

His words rose above the waves of ecstasy enveloping him:

I give myself to one Truth. To the Divine Mother who nourishes all that breathes,

One Earth, the Mother of us all, and in one Womb wherein all are begotten, and wherein all shall rest,

Blessed in the living season: Her fruits in abundance, Mystery of Mystery: in Her name, and in the Serpent and the Lion,

Mystery of Mystery: Light, Life, Love

The drummers held the rhythm as the dancers moved in unconscious synchronicity that was a community default position shared with termite nests, flocks of birds, schools of fish. There was one common flow, one common breath inherently interwoven and interdependent, forming together the one nature, being and non-being.

Sacred Union (Pythia)

As Pythia spun to the percussion of drums, a golden thread of light grew bright, chasing her, circling her, turning her around and around, faster and faster until it spun a cocoon of light around her, eclipsing out the shadows and colours and textures of the world. Spinning, circling, swirling, until she became a quiver of golden glow. As she slowed her pace, swaddled in woven light, she gently, as a fluttering ribbon, folded down into the soft cushioned palm of the Mother, who, closing Her hand into pillowed flesh, formed a clenched fist. Safe and protected within strength and might, the light slowly dissolved, rippling lightly away on an ethereal breath.

When Pythia opened her eyes, it was to a softened pre-dawn. Beside her sat her Scribe. She smelt the perfumed flowers lightly crushed under her. She breathed in their scent, blissfully unaware of the night's celebrations and revelry.

The smell of flowers was strong then, strong now. Pythia inhaled the pleasing whiff of wild thyme as the heat-soaked soil gave up its perfume bruised from the day's warmth. The last pink hue of the sky morphed into deep purple and the sun slipped through satin haze. The moon was only a promise away.

One more promise, Pythia confirmed. The Great Mother's work will then begin.

Pythia stretched, creating space for contentment. She was ready. From the time of Vrados' return, her preparations had begun in earnest. As the closure of day settled into dusk, Pythia closed her eyes. Her heart warmed as she brought the smiling face of a young child to mind. Ashtar had played an important role in those preparations. From the very outset, the Mother had plans for Ashtar.

CHAPTER EIGHT

Ashtar

Ashtar woke to hushed tones interrupting nightfall. Ashtar's lids creased into her cheek, too heavy to keep open to listen. She did not sense any tension or urgency. Mam's soft step roused her. Ashtar tasted nectar on her lips and heard her Mam's gentle reassurance. Sitting up, she rubbed her eyes and got out of her cot, as asked. Mam reached for her cloak.

"And your sandals."

Ashtar saw Pythia cloaked for travel standing by the door. Now dressed for the night, as Ashtar walked towards her, Pythia turned and left the house. Ashtar looked up at her mother whose smile did not quite conceal her anxiety. Ashtar followed Pythia, quietly closing the door behind her.

She struggled to keep up with the long strides of the tall, slender woman, only managing to catch up when they reached the harbour. Bobbing alongside the dock was a small caïque, and Ashtar could see a hooded figure. She stared with naïve curiosity.

"Come."

She did as told and stepped into the craft. The dark night held no whisper of wind. The oarsman was strong and soon the rhythm of movement lulled the girl back to sleep. She snuggled into the flowing folds of Pythia's cloak, resting her head in the older woman's lap.

Ashtar woke from a gentle but persistent shaking. The soft pink and yellow tinges of dawn had just slipped through the night's disguise. Ashtar could see the shadow of land to her right. Land mass rose high, alluring, magnificent. Pythia touched her shoulder and then quickly, with a small stretch of cloth, bound her eyes.

"You need to become familiar. It needs to be done quickly," Pythia instructed.

Ashtar sat blindfolded, allowing her other senses to come to the fore. The craft had now changed direction, and Ashtar could feel a slight swell helping the boat move along. An amiable breeze offered coolness on the somewhat balmy morning.

The small caïque dragged its bottom along grated sand and came to a stop. Waves, small as the movement of milk licked by a kitten, responded lazily to the south wind's call and lapped the shore.

Pythia stood Ashtar up and slipped off her cloth dress. Strong hands from behind effortlessly lifted her up then lowered her beside the caïque. The hands were large and patient, waiting until she had gained her footing after the cool impact of water. The height of the swell came up to her knees. The sand was gravelly underfoot with a few larger pebbles, smooth from a lifetime of the water's persistent rub at their edges. She sunk further into the stones, almost tumbling between current and shifting sands. Regaining her balance, Ashtar walked through the sinking pebbles onto smaller sand grit. This too was not capable of holding her weight so she continued walking further up until the dampness gave way to a small shelf of larger pebbles. Still smooth and cool but no longer wet or slave to her weight, Ashtar was able to walk without sinking. Two steps past the pebbles she was on firm dry sand.

'All in all,' Ashtar concluded, 'five steps to tide.'

Even without sight, Ashtar knew that the landing had taken place in a small cove with black sand. Some rocks, yes to the left of the cove, but maybe not enough to threaten craft. She waited on firmer ground. She felt Pythia beside her and the dry cloth of her dress handed to her. She slipped into it.

Ashtar felt Pythia's hands around her waist leaving the weight of a thin rope on her hips. She waited. She could hear the caïque dragged as far as the tidemark. She heard the oarsman walking up the slope of the shore, returning with a lighter almost silent step. She felt a small quick tug at her waist and stepped forward in its direction. For a while, she held onto the rope with her small hands trying to feel the rhythm of the walking motion. She did not want to be pulled like a hesitant donkey. She aspired to predict or sense the pace and direction and to lessen her reliance on the rope. Up the sand hill until it levelled out and then turning to her right, land on her left, she walked around the curve of the shoreline.

Ashtar knew counting steps was a waste of time. The craft

could land anywhere along the small cove. Her feet were to be her eyes and the song of the sea, her direction. Sand gave way to smaller rocks and some pebbles. The pace slowed and the rope became aligned vertically rather than horizontal. Higher, she was walking higher up from the shore. Ashtar put her hands out to feel into nothingness. The side of her foot scraped on an unseen boulder. Slower now, along a flattened stone with, now and again, larger stones that bit at her feet. The rope guided upwards, winding along into a deeper darkness — the shadow of the land and the coolness of condensation.

She had learnt if she kept the rope directly central, taut and straight, it was less painful. She had already stumbled over jutting rocks. Many, many journeys would be required to teach her. She hoped she would not disappoint Pythia or Great Mother.

The slope grew steeper into a cliff front with a wall of solid rock to her left. Small shrubs scratched at her ankles. Thyme: she inhaled deeply, breathing in the scent. As she walked, she listened carefully to the waves confiding the range from the cove. Eventually the conspiracy of land and distance muffled their sound.

Ashtar felt the trees before she smelt them. The sun was not yet high enough to cast shadows, but she felt an intangible presence of cool comfort. She inhaled deeply and a cleansing savour of pine replaced the ocean's saltiness. Pine needles underfoot were a welcome change from the harsh path of rocks and stones.

The rope slackened and Ashtar lingered. The trees, aware

of her intrusion and unfamiliar with humans, initially held tight their murmurings. Ashtar opened her heart revealing her vulnerability. Recognising the Divinity within her, the trees shook out their glittering leaves and shyly began to share their stories. They confided of the bees that rarely ventured this way but would spread their dust of other far-off wanderings when they did. Of the wild long horned goats who stood on two legs in search of sweet leaves with their tongues twisting around and devouring their lowest branches, and who drank from the source and the purity of Mother's blood, which nourished and nurtured them from sapling to crone. Lastly, they shared the secret that lay deep at their roots in the womb of the Mother. Ashtar stood quietly, respectfully listening to their gentle conversation, lulled into a blissful state, happy and content, despite her bloodied feet.

The rope remained limp as she and Pythia walked as one. They turned around to walk along the secret path of the trees, down a slight gully until Ashtar could hear the soft underground humming rising to the surface as a spring of life. She dipped her hands to receive the Mother's blessing.

Ashtar waited for guidance. As Pythia removed the cloth, she blinked into the sunlight and looked around. To her left the cliff rose high, not as steep as earlier but now with pine and cypress trees dotted around large boulders and rocks. To her right the land gently sloped, giving distance to its own descent into a gully, another hill and finally, as Ashtar already knew, the sea. This area was sheltered. Pine needles

strewed disorderly on the ground, the wind held at bay by
the curve of the land.

Ashtar took the flask Pythia offered and filled it with the
cool sweet-water. Once done she followed Pythia back along
the track to where they had begun their journey. She greedily eyed her surroundings trying to match the physical sensation with her sight. Returning to the cove, Pythia bound her
eyes again. With the rope at her waist, Ashtar repeated her
training practice on this first section of the trail several times.
On the last trip from the spring, Ashtar stumbled more often,
exhaustion dictating her stability. She was happy when they
returned to the caïque, and gladly accepted a piece of bread.
Munching quietly, she sat concentrating, retracing her steps,
the path, smells and sounds. She was grateful the trees had
shared their confidences.

On the homeward journey, Ashtar remained alert despite
her tiredness. She marvelled in awe of the cliffs propensity to rise directly out of the sea; brutal, sheer, rock-face,
wrinkled only by the worn paths of wild goats. Green shrubs
hugged on tightly with roots that spread wildly to maintain
a semblance of stability. They passed tiny pockets of beaches,
some pebbled, some sand, many at the mouths of huge gorges,
splits in the land, many offering possible entry into the vast
coastline.

Looking back westward beyond the cove where they had
beached, she saw layers of promontory lining up, each reaching further than its predecessor out to sea, each becoming a
lighter shade of blue until the very last point was lost into the
sea mist where horizon and sky melded. The setting sun sent

sparkles racing across the ocean. Ashtar shielded her eyes as her gaze travelled towards the horizon and back to the land. The mountain crags to her left with their hidden gorges and caves remained stoic against the slight onshore breeze.

Ashtar sighed. She hoped she had pleased the Great Mother, but even at her tender age, she knew there would be more challenges. There were new scents to learn and a heightened sensing that, with the language of the rocks and trees, were all needed to be known to become firm friends. This would take time and patience. Despite praise, her stubbed toes and bleeding knees taunted that she had not been good enough. Only the residue aroma of oleander now remained. She lost herself in the fragrance as the craft slid along the water's surface.

It seemed to Ashtar the caïque was heading into the tide, but the oarsman was strong and the journey, though long, was swift. Ashtar watched as he ploughed through the water. He had not spoken once throughout the journey and remained hooded. She saw how his muscled arms worked hard, a slight twitch and a release before tightening again as he rowed on. She did not dare to stare too long. Child as she was, there were still the necessities of respect.

She knew from the scars on his arm he was one of the Great Mother's Galli. That he had sacrificed his phallus to Her, buried it deep within her womb to nourish Her, and despite never seeing him without his hooded cloak, knew that he was hairless as an ongoing statement of his life's pledge.

Ashtar had witnessed the sacred ceremony of the Galli held two suns after the Ritual of Sacred Union. On the Day of Blood, the Galli who led the ceremony drew blood from his arms as an offering to the Mother Divine. Other young men whirled madly to the music of cymbals, drums and flutes, slashing themselves to splatter Her altar with their blood. Ashtar had stood with her mother and other Temple women clapping hands accompanying the rite. She had watched stunned as men castrated themselves during the frenzied dancing. Many threw their testicles as an offering at the foot of Her statue.

Ashtar's mother explained that their act of sacrifice was like the bee. When the bee drone had finished coupling with the queen, his organ was torn from his body as he pulled away. The drone died of his wounds. These men, after Sacred Union with the Mother, tore off their phallus in respect to the Mother, surrendering their coupling to only Her. The honour of Sacred Union was great and many men died like the bees, with their flesh and blood fertilising the fields. Some however survived and lived to serve as Galli. Like the oarsman. He devoted himself to the Great Mother. Ashtar had already seen that he seemed able to converse with the Great Mother through Pythia. Between them, they did not need words to communicate.

Ashtar never learned the oarsman's name, nor did she ever speak to him, even though he accompanied her to the cove every second night of the moon cycle. Once familiar with the journey, she often rowed herself the distance. Her main task was to become intimate with the new land, to learn its language of rock and beast. Then she would be responsible to teach the route to some of the Select and to start transporting supplies under the cover of night. Male elders would not miss the presence of a young child.

On this first night of Ashtar's training, Pythia had sat in the craft and observed the young girl lost in her thoughts. Without exposing the stirrings of her heart, Pythia felt blessed that the Great Mother had selected Ashtar. The child was smart, quick to learn. She had stumbled many times and now bore the markings of failure on bloodied knees. She had not cried out, but stood up, re-focused, smelt for any fragrance in the air and listened.

Pythia noted that the child had waited patiently until confident to move on. At one point, Pythia observed Ashtar picking up a rock. She had rolled it sideways listening carefully to its journey over and down the cliff face. Her face had paled when she understood the distance down the gorge. However, she composed herself and refused to let fear dictate or confine her learning.

'Yes,' Pythia thought, 'the child will do well.'

Cressida roused. There was a sense of familiarity she did not understand. A wave of disorientation set her adrift momentarily. Confusion furrowed her brow. With no explanation to hold her attention, she slipped easily back into drowsiness, but not before noticing a faint outline of a dream emerging.

Oh no, not this.

Ashtar used all her strength to push the small craft into the water, then jumped in and started rowing the boat. Her arms still ached from the repetition of this task. The caïque was laden with woven baskets filled with livestock to take to the new site. They weighed the craft down onerously and although the ocean was presently calm, Ashtar fervently hoped she would get to her destination before the storm hit. At her tender age, she had however miscalculated the difference a heavy load would make. Regardless of her pleas for a stay of conditions, or her mighty effort to navigate the craft to the cove in good time, she found herself desperately clinging to the oars trying to maintain balance while being tossed around by the mounting fervour of both sky and sea. Her arms burned as she rowed as hard and fast as she could.

The huge swell of the ocean rose to taunt the sky as the elements competed against each other. She was insignificant flotsam to their force, stuck amid their escalating battle. Wave upon wave of water and shrill surging air locked together in a haphazard, volatile embrace, screaming and sneering in rivalry. The caged birds and animals screeched in terror and their frantic movements threatened to overturn the small craft. Ashtar hung on tightly, knuckles white, sweat of her effort lost into salty drenched air that she would breathe in only to spit out into the rising crescendo of spray and rain. A lurking fear of uncertainty grew bolder. Finally, riding high on a foamy crest, she glimpsed the familiar cove looming ahead. The sight renewed her strength and, despite feeling overwhelmed by the immensity of the storm and the size of the waves catapulting her around, Ashtar gained confidence.

She prayed to the Great Mother to help guide her through the tempest. Relying on faith and sheer determination, she managed to navigate between the massive outcrops of rock that threatened to smash her craft as a mere afterthought.

In the relative safety of the cove with her strength draining, she struggled to row to the shore. The caïque, like a nag, knew the way home and rode the waves to safety. When Ashtar finally felt the seabed and craft gravel together in greeting, she jumped out. Using her last reserve of energy, she pulled the craft further up from the tide line before collapsing, drenched and gasping for air, exhausted and grateful to feel the wet black sand beneath her.

Cressida moaned. The silky tones of the woman's lilting rhythm did not falter and flowed effortlessly from one narrative into another.

Our separate stories are a common story. I know your story by knowing my own; I know my story by knowing yours.

It seemed as if the images on the cave walls shimmered around her.

The crackling of pinecones opening in the heat were enough of an enticement for Ashtar to pause. The earthen pot she carried was heavy. She wriggled her shoulders to adjust the pot strapped across her back so she could better manage the climb up the cliff face. The route had become easier as it had become more familiar. Sometimes, if her load was light, she would feel like she had just started out on the path, only to arrive at the site before even the raptors caught a whiff of her travels. She knew every turn and scramble. She knew how to pace the flat sections with those that were ascending. Reaching the larger rocks, she turned northward, knowing the village site was nigh. Ashtar could recognise if there had been a wind since her last visit, or if there had been any rain or even goats wandering the path. It held its own narrative and Ashtar delighted in its stories.

With her training complete, Ashtar and a group of young Select would beat a steady path to the new village site, carrying supplies in earthen jugs and vessels. Ashtar would try to guess what was in them by their weight and knew to be cautious if it were liquid. Several of the young women had over-balanced and almost fallen down the cliff from the weight swilling around. Oil was especially heavy. Ashtar had carried oil and cloths and ropes, as well as saplings for the orchards, olive trees, orange, lemon, laurel and sycamore figs. The saplings and herbs all had their sacred purpose be it for oils, medicine, teas or resin.

There was an air of excitement amidst the secrecy in

setting up the new village. Pythia had mapped it with detailed consideration and Ashtar walked the layout by heart. In early days of settlement, many of the caves in the cliffs would provide shelter for sleeping and sacred space for rites. Already meeting-houses and bathhouses requiring access to water ducts were charted alongside the river. There were also plans for an intricate system for waste.

The Temple and Temple compound were central to everything, and the Galli had worked day and night cutting and chiselling rock brought down from the heart of the gorge. It was almost complete. Surrounding land boasted of newly laid stone terraces and Ashtar had helped plant groves of olive trees within this design. There were stone pens and holdings ready for livestock. On one visit, she had sat and watched some women set up five new hives. The domestication of bees was a new skill, but the women had learnt quickly and Ashtar had licked her lips in anticipation of the sweet nectar they would produce.

She loved the new site. It felt different from the old village. This land was strong. It was honourable and gracious. Although Divine Mother could be brutal and harsh, She provided much nourishment. Her blood flowed generously with fresh springs, blessing the site and feeding into a languid river. Ashtar was sure it would become a raging torrent in the cooler season with the snow of the mountains transforming into Mother's milk. The Divine Mother also provided sustenance. There were abundant wild goats, birds and fish. The pines already growing at the site would provide most of the resin as well as cones for rites, pine nuts for roasting as well as the desperately needed shade and coolness to stave off the seasonal heat.

This is going to be such a good home.

Ashtar felt content. The smile froze on her face as the scene in front of her slowly dissolved. She blinked, rubbed her eyes. A fuzzy image grew in her mind revealing another site. Ashtar squinted to focus. It was far away, over the sea toward the setting sun. She saw a river flowing from the foothills of a mountain. A Temple nestled in the fold of a small gorge. She saw herself sitting in the centre of the world speaking the words of the Great Mother.

The image brought a wave of dizziness. Time became tangled. Her surroundings faded into vagueness, and she stood entranced. A trickle of sweat dripped down her back. Then another. The weight of the torturous sun threatened to consume her.

Her? No, not her. Another.

Ashtar watched as a young woman with cropped blonde hair sat in the shade amid fallen stones laced with the residue sweat of past Oracles. Ashtar sensed the young woman's confusion, witnessed her tear-stained face. She could feel the young woman's frustration at her lack of understanding. Ashtar smiled. Truth was glorious in all its secrets.

The image distorted as an unknown force propelled Ashtar back into her present. Opening her mouth, words tumbled forth unleashed. While she did not comprehend the words she spoke or understand the tongue, she could hear the future, crying its pain of torment. She recognised the inspiration that guided Pythia. She stood tall, sourcing power from below her feet rising up her spine. She raised her arms and prophesised into the ether:

"From wise sage, human interpreter of the Divine Will of the Mother, to one no longer respected, but hated, feared, doubted, ignored. Blamed for the disasters about to befall Humanity".

A huge vibration surged through her, shaking her off her feet. Overcome with the need to sleep, Ashtar remained where she fell and curled up.

Waking somewhat later, Ashtar felt pleasantly light and weirdly buoyant. Her hearing was acute, almost painful. The air around her a veritable jungle of discordant noises, and this cacophony made it difficult to adjust to her surroundings. She closed her eyes, but in doing so saw unimaginable colours and images shooting through her mind. The visions filled her head and she had an impulse to empty it. Opening her mouth, a most wondrous verse filled the air around her. Overwhelmed by a sense of carrying the most extraordinary powers, she shook with the very forces of existence, perceiving events and meanings of past, present and future. All flooded her senses with great clarity and comprehension beyond her tender years. Gentle stillness descended.

She coughed, choked by an urgent need for water. Her tongue felt fat as if the words had sucked all the moisture from her mouth, from her body. She drank greedily from her flask.

Looking around, Ashtar realised she had slept for a long time. The sun was bidding farewell, its softening light bringing a soothing timbre to the end of day. There was no one around. Ashtar knew the locations marked for delivery of the supplies accorded to content or purpose. The pot she carried was to be stored in the Temple.

She walked into the deep cool of the Temple's entrance, carefully set the vessel down and stretched out her weary muscles. She sipped from her flask again. Transporting the pot was tiring. The combination of weight and movement required concentration for most of the journey. She could afford to relax now.

The Temple was Ashtar's favourite building. She went into the main altar chamber and lightly stroked her fingers across the stone hewn platform. The rock was solid with shades of white and black marble rippling through.

Beautiful.

Walking around the altar, she spied Pythia's chamber behind the altar. She hesitated before entering. As her eyes adjusted to the dim light, she saw that Pythia had slept there at times. She yawned, succumbing to an unspoken invitation to rest awhile longer. She lay on the rug intending only a few minutes respite.

A slither of moonlight streamed through a small crack in the wall, enough to shine sleep away. A soft sensation rustled close to her ear. 'Soft, mmm silky,' she thought drowsily. She closed her eyes aware of a hushed sense of touch. It washed through her, inside her head; a calm, gentle shhhhh, a gentle hiss like the fluttering of a butterfly's wings. She held her breath, listening to the newness of the sound, trying to discern what it was, this unknown sensation. It was vaguely familiar. Realisation came with a sharply drawn breath. Serpents!

A wave of fear took hold before she could prevent it and her rigid body drew sharp hisses of protest around her. But they did not strike. Not then. Ashtar's head felt like it was swimming in an ocean of writhing snakes, entangled in her hair, whispering their secrets into her ears. She concentrated on quietening her breathing, slowly, slowly, breathe in, breathe out, placating the snakes. They were small and moved in a quivering rhythm, winding this way and that with their cool, smooth forms over her matted hair and warm skin. She lay still, drawing quiet breath, and when she could no longer sense their presence around her head, she sat up, only to experience a high pitch vibration shaking inside her head, inside her ears.

High, shrill, an unfamiliar fuzzy shuffling of sound filled her head. She quickly lay down hoping to stop the piercing. Unknowingly she placed her head directly into the lap of a large serpent who reached out and bit her neck. Ashtar screamed from the shot of pain. She bolted upright, as the serpent glided quietly away through the darkness of the chamber.

The poison spread quickly through her body, up her neck flooding her head, skull, eyes and ears. It flowed down through her chest and arms and into her legs; its cool silver stream dancing through her warm-blooded veins. It stilled the noisy chatter and ringing in her ears, bringing instead a tide of soft whisperings.

The poison pulsated in time with her heartbeat. With the first flush of fever, her body tried to fight off the icy coldness attacking through emotions of conflict, aggression and fear. Her fight weakened as the cold toxins took hold and roamed with arrogance through her veins, spreading raw biting sensations. She felt outside of herself, removed, aloof, watching from far away. Then, without warning, flung back into her skin. Her feet prickled and tingled, her ankles swelled. Her whole body started to expand, ever so slightly at first, swelling, pulsing, creeping. Her skin felt stretched as if she had outgrown herself and needed to shed it.

Ashtar broke into a pant, drawing in air, swallowing and gulping. Urgency set a pace racing away from conscious thought. Her tongue darted in and out seeking moisture from the air. Perspiration streaked down her cheeks. The whispering in her ears was incessant, insistent for release, becoming louder and louder until finally exploding out of her mouth, forcing and freeing sounds and words that had emerged from inside her ears. She remained in this flux throughout the night, her body alternating between hot and cold. Her ears continued to pull in the voices of the earth, the language of plants, rocks, trees, water and animals, and she a conduit, released words as fast as they formed, streaming out of her mouth. Ashtar did not know what she said, and it did not seem to matter. The Earth sought expression, urgent with desire for articulation, all energies speaking through her. Her ears did not hear her voice or the content of her words, only the language of the Great Mother.

It was early dawn when Pythia came across Ashtar's spent

body. She saw a faint familiar trail in the dirt and noted the peace surrounding the sleeping child.

This one is kissed.

She returned with a jug of spring water and a bowl and cloth to wash the young girl's face.

Ashtar shuffled, slowly awakening. Her sleep had not revived her energy. The whispering in her ears now sounded like Pythia's lisp.

"You have been licked by serpents, child. Your destiny ordained."

Dazed and groggy, Ashtar sat up. There was a calm silence in her head as if she had bathed in lavender and rosewater. The blanket dirt of noise washed away. Overwhelmed and still slightly feverish, she stood on unsteady legs. Pythia picked her up and held her close.

It had been an auspicious night.

CHAPTER NINE

Pythia

Pythia stood up and placed a strand of hair behind her ear. 'Enough', she thought. 'Enough now. It is time.' Happiness and sadness vied for status. By leaving with a select number of women, many more would suffer from the malignancy spreading through the village. However, she could not deny her relief in going. Everything was as the Oracle had predicted. Pythia surrendered a sigh. She lit a small clay lamp to guide her path down the hill, and left the cave without looking back.

The women were ready. Adorned in travelling cloaks they sat in small groups waiting for Pythia. As she arrived at the Temple, a loud boom bellowed into the early evening's still-ness. Confusion and disorientation rode the sound waves, startling the women. The noise swallowed the silence of the land. Pythia quickly led the way out of the compound. The Mother was calling. It was time to leave.

From the top of the path leading to the harbour, Pythia could see the Great Mother's moan reverberating up the hill. The ground rippled like water. She felt the rolling of earthy layers beneath her, as if she was already on the caïque in choppy waters. Balance was precarious.

Rock and crust screamed in protest as solid earth tore apart: a raft of tremors spewing, belching, spluttering from Her core, rising to the surface, coming again and again and again. Stone walls shattered as easily as earthen vases, swept aside like the flimsy veil of a Select's first Sacred Union dance. Some of the children whimpered, tasting fear. Everyone held hands and continued a steady pace down to the sea. There was mayhem all around them filling the air; dirt and dust, rumblings, cracking, crashing, screams and crying.

The women and children entered the harbour unseen, the destruction of the village masking their escape. Several caïques manned by Galli lined the dock, waiting for them. The turmoil of the land filtered into the impatient sea and the caïques rolled about, restless to be out in open water. Finally, with everyone boarded safely, the Galli began to row. Pythia breathed in time with the rhythmical push-pull action of the Galli's strong toned arms, bringing the oar toward and away from his chest. He ploughed through the water with hard, determined strokes, each creating distance to separate the two worlds.

Night clouds drifted across the darkening sky, mingling with dust. They were not so thick to obscure the rising moon but produced enough shadow to aid the refugees.

A loud explosion shattered through the debris of noise and chaos. The women sat aghast, watching in horror as the village burst into flame. The Galli rowed on, everyone a silent witness. As the glow of the burning village and stench of charred flesh diminished through distance, the women tried to relax into their journey. Some slept, others talked quietly.

It was after dawn when they landed in the small cove, sheltered from burgeoning winds and sea surge by its natural crater shaped harbour of basalt. It had been carved in even more ancient times by a volcano, who had now slept too long to be disturbed by any travellers' plight. Pythia gave thanks to the Moon, pale and dainty in the morning sky.

She stepped out of the rocking boat into soft shallows. Small fish darted around her feet. A series of gentle splashes followed, as one by one the women assisted each other in disembarking and pulling the boats onto the shore. Once beached safely, the women assembled where Pythia awaited them. Sleepy children lay on the dry sand, resting with the most pregnant of the women.

Pythia looked at the weary women. She spoke to them, sharing the oracle.

"We live in a time of enchantment. We are midwives to hope. Disenchantment will follow, denying our existence, forgetting our stories. There will come a time for re-enchantment. Our children's children will gaze upon Great Mother with new understanding. It will be in their blood."

Despite their tiredness and concern for those remaining in the village, the women glowed with anticipation. A collective joy radiated and her heart warmed.

"Welcome sisters," she continued, "Our new life awaits us. We shall strive to manifest the natural harmony and balance offered by Divine Mother, on whose body we tread and whose milk we drink."

She breathed in the power she felt. The Mother was strong here. The women, also feeling the strength, knelt and kissed the ground.

"Follow the dictates of your guiding light, dear sisters, for we have the hero's journey before us."

Pythia turned toward the caïques. The women followed. Everyone worked together off-loading the cargo and strapping larger vessels to their bodies with long woven cloth. The sheltered cove, while perfect for their early morning landing, did not offer any safety from marauding travellers or pirates. Nor did it protect or hide them from the spurned Vrados. Pythia encouraged haste. Ashtar took the lead as trained, and with six other Select interspersed among the women and children, set off toward the site of their new home.

The women walked in unison, as if in ritual, attuned in movement. Synergy flowed with one breath moving in one flow. It was a long walk and many women felt unprepared. Many were in varying stages of pregnancy and bore the morning heat with impatience.

One foot, then another. Another, then another.

Collective feet hurt. The woven slings dug into their flesh and rubbed raw. Small welts bled.

One foot forward, then the next. It was all many could do to stop crying.

Their last spot of rest was by a small trinket of a river providing fresh sweet water from mountain sources. Onward, one step, then another, and another:

A woman shifted the sling on her shoulder, hoisted her load a bit for a moment of respite from its weight.

One woman's legs ached, especially the left, down her hip. It was a weakness she carried and the overloading danced with pain.

The balls of another's feet felt like they were burning.

Sweat lingered, then dripped down her nose, and hers. Dripped down their faces, attracting flies. The women ignored them for as long as they could.

They all flinched, but kept going.

Every move invited pain, inflicting cruel intentions on weary bodies. No one dared break stride more than necessary. Everyone kept moving; no one hesitated or cried out. Not even the children. In mutual silence, they shared the agony of the physical journey, the exertion and sheer determination to keep mobile, and the strain of bravery and courage. Everyone was tired and hurting.

But, they were the blessed ones. They would not dishonour through complaint or weakness.

They arrived at the remote site well after the sun had reached its peak and its observance of the women curtailed by the side of the gorge. Elation soothed their weariness. Pythia strode through the dusty tracks towards the Temple compound. The women would reside here. The Galli would initially sleep in the caves adorning the cliffs. As the children discovered rich reserves of energy and ran freely exploring the site, the women settled in.

CHAPTER TEN

Cressida opened her eyes. She did not know if she had slept or even if she was still asleep. It did not seem to matter. She remained motionless except for the gentle rise and fall of her chest. Serene and calm, she felt held within the lap of narrative. She watched as Pythia traced her fingers along a series of images on the cave wall.

'Please don't stop,' Cressida silently wished. No voice, no sound just thoughts that streamed like a ribbon in the breeze.

Pythia smiled.

"This," she said, pointing to a section that looked like women sitting around a fire. "This is Harrownight."

Cressida closed her eyes again as the tinkle of Pythia's voice suspended in air, slowly faded as an image of a night sky set alight by thousands of shimmering lights swam in infinite darkness.

Pythia looked up at the night sky. The flecks above beamed strong and vital, fit to burst. Her skin tingled from their energy. She noted the change in direction of two of the brightest stars, auguring a commensurate shift in the moon phases to come. She nodded. This was a shift from tension and conflict to a more reflective orientation. The timing was perfect. She sensed a calling to contemplate the Divine within, to get closer to actual, timeless truth. Deep reflection would offer powerful insight for those prepared to open and surrender to the Mother. Alignment of the stars illuminated the promise of inner freedom.

Pythia returned to the Temple with a bundle of twigs. A small woman approached her and asked tentatively, "Harrownight?"

Pythia replied gently, "Yes, Nefeli, Harrownight."

Pythia continued to the compound square where a large pit already held tinder. She added her armful of twigs.

"Can we risk it?" Nefeli asked, having followed Pythia to the Platia. They had settled in the village for only a few full moons and lighting a big fire could be dangerous if seen from the ocean.

"Can we not?" Pythia answered.

Nefeli nodded, concurring, and then set out across the south end of the compound. She returned shortly with her arms laden with sticks. The two women at task attracted attention and word of Harrownight quickly spread. Some women set out immediately to gather their wood, others preferred to spend some time reflecting on the challenges the night would present.

One evening, after several suns had passed and the stack of wood was measurable, a woman approached Pythia.

"I am afraid that I do not embrace the task at hand," she confided.

Pythia read her anxiety and replied tenderly, "Harrownight will not commence until you are ready."

"I fear for my younger sister. She is at first blood. Do you think she will be ready, truly ready?"

'Were we ever truly ready?' she thought. At their former village, Harrownight had become a regular feature in seasonal cleansing after Vrados had introduced his new edicts. Many men wishing to emulate his foreign lifestyle had enticed women to leave the Temple compound and live in smaller compounds. This isolated women from their sisters and there were many dire consequences resulting from this simple living arrangement.

She reassured the woman again. "I have seen your sister embrace this task, believing perhaps this will confirm her connection to the Divine Mother. She also harbours deep ignorance that the hand of her mother's lover upon her was acceptable practice. Harrownight will be deeply challenging to that one, but I am content she demonstrates her will to learn to become woman of the Mother."

Once all the women had contributed to the pile of wood, albeit some with trepidation, others more eagerly, Harrownight was scheduled for the next full moon. In the preceding week, the women began sharing concurrent dreams and their sensitivity intensified that they started experiencing each other's feelings and physical tensions and pain. Harrownight would free them from this.

Ashtar could barely contain herself within her skin. Her excitement burst through her pores as the thrill of the morning birds' song woke her into realisation. Tonight was Harrownight. As a child, not yet maiden, Ashtar was not able to participate in the full ceremony, but Pythia had invited all the young girls to attend. She looked over to where the precious labrys lay next to her cot, blessed with the qualities of the butterfly emerging from the chrysalis, transformational and regenerative. Her eyes glowed, lifting the corners of her mouth up into her cheeks with anticipation. The dance of Harrownight belonged only to the women. It was an ancient spiral path, danced to summon the Mother. And it was tonight, and she was going.

Ashtar had seen the dance once before. She had marvelled at the women weaving along a path ingrained in their hearts and ancestral blood. It was a dance of eleven cycles. The women would weave in close to the centre and then out again. The women danced away from the outer world toward self-knowledge and truth, guided by the Great Mother's thread; for the knowledge of the spark of Divinity lay within the very core of every woman. They danced toward the centre of their destiny. For at the centre lay their darkest fears. Their dancing did not seek to conquer their fears, but to accept them. Acknowlegment of ones shadow, where fear, darkness and loss resided was necessary to realign ones self with the harmony of life. The Great Mother bestowed this healing gift. Ashtar had watched in awe, as the women appeared to shimmer.

Tonight, Ashtar would hold the space for the women who

danced the thread of their destiny, to be reborn and birthed, healed through love, compassion, kindness and forgiveness.

As the western sky blushed rosy with salutations from the setting orb and the Moon peered over the gorge's cliff lip, the women gathered around the large pit. The pile of wood rose as a towering monolith of dedication. Positioned off to the side was a raised platform. Here, Nefeli lay on a pile of woven rugs. Beside her sat another woman holding her hand.

Pythia stood facing the pit holding a flaming torch of twigs. She spoke slowly, looking around to address each woman.

"If we hold back from any part of our experience, if our heart shuts out any part of who we are and what we feel, we fuel the fears and feelings of separation that sustain the trance of unworthiness. Feelings and stories of unworthiness and shame are perhaps the most binding element in the trance of fear. Trust the knowledge that comes through the body and speak truth. Turn towards pain, not from it. Become acquainted, intimate. Surrender to cleanse and integrate those experiences that prevent connecting with the Great Mother. Your perseverance, courage and patience will align heart and body with the Earth."

She received a cup of wine held out to her. She raised it to the sky and then tipped half onto the earth before taking a sip. She passed the cup to the woman beside her, who took a sip and passed it on. Each woman shared a sacred sip. Pythia spoke again.

"The power of forgiveness is a miracle from Great Mother, a shift in perception from world to spirit, from past to present from fear to love. It is the Mother's greatest gift and your greatest power. Your willingness to forgive is your refuge and your strength. Forgiveness is not condoning. Surrender your darkness. Pour forth your light upon it."

Pythia threw the torch into the tinder. As it burst into flame, she introduced Nefeli's story.

"When Nefeli sat in the circle of her first Harrownight, she was distressed. She explained that on coming to the Temple she had found herself wandering up behind the goatherd who was leading two goats away from the herd. She knew they would be slaughtered and felt their distress.

"'You are placing your own grief on these goats,' a Select advised. Nefeli disagreed."

"It was the goats. It was not me," Nefeli said. As she described the goats in more detail, the women around the fire started to experience her feelings of pain and anguish. Women sobbed, others hugged themselves.

Nefeli said to them, "At times I feel as if I am spread out over the land and inside things, in the splashing of the waves, in the clouds and the animals that come and go, in the procession of the seasons. There is nothing with which I am not linked. Here," she said, touching her heart, "everything has its history."

Pythia touched her heart as she explained. "Everything from Mother Earth, animate and inanimate has within it spirit, and communicates in spirit to all that will listen. Tonight, we learn from Nefeli. Speak to be heard. Listen, so you may hear. Retain your openness and heart for the soul of all who share our world."

Pythia knew Nefeli would incarnate as Divinity. Through embodying the living presence of the Great Mother, this small woman enabled the women to reconnect with the healing power of the Earth. Through love and compassion, Nefeli opened her heart to receive the physical and emotional trauma expressed around the Harrownight fire. By connecting energetically, Nefeli would guide each woman to well-being through sharing her own energy strength.

Pythia spoke into the fire. "The souls of our children and children's children, receptive to unresolved traumas, need us to be cleansed or they will carry these into their own psyches. Your trauma can reverberate through the soul, entangle in your child's fate, and assume the suffering of others. Through the Divine Mother we seek wholeness and balance."

Cressida stirred. The power and intensity of Pythia's robust words reached through time and consumed her. She could barely breathe. A wave of sensation swept throughout her body, which Cressida thought — or felt — she was not sure, had been slumbering and was now rising through her. It brought a vision and she saw with horror that something seemed to be missing from her heart. She saw a tight band clasping her heart. Looking closely at this band she saw it was hollow and that it spiralled around and down her spine. Then with crystal clarity, she saw a tunnel opening out the end of her spine. It was beautifully faceted with a stone vault. This tunnel led down into the depths of the earth, but it seemed overgrown and blocked. In her entranced state, Cressida reached to touch her spine and scratched her finger on a small sharp rock. She winced with discomfort before mindlessly squeezing it , dripping blood onto the earth.

When Pythia spoke again, her words filtered through Cressida's transgression. Cressida relaxed. Pythia's words, seemingly spoken simultaneously from inside the cave and from around the fire, lapped over each other, until once again, Cressida became enmeshed in the weaving of narrative. She watched as the women stood up around the fire. She heard their words without sequence; she could not tell who said what, but as she listened, Cressida heard the plaintive cry of abused women.

"It's not like he punched me — he just slapped me with an open hand."

"It's not just name-calling, or things said in anger. It was the constant undermining and criticism. It could be loud and overt, or the little whisper in my ear at a celebration: 'They're not laughing with you, they're laughing at you.'"

"He sometimes tied me up so I could not perform the rituals, especially Sacred Union."

The women nodded, yes, sometimes it became too hard to participate, the arguments were not worth it.

"It was only when Pythia asked me simple questions like,

'Does he raise his voice, does he yell, call you names? Does he swear, does he throw things? It was yes, yes, yes. I had always thought I was to blame for his behaviour."

"I am the strong one. What he did was something I simply had to withstand to help him overcome his daemons. I believed, with the Mother's blessing I was the only one, the only person who could protect him and help him become a better man."

"I was being manipulated. I never saw it."

"But in the village. He was smart and strong. His craft provided the perfect cover: who would believe such a decent man could be capable of such behaviour?"

The women looked at each other, sharing the one thought, 'Have we been coupling the same man?'

"I talk to women who say, 'Oh, the first time a man hits me, I'm out of there.' Well, it doesn't start that way. What happens is, he throws a jug across the room and intentionally misses."

"He never hit me. It was his words."

"I lost myself in being us, not me. I lost myself in trying to help him, make him happy. I thought that made me happy too."

"The healer told me I cannot birth for the Mother because of his beatings."

There was a strong intake of collective breath and an immediate stillness around the flickering flames. The heaviness of these words demanded space. Such was this atrocity. The women bowed their heads in mutual sorrow for this young woman's plight. The Mother was birth, death and rebirth of the natural and human worlds. Their bodies were the direct incarnation of waxing and waning, life and death cycles in the universe. Birthing was their right and gift from the life creator. A few women sobbed. A respectful silence descended until once again the release of Harrownight bore words out and into the night air.

"It was little things that made me begin to question myself. Words became twisted. My sisters had faults. Why did I trust them?"

"I found out I was with child. I told him. I remember his face changing. I remember everything becoming dark and the joy I felt, trampled. Mother took the child early."

"There were times when I really think he enjoyed being violent. I think he despised my shyness, thought I was weak."

"He was not the man I thought I knew and loved."

"I had made him angry, he said. I had made him angry? How? I made him hit me? Kick me?"

"I let him touch me so he wouldn't hit my mother."

Pythia sat quietly until the weeping and sobbing subsided. She addressed the women.

"Every day I would hear your stories. I saw your injuries, your black eyes, fractured and broken limbs, burns and welts, battered hearts. I asked the Mother, 'Why were these strong glorious women remaining within such walls of brutality, why do they not stay at the Temple, why endure this treatment?'

"She responded: 'You wanted to protect him, did not want him to get into trouble, you were embarrassed, you did not want to make a fuss, you feared you had angered the Mother, felt guilty, or you did not want to upset the children. You loved him, you were ashamed, scared, thought it would not happen again, did not want to make him angrier, and did not want anyone to know. You felt you asked for it, no one would believe you, were afraid of the repercussions. His poison flowed into your veins and you lost clarity. His toxins spread, the pus of revulsion, the need for power.'"

Pythia started clapping a rhythm borne from the heart-beat of tidal seas. Her beat navigated the twilight between consciousness and matter.

"Overcome any bitterness that may have come because you feel like you were not up to the magnitude of the pain entrusted to you. Like the Mother of the world who carries the pain of the world in Her heart, each of us is part of Her heart, each of us is endowed with a measure of Her pain. You are sharing the totality of that pain. You are called upon to meet it in strength instead of self-pity."

Slowly each woman picked up the beat and clapped as they started to circle the fire. The rhythm moved into their feet and soon all were stomping and clapping, then dancing and spinning. The heat and emotion spun them into a shared breath of brilliant light. A boiling force erupted and flowed up and out through their heads causing them to soar over fantastical terrain, re-aligning themselves with the stars, with each other. Amongst the flickering of starlight, they danced towards infinity. They drifted in and out of focus, bathed in bliss, until gently returning to earth. Fashioned from the clay beneath them, feet connected to home.

Pythia glanced at Nefeli. Her silent writhing, convulsing and shuddering that had accompanied the women's stories had ceased. The woman tending her small body wrapped protectively in a rug, rocked her as if a small child. Nefeli was spent, the women cleansed.

Pythia spoke, "Boys will copy the buck. Our teaching is undermined if the man has established his poisoned pattern. Our service for the Mother is clear; we need to wean the venom, to infuse hope and integrity of the Mother's love. She is to be sustained through darkened cycles."

Pythia felt the lightest flutter of a butterfly wing of pure air wisp over and through her body. She breathed in the purity, feeling her skin tingling to the depths of her core and she raised her arms up to greet the Light. Arms akimbo, the Mother spread through her vessel, and words rode upwards amongst the embers and smoke. The words carried a deep ancestral comprehension of roads to be travelled:

Eternity is the day, and everlastingness, the night. It is the heart, which makes all come forth, it is the tongue that repeats it.

Pythia poured perfumed oil on the fire and the scented coals leapt star-ward, bathing the women with its smoke. She pulled out a small dagger and cut into her arm. She passed it around the circle and each woman made a slight cut to drip blood into the fire. Pythia admired these courageous women. Their words now expelled, no longer threatened to cause disease in their bodies.

In completing the Ritual of Harrownight, Pythia led the women in a final sacred prayer. Standing and holding hands upward, the women walked around the fire, slowly picking up pace until they lightly skipped, each step lifting them lightly and joyously in a simple movement of release. Together they chanted, firstly for the Mother and then to the Mother residing in the perpetrator:

"I am sorry. Please forgive me. Thank you. I love you."

The fire swooned, licking at the circumference of the pit edging towards its slumber into embers. The women returned to their beds to sleep deeply in the bosom of the Mother. The women held each other in their thoughts and dreams.

CHAPTER ELEVEN

One more.

Words whispered into the space. Cressida snorted in her sleep, the only evidence of life.

It was mid-season of the Sun when the long boats arrived. It was a day when the line between sea and sky blurred with heat and sea mist, two shades of blue creating a muted hue affirming the mystical and wondrous. It was a while before the glimmer on the horizon identified as craft and not resident of ocean depths.

"Tribal Women," Pythia informed the gathering women. "This auger's well."

She turned to them, "Come, they are making good time and we are behind in our preparations to receive them."

There was a flurry of activity as Pythia instructed the Select to set up bedding, basins, oils and fruits for their guests. The energy in the compound heightened with an eagerness tinged with nervousness. The reputation of the Tribal Women preceded them. These were women of great stature, great honour, strong, vital and powerful. And, Pythia hoped, of great heart. An alliance with these women was integral to her work and she prayed for the Great Mother to guide her in her dealings.

In the final throes of her preparation to leave the village, Pythia had a dream of dancing entwined with the Tribal Women and awoke with the realisation that the community's survival depended on an alliance. Under the Mother's instruction, she had sent out an invitation, risking a Galli and a Select. The Tribal Women had responded quickly and she prayed this boded well.

With arrangements underway, Pythia and many of the women and children headed to the shore. The Galli remained behind in the compound with the male children. They were to move further up the gorge, sheltering in caves and completely out of sight for the duration of the visit.

The Tribal Women's arrival in the long boats gave Pythia hope that they deemed her proposition worthy of consideration. A conch shell sounded across the waves. Hand-drumming serenaded the boats into the cove.

A small craft set off from the first long boat. It was the Galli and Select returning unharmed. Another small caïque followed. In this stood the Tribequeen, an amazon of a woman wearing skins decorated with gold and fur. Her bronze dagger gleamed at her hip. Her headdress cast from bronze was inlaid with gold and precious jewels. It served as part-crown and part-armour. It blazed in the sun reflecting light that splattered across the many faces watching in awe, and making all turn and shield their eyes. More small craft followed the Queen.

Conch shells continued trumpeting, and on shore, the drumming was accompanied by the floating notes of seashell flutes, shell percussion and the drawn-out droning from a bag made of goatskin. The formality of welcome soon gave way to an informal riff, and the laughter of children accompanied their improvised percussion. Then a single note of golden honey wove in and around all women, harmonising with the earthy instrumental music. Blending matter with vibration.

Daphnis, her eyes closed, her arms out at shoulder height bent at the elbows with palms forward in Pythia stance, sang her sound of sunrise and dew drops, wild thyme and marjoram. She sang a harmony which, flowing delicately on the tips of speckled air, became velvet-smooth, soft, rich and deep; a conduit for consciousness.

The women on the shore and in the boats swayed, entranced by sounds of exquisite pleasure, until they too brought their voices into play. There was calling out and responding, entwining sound and breath. It was playful at first, the acoustics uniting to create music unknown to either tribe but borne from every heartbeat.

Every woman and child found a place for their voice, their song, and became part of a larger overture, a cacophony that grew spontaneously, without lead or instruction. The playfulness shifted, morphing into harmonised frequencies of mourning, grief, birth, love and joy; life expressed through song. Never had any of the women experienced such undulation of spirit and the coming together as one soul. The women glowed, awash from sounds of purity, generosity, courage and kindness.

They all felt it, felt the connection as they breathed together, sung together, sounding out their lives and memories through pulsing, beating, throbbing, wafting sounds as one, united in the Divinity of the Great Mother. Pythia held a wavering pure note of her love for the Mother and offered this to her counterpart. She raised her arms, serpents entwined, and as the Pythia of the village, the spiritual leader of the women, started to dance and twirl. Tingling energy fed her body. Truth glistened in the perspiration glowing on her skin.

The Tribequeen responded by lifting her face to the heavens releasing a long deep guttural howl that called on the blood of the Moon, the flow of tides, the screams of the dead and dying. Her sound sang of battles and victories, of valour and honour, of blood and sacrifice and the darkness of shadow.

A tear of pure joy traced the scar down Pythia's cheek. The spontaneous outpouring of heartfelt greeting had swept up everyone, and she recognised these women as sisters. The women on the shore raised their arms in the collective spirit of the Great Mother and twirled before running forward to embrace the Tribal Women as they came ashore. Women hugged their sisters in a physical manifestation of their shared song. Hearts lifted, laughter rang out and a deep cleansing was shared by all. It was a greeting of old friends, of lovers and kinswomen.

CHAPTER TWELVE

S tillness adorned the cavern with silence. Time slept until a shattering roar erupted.

Cressida woke as the ground shook. She opened her eyes and blinked. She was alone. She lay groggy, sleepy, not wanting to move. The stillness returned and she closed her eyes, returning to the darkness as a dreamless sleep blanketed her.

The second roar seemed to come from beneath the floor of the cave, deep down below her. As the ground shook, Cressida jumped up in fright. Eyes wide, she looked around confused. How long had she been here? Had the storm finished? Was it over? Was she safe? Was she safe?! She hesitated, her question hanging in mid-air. Well, was she? An answer came from a deep guttural roll, like some sort of internal thunder, way down in the vicinity of what she had thought was an explosion. She looked around, trying to gather her scrambled thoughts. It was a lesson in herding cats.

Tremor. The word fluttered.

Safety. Escape. Urgent thoughts stressed action. *Do something, anything that makes sense.*

Fear crept up her legs, freezing her with horror. The ground, the solid ground she was standing on, right there under her feet, the stable and reliable earth she had always known, was moving. The ground was moving. Impossible. She swallowed. It shook harder. A deep hum came towards her through solid rock, crust, dirt, and ground.

She could feel the strength and power of an unknown force that was literally rising from the earth's core. She could feel it, and it was growing. As it grew in vibration, it became louder. She realised she was trembling in unison. She dropped to her knees to try to hold on to something solid.

Ohmygodohmygodohmygod. Fuckfuckfuck.

She clutched at the ground. The guts of the earth churned for what seemed an eternity, shattering any faith Cressida may have had that the ground she had walked on for twenty-three years was ever to be trusted again. Nothing had prepared her for this. It defied everything she knew as truth. The explosion shook out belief and filled its place with confusion. As abruptly as it started, it stopped, leaving in its wake a sense of nothingness. Nothing transitioned back to stillness; a heavy weighted claustrophobic stillness. A pervasive feeling of dread lurked in the shadows.

Cressida remembered only one thing about earthquakes; aftershocks. Her one defining feature borne of this knowledge was the speed in which she determined to get the hell out of there. Fearing another episode woke her with purpose. *Get out! Now.* Her new mantra picked up speed. Cressida grabbed her phone beside her knees and scuttled back in the direction she had entered the cavern.

Returning to the large rock, she squeezed herself through the narrow gap toward the light illuminating up ahead.

'Thank god,' she thought. She had envisaged a rock fall prised loose from the shake, blocking the entrance. No one knew she was here. Clambering up the incline took several tries and a good dose of sheer will and determination. Once at the gap she crammed her body through its slim crevice. On the ledge, she was grateful to see the last hint of day.

While the storm had cleared, a howling wind remained. Cressida shivered. She could see the moon, pale, almost insignificant behind retreating storm clouds. She slid her way down the cliff face, scraping and banging her weary body against rocks. It was surprising how high she was from the river. Water flowed along its trajectory, less angrily but still with a strength she didn't want to test. In the intermittent light and darkness and accompanied by the constant rumbling of the storm tormenting those in its path out to sea, she made her way back to the mouth of the gorge.

Her journey back was further than she expected. She faltered often, floundering too many times to keep her tears at bay. She wept her distress. Life and death had never seemed so close, no longer opposites of a spectrum — a beginning and end — but twins of the same mother, with only a translucent veil of misty incomprehension to delineate any sort of line or boundary.

When the gorge finally discharged her to the shoreline, she stumbled and lay, trying to breathe, desperate to regain her breath. The problem of escape and death had dominated everything since the tremor. She lay gasping in the dirt.

CHAPTER THIRTEEN

Storm, tremor, possible tsunami; the warnings were laden with apprehension. Angela sat alone during the first tremor. She had lived through a quake in another time and place and felt paralysed with fear. The shake released adrenaline that coursed through her body and her heart. It was exhausting and terrifying. So why was she outside? Why go to the gorge on the day after havoc had wreaked itself on the village? She questioned her sanity.

Her aunt lived in the old village and despite her fears, Angela wanted to make sure she was okay. She did not fool herself; she knew it was the comfort and reassurance from the arms of her mother's older sister which she sought. As she had known, her aunt was fine. The old woman had lived through many storms, many tremors. She had read the signs and had been prepared.

They sat through the second tremor together. Once it settled, her aunt bundled Angela up, sending her back home before darkness fell, with a backpack full of soup, fresh eggs and cake. As Angela left the old compound, she saw a bedraggled figure staggering out of the gorge heading towards the shore. She recognised her as the *gynaika*, the young woman she had seen out walking.

Angela watched as the young figure propelled along the path haphazardly, possibly drunk. She saw her fall and not move. Face down. Angela hurried over to her. She was still lying on the ground when she reached her. Angela knelt, "*Tis kanis*? Are you okay?" she asked. The young woman was dirty and wet and smelt of piss and vomit. She was clearly distressed.

'*Oxi*, no, not okay.' Angela helped Cressida to her feet, half carrying her back to her home.

It was a bit more difficult than she had anticipated as the young woman stumbled often and seemed to be in shock. She was a mess. Angela wondered if she had some sort of mental condition. She was blubbering incoherently. Slowly and awkwardly, Angela got her back to her small home, her mother's house. The young woman was messy — clothes in disarray, hair matted and smelly, very smelly. Angela grabbed a blanket off her bed and wrapped it around her. She sat the woman on her couch and retrieved the soup from her bag to heat. Standing at her stove, she watched the young woman curl up on her couch and fall asleep. She took off the soup, made herself some tea and sat on a chair watching the woman sleep.

Cressida opened her eyes. It was dark. Again? Where was she this time? There was a dim light from a small lamp in another room. She lay still, assessing her surroundings. She was inside, but not a cave. So far so good. She was warm

— even better. She saw a figure in a chair and swallowed. Had she been kidnapped? Raped? No, she was not naked. Okay. She coughed and the figure stirred. The figure sat upright. Cressida saw it was the woman from her walks. She sighed with relief and slowly sat up. Groggy and, ewww she had pissed herself at some point, oh how embarrassing.

"*En daxi*? Are you okay?" the woman asked.

Cressida nodded.

"Would you like a drink? Some soup?"

"Water, please."

The woman stood up and returned with a glass. Cressida guzzled it down and the woman refilled it. How long had it been since she had any water? Or food? How long had she been in the cave — her thought trailed. Cressida felt a wave of tears rise from behind her eyes and before she could stop herself, started to cry. Again? It felt like she had been crying forever.

The lovely woman spoke again. "Why don't you have a shower, you can borrow some of my things and have some soup and sleep here till the morning. You can go back to your place then, but for now, let us get you clean and feeling a bit more like yourself. *En daxi*?"

Cressida wanted to hug her. She stood up and followed the woman to a small bathroom. She stood useless, watching the woman pull out a big, oh yes, a big fluffy towel from a small cupboard. She went out and returned with a clean set of, oh my god, the perfect set of flannel pyjamas.

'I love this woman,' Cressida thought, still too mute to offer anything more than a simple 'thanks' when she was being given the world. The woman left, closing the door quietly behind her. Cressida looked in the mirror. She looked back, yes it was her in there, tear streaked face and somewhat dazed expression, but her. She ran the water and stepped into the warm, cleansing stream that washed away the dirt, grime, fear and anxiety. Here she felt safe.

Cressida stayed under the running water longer than was necessary but in good time to let the heat warm and comfort her. She left her disgusting clothes in a pile and entered the small living area. The woman had set the table with some soup and bread. Cressida could have kissed her.

"*Me lene Angela.* I am Angela," said the woman offering her hand.

"Cressida."

Big, kind, brown eyes.

"Thank you."

"*Parakalo.* Here, sit, eat."

Cressida and Angela sat together and ate in silence.

CHAPTER FOURTEEN

For six days the skies cried with a raw brutality. Back home in England it would rain with a frigid intent to divide and conquer. But here in Crete, standing in her bikinis squinting into the downpour, Cressida felt an unleashing of her pent-up emotion, which felt cleansing.

The ferries had given up any attempt of a timetable and life in the village hit the pause button. The old folk muttered, shaking their heads, unable to recall a deluge like it in their collective memory. There was however, tangible relief that there had been no further tremors.

"Catastroph," grimaced the old men, still managing to gather at their favourite Kafenion to cast dispersions as to whose fault this was. Usually the government shouldered the blame, but this was debatable: the intervention of weather gods favoured the odds. Only the taverna owners remained cheerful, selling their personal stock of retsina and raki once the beer had run out. On the seventh day, emulating religious fervour, the rains decided on a day of rest. The Sun made its appearance, faking an innocent smile as large as Alice's cat, and shone throughout the afternoon as if there had been no disruption to its summer program.

The ferries cautiously returned and relieved the village

of hordes of frustrated and somewhat sodden tourists, who despite the overwhelming hospitality of the locals, were disgruntled at being stuck in the village instead of else-where in the sun. Holiday brochures had not forewarned of inclement weather. Supplies from the ferries were quickly exchanged with human cargo boarding en-route to escape. There had been a communal phone order for mops, buckets, disinfectant and shovels. The village came together to clean the mess left behind. The winds quietened to a companion-able breeze and columns of sheets, towels and clothes flapped in the now, buoyant, unapologetic sunshine.

Cressida baked a cake to celebrate, and the following day took it with the freshly laundered pyjamas to Angela's house. Angela greeted her warmly. She had returned from her office at the park gates to the gorge, where her manager had deter-mined it was still too dangerous to open the park to tourists.

"Come in," said Angela, "please let us share your cake over a coffee."

As simple as that, a friendship began.

"I work in Parks Management during the season," Angela said with her mouth full of orange poppy. "In the off-season, I work for the museum. I am trained as an Archaeologist but given it is poorly paid, I work as a conservator-restorer. My job is to preserve artistic and cultural artefacts."

"What does that mean?"

"I analyse and assess the condition of things like pottery or relics. I look for evidence of deterioration, and then plan for the care of the museum's collections to prevent further damage. Or I carry out conservation treatments. I also do research when required. I used to work in the field, mainly interning or volunteering on digs. I had a couple of jobs as a site assistant, but I could only do that when I had saved up enough money. I am too old now." She laughed easily. "I like my creature comforts."

Cressida mused over this information. While the rains had provided time to think, she had not reached any conclusion whether or not she had been delusional in the cave. In the past, some of her panic attacks had bordered on psychosis. Although this had felt different, she was not confident to say what had really happened. A woman talking to her, in a cave? Yep, that was a winner. Cressida nibbled the nail on her little finger. The glint of a thought flickered. She held a trump card. She had photographic proof that the paintings were real. The photos were not too bad given the lighting. In fact, they were pretty good, which was lucky since the video was too dark. Moreover, some of the pictures seemed to fit the story, the bits she could remember anyway. It was like being a kid with a picture book; she couldn't read the words but knew the story from the pictures. How else could she know the story? Maybe she should go back to the cave. The question seemed stark in the warm kitchen. Back? Cressida flinched, she did not want to go back, and definitely not alone. No way. She looked at Angela.

"You work for the Park?"

Angela nodded, a mouthful of cake preventing her from speaking.

Cressida nodded with her. Yep.

"So," she hesitated, then led with what she hoped was an

innocent question. "Do you know of any caves in the gorge? Like, are there caves?"

Angela swallowed before answering. "Heaps," she said licking her fingers. "There are caves right the way through to the start of the gorge in the mountains."

"Have you mapped them? Do you know what is in them?"

Angela chuckled. "Oh no, Cressida, there are too many. The older folk would know more about them; the bigger ones or those used for shelter in the past, especially during the war. But they have not been mapped, more left to local knowledge."

"And cave paintings? I mean umm, frescoes."

Angela put the last bit of her cake down and eyed the young woman. Cressida felt she had said enough and focused on sipping the last of her coffee. As she got up to leave, she tried another angle.

"Your work in the museum, do you need to know about Greek mythology?"

"Aside from being drip-fed on a diet of myths as a child? *Nai*. Yes, of course. It is integral to my work," Angela answered. "The ancient stories of the island are generally sourced from ruins, artefacts, things like pottery and vases."

"Do you know someone called Pythia?"

Cressida stared into her cup, a crash course in reading coffee dregs, not daring to look at Angela. She did not want to expose her anxiety at even saying the woman's name aloud. Despite all the myths read when young, she had never heard of Pythia. She desperately tried to be nonchalant. Like, this was not important — not at all, not in the least.

Poker was not her game and her discomfort shone like a

neon light. Angela picked up her laptop averting her gaze, taking her time.

"Pythia? *Nai*, yes. It is an ancient title, sort of a High Priestess. Let's see if there is anything more specific."

She tapped the keys, then looked up briefly from the screen.

"Paraphrasing Wikipedia," she joked. "Pythia is an ancient Greek word. It was not a name per se, but the title given to the Priestess of the Temple of Apollo at Delphi. The Pythia was the Oracle of Apollo, god of prophesies."

She clicked on another link.

"Pythia was defined as the House of Snakes. Derived from Pytho, which in mythology was the original name of Delphi. According to early myths, the site was initially sacred to Gaea. You've heard of Gaea, I assume?"

Cressida nodded. "Mother Earth Goddess."

"*Nai*, you know this. She was the personification of the Earth, the ancestral mother of all life." Angela scanned the document then chortled out loud.

"Oh, listen to this, about Delphi. Diodorus..." she looked up grinning, her words dripping sarcasm. "Oh, you know, Diodorus, that historian around 60 BC? Sure, you do. Well, he said initially the Pythia was an appropriately clad young virgin, for of course, great emphasis was placed on her chastity and purity, which was reserved for union with Apollo. Well, he said, and I quote," she paused, and then with deriding pompousness continued, "Echecrates, having arrived at the shrine and beheld the virgin who uttered the oracle, became enamoured of her and carried her away and violated her. The Delphians, then passed a law that a virgin should no longer prophesy, but an elderly woman of fifty, dressed in the costume of a virgin, would declare the oracles."

Angela looked up from her computer with a grin. "Does this help?"

Cressida nodded, kissed the older woman on both cheeks, and bid *kali nichta*, goodnight.

CHAPTER FIFTEEN

Within a week, the rhythm of the village returned to its well-rehearsed tourist tango. The seas washed themselves clean of the silt and mud that had ventured from inland, recovering its default position of pristine clarity. Tourists returned, flocking through the gorge and refuelling at shoreline tavernas. Cressida embraced her working routine, finding its steadiness reassuring. Forgoing her late-night antics, she now woke with the roosters and responded to the song of the sea.

Cressida loved the village beach. Its shallow entry enticed the swimmer to enter farther and farther from the shore before dropping away abruptly, as if to say, 'swim now.' The water's temperature epitomised the Greeks: always inviting, always hospitable. Here in the cove, there was what the locals called sweet water, where the springs from the mountains travelled underground into the ocean. Sometimes the trickle was more persistent and Cressida could see where it entered the body of water in a hazy tell-tale blur, exposing secrets of internal waterways. Reminiscent of a heat haze on land, it blurred the seascape like translucent silk beneath the gentle swell.

Cressida remembered being told 300 strokes was the

equivalent of 10 laps of a pool back home, so she created her own ritual of swimming 150 strokes out to sea, 50 further out than the buoy anchored to the seabed, and 150 strokes back in. Ten laps a day was her goal, every day. When the ocean behaved as a gentle lover, she felt caressed and supported. Enveloped in liquid blissfulness, the boundary between her and ocean was almost permeable. She could hear the sea whispering in a language unknown, offering resolutions rising from the depths, murmurings from the mountains, from the gorge. At other times, it was volatile. It would slap her around, forcing its way into her through the breath she took with each stroke. Waves pushed her sideways and spray pissed into her eyes. No longer the languid playful lover, it was a brutal, angry bully. Regardless, she swam in all its moods.

Now in mid-summer, the morning temperature of the water was slightly more comfortable than refreshing, but perfect for Cressida who sought to swim out the clatter in her head. Ever since the cave, the noise inside her head had become more persistent. Crazy thoughts, questions, worry, all leading her down a well-trodden path toward panic. Swimming helped to dissipate this somewhat — one hundred and forty-six, one hundred and forty-seven, one hundred and forty-eight, one hundred and forty-nine, counting her strokes until she stopped, way out from shore. She floated, retrieving her breath, allowing the gentle sensation lull her.

Held afloat, her weightlessness calmed her pulsing heart. Her puffing soon settled in accord. She looked through her toes at the huge cliffs surrounding the white painted town. Big, craggy, majestic and strong.

'I am the colour of the mountains, of the land,' she thought, casually comparing her tanned legs to the landscape. She let the thought drift, leaving a residue of peace in its wake. She sighed into the ether, no need for thinking; simply letting the ocean hold her in nothingness, freeing her from the plague of pent-up fear and confusion. She held no expectations that the sea would be anything than what it was; fluid, moving, always changing, never still. This was comforting. The tremor had literally shaken out her sense of solid stability. Lying at ease in the water made all things possible again.

"Yes," she informed the overhead white flimsy puffs. "Yes. I will accept a woman came from out of nowhere and spoke to me. Yes. She was there and I will believe it. I choose to believe it. All of it. Yes."

Resolved of this weighty concern, Cressida swam back to shore, completing her ten laps of local pool. As she emerged from the water, the sun had already made shadows on the sand, greeting the village from over the eastern cliff.

Perhaps another walk to the gorge?

She shook her head — nope, not just yet. She dried herself, famished and ready for a good cooked breakfast, mmm pancakes.

She knew what she needed to do.

After breakfast, Cressida went to Angela's house. By then her calm resolution had become fraught with doubt and misgivings. She knocked at the door, bustling past her host, pushed on by a sense of urgency. She was scared she might change her mind if she paused too long.

"I am really sorry. *Lipame*. Really, I am. But I must believe this and well, you work in the Park and the museum, so you — you are the best one — well, possibly the only one, but please, please help me. I am not crazy. Damaged maybe, slightly broken, but I am okay. Promise me you won't think I am crazy."

Cressida sat down on the couch and accepted Angela's offer for coffee.

"No sugar, umm, *oxi záchari*."

Sipping from her cup, she told Angela everything. Everything she could remember. When she finished, Angela asked to see the pictures. Cressida opened her phone and handed it to her.

Cressida watched as Angela slowly scrolled. Silence lay heavy. She couldn't work out what Angela was thinking. It seemed like an eternity waiting for her response.

"These are all from the cave?"

Cressida nodded.

"Can I upload these?"

Angela connected Cressida's phone to her computer. They both stared in silence watching the screen. When finished, she handed Cressida her phone.

"Tomorrow," she said, "I will print these off."

That night Angela gladly exchanged sleep for wonder. She spent the dark hours glued to her computer screen, closely examining each image, awed by what she saw. She had cleared her table and sorted through her bookcase, retrieving several reference books. She felt almost sick with the level of adrenaline pumping through her.

Initially she tried to interpret the paintings as a linear narrative, but the range of unfamiliar images hampered this approach. She could not confirm whether they were literal, representative or symbolic. She recognised some images, mainly those already known as sacred items, rituals or aspects of community life. Reconstruction of Minoan culture, mostly based on archaeological remains rather than text or images, limited her knowledge base. She kept her books close for support.

Given the enormity of the task, Angela decided to divide Cressida's images into sections, almost small vignettes, and fervently hoped she wasn't dissecting them inappropriately. She numbered the images and set up a classification spread-sheet. Then she sat back to think.

She would need help. If Cressida agreed, she would send some images to a couple of colleagues for their appraisal. People she trusted. There was no denying the photographs were incredible. Cressida's story was intriguing, almost fantastical. She turned the word fantastical over in her mind observing its transformation into the words fancy, fanciful. If they were unable to verify the images, people might ridi-cule Cressida, her story dismissed as mere fancy, the active imagination of a hysterical young woman suffering panic attacks. Angela felt a pang. She wished to spare the young woman any undue criticism, judgement or derision.

Something Cressida had said stayed with her. Damaged — Cressida claimed she was damaged, slightly broken. What had she meant by this? Was it this sense of brokenness she identified with? She liked the young woman and admitted feeling protective. She returned her focus to the screen and flicked through the images. A lump lodged itself in her throat. She needed to get to the cave. Tomorrow? Angela checked her diary. Once she could verify the authenticity of the paintings and estimate their age, she would need to notify Parks Management. And the museum. She sat up. The museum, yes, she would need to inform them.

Angela tried to swallow the lump taking up residence in her throat. This was an incredible discovery. It would certainly be the highlight of her career. Would the Director of the museum support an investigation without solid evidence, preferably artefacts? She knew the answer to that. If he were to finance it, she wondered if she would remain part of the exploratory team. She was not convinced. They had not always seen eye to eye on aspects of the mythology of the island.

She remembered an earlier conversation about Goddess worship and matrilineal descent, where he revealed a rather orthodox bias.

"The modern scholar categorically accepts that female rule is inherently unlikely," he had said. "The burden of proof rests with those who claim that female rule ever existed. If it cannot be proved, we may assume it did not exist, as it is after all, most improbable."

He reminded her that her predecessor had misconstrued her task as one of elevating women to a level equal with men, which he firmly dismissed. He had rationalised, "To be realistic, this is exceedingly difficult due to the reality of female biology and the universality of male dominance."

Bitter distaste flavoured her recollection. She wondered how he would take the news of this discovery and the strong female presence suggested by the images. 'The power of the interpreter,' she thought wryly. She looked back at the screen.

She was unaware she was nodding. She would need to be cautious about any interpretations she offered Cressida. It was important to create space for the stories to unfold without prejudice or direction. At this point, she could offer Cressida a mix of her training and research. She grinned; the task ahead was exciting. She could hardly wait to go to the cave.

CHAPTER SIXTEEN

"Are the paintings like Egyptian hieroglyphics?" asked Cressida, looking through the pages Angela had printed.

"Some might be. Others, I am not so sure. But, because the Minoans traded with the Egyptians, we have records that can help us reconstruct some of the images."

Angela selected a photo as an example. "The Crete-Mycenaean cultures share some recurring symbolic characteristics like Egypt and Libya. But what we have here," she placed an image on the table for Cressida to look at, "is possibly a form of writing called Linear A. It preceded Linear B from when the Greeks first came to the island from the mainland. So far, the experts tell us that Linear B mostly deals with administrative issues and lists. Unfortunately, they do not give us a picture of the political or religious landscape, let alone women's history or experience. The earlier ones, Linear A, are thought to be Minoan." She frowned. "These are yet to be deciphered."

Angela pulled out some photographs she had grouped together.

"There are things we can identify. Look at these gorgeous spirals, there are so many of them, and these here," she said, pointing, "are possibly boats on water. The double axes here are specifically sacred. They were ceremonial tools. Look closely."

Cressida squinted.

"What does it look like to you?"

"It could be a butterfly," she suggested hesitantly.

"Correct," said Angela. "Though, I didn't mean it to sound like a test. *Nai*, it looks like a stylized butterfly, the symbol of transformation and regeneration. Does it remind you of anything else?"

Cressida shook her head.

"Don't you think the blades resemble a woman's vulva?"

Cressida stared at her, surprised an older woman would be so blunt. Angela continued.

"A woman's vulva; with labia both sides and the clitoris down the middle. When you look at the axe with its long handle," she paused, "Long handle, phallic symbol, *nai*?"

What an odd conversation, but Cressida could see what Angela meant.

"It represents the male/female union — the source of life itself. Labrys is part of the word labyrinth, which translates to 'house of the labrys, the double axe.' The labrys is a symbol of rebirth and initiation that took place in a labyrinth. The individual would be facing her deepest fear — those that prevent moving forward in life. Then, as now, initiation involved a losing of the self, a symbolic death followed by spiritual rebirth. Spiralling was part of initiation ceremonies in some form."

"The labyrinth? Like the myth of Theseus and the Minotaur?" Cressida was on common ground.

"*Nai*, but so many points of contention," Angela answered. "For some, Ariadne was the Great Mother Goddess of Crete. She spun the fate of mortals, each individual's path with her thread. As you know, conquerors or occupiers would often reduce the deities of the conquered to demi-gods or legendary mortal figures. The Mycenaean imposed mainland Greek pantheon on Crete's culture. The story of Ariadne and her sacred labyrinth of initiation is one such casualty. They reduced her status to the daughter of the supposed King Minos. It is a story told through Greek eyes that adore their young hero. In the legend of Theseus, he follows Ariadne's thread, his destiny."

Cressida was intrigued. Angela had such a gift for storytelling.

"We must remember there were no Kings who lived in Palaces in Crete. These were Temples. Theseus went to the Temple where he met the Goddess Ariadne incarnated as a Priestess. Ariadne was the Mother Goddess of Initiation and Healing."

Awash with delight at this unknown version of the myth, Cressida scanned the images closely.

"You saw the horns at Knossos?" Angela asked.

Cressida nodded. She had visited the famous ruins of Knossos when she first arrived on the island, after her visit to Artemis' cave. Knossos was the renowned Palace of the Minoans, discovered and excavated by Arthur Evans — a destination, Cressida soon learnt, visited by hordes of tourists. She had avoided the many guides herding groups and walked quietly around the huge site by herself. The tourist brochure hung limply in her hand. There were tumbled rocks and stones, paved paths and amazing re-constructed temples and other buildings. Coloured paintings, 'frescoes,' corrected her brochure, gleamed in vivid colours. A massive stone bull's horn held court on a wall. The excavation was spectacular, but it had been confusing, too much for her and she had had to sit down, overcome by queasiness. She'd held her head and felt like crying. None of it made any sense. She had left the brochure on the seat.

"The horns honoured the Bull. The museum also has some bullhead pottery artefacts used to pour wine. There has been some debate that toward the end of Minoan society a cult of the Minotauraus, worshipping the Sacred Bull developed into a monotheistic tradition."

"Mono?"

"Belief in one God," explained Angela. "Oh, look here, the Moon and these are triads, more spirals, lilies, omphalos. They are all symbols of the Goddess. Oh, look at this one." She pulled out a photograph she had relished the night before. "This is simply stunning. It is the Tree of Life."

"Goddess," confirmed Cressida. "The Great Mother was a Goddess."

Angela nodded but quickly added, "I use the word in the same way Marija Gimbutas defined it. The word 'Goddess' can be problematic if you tend to imagine a female version of a transcendent Father God. Gimbutas termed 'Goddess' as, and I love this quote, *the infinite powers and patterns of nature expressed through plant, animal, and human life.'* Gimbutas was one of my favourite archaeologists."

Cressida held out a photograph. It seemed vaguely familiar. "Do you think this is the Goddess?"

The image was of a woman sitting on a tripod surrounded by animals and plants. There were lilies in her hair and she was dressed exquisitely with large golden hoops hanging from her ears. She wore a necklace of dragonflies and ducks.

Angela considered it. "Mmm, I'm not sure. She is older than how the Goddess is usually represented and, here we go, this one is the Goddess. Well Priestess as the incarnated Goddess." She put another photo in front of Cressida, "See how young and beautiful she is?"

"What is that next to her? That with its bird head on the body of an animal. Lion?" asked Cressida.

"It's a Griffin," Angela explained. She pointed out another example of a young strong bare-breasted goddess flanked by two lionesses. "These are simply breath-taking. I have seen some of these portrayals on seal stones at the museum. You should go sometime. And you should read some of Marija Gimbutas' books. I can loan you some. She has written about hieroglyphs as a series of pictorial symbols, sort of what we have here."

Before Cressida left, the two women checked their schedules and agreed to go together to the cave on Sunday.

They set off early morning with the luxury of access before the gates opened to the public. Cressida walked quickly so as not to change her mind. It was one thing to find the cave; it was another to think about entering it again. Walking up the gorge was freaking her out. Angela followed closely behind, carrying a backpack full of camera equipment, lights, rope and other archaeological incidentals. They walked for a while; the river was mostly dry, save for a few puddles caught up in large flat rocks.

Certain areas of the gorge had been roped off from the public, where rocks had fallen and landslides had created monumental grey, brown and slate-blue abstract fountains foaming down from pinnacles. Nothing looked familiar.

"I am so sorry," said Cressida. "I just don't know. It looks so different."

Even when she reached a bend in the river where she thought she might have been running at this point, the topography was not as she remembered.

They walked as far as the ancient village, which was further than Cressida had managed to reach on the night of the storm, and slowly re-traced their steps. Angela fired off a volley of questions. "Was there much space between the cliffs and the gorge and the riverbed? Were there trees or shrubs around? Can you remember reaching the big boulders? You passed the bridges, right? Did you climb up rock, or dirt or scree?"

"Not scree."

"But you saw the scree and sought elsewhere? It was definitely on your left, heading up? How high had the river risen? Were you on the path? How high do you think it was from the riverbed?"

Cressida sat down on a large rock. "I feel like an idiot," she said. "I cannot believe I have no fricken idea." She looked up at Angela. "You do still believe me, don't you? Even though I can't find it?"

She wanted to cry. She could hardly believe herself so why should anyone else. They stayed in the gorge for several hours, walking up and down various sections with neither of them wanting to give up. They eventually had to accept defeat and left the gorge deflated.

It was yet another wide-eyed night. Cressida stared at the far wall of the room. Sleep was supposed to be natural; it seemed anything but. She turned onto her right side, having heard it tilted one side of the brain into acquiescence, then sighing into the night, turned back in frustration. Even meditation; breathing in, breathing out, was to no avail. Two seconds was not going to cut it. Her mind buzzed, holding its own inquisition, seeking blame and retribution.

Was it her fault? The question loomed large before looping in a continual roll. She reviewed the narrative in her head and listed her points of reference. Okay, she would describe herself as an introvert; she has no interest in talking, talk, talk, talk, all day about just anything, with anyone. She found group stuff difficult. This was not wrong. Was it? The world around her was big, and she could feel its tension, and its tightness, but just because she felt this, was a part of this, did this make her responsible? What role did she play in this? Was what she felt real? Was her perception true? Truth? Hah. Now there was a big question. She wished she could see herself how others did. Perhaps glean something hidden that she could not see — about her, about how she was in the world. Look with open eyes, to answer her question. Was it her fault? He said it was. That is how he saw her. But he was a bully, charming but ultimately a bully, and so he, he saw her — as what?

His energy remained like a ghost, pervading her space, haunting her in her sleep — if it would only come — and in her waking moments. She was alone in her torment. She was alone now, just as she was then. He was insidious. How clever he was publicly portraying a persona of good cheer and witty repartee. She knew he was ruthless and snide. Undermining her in ways too slippery for others to see, forcing her to defer; to accept the power and intent of his words without question. Did he ever question himself?

Small and inadequate — that was her truth. Survival resorted to a pathetic line of defence, of closing down; to ignore him as much as possible without enraging him. He could be charming and she was compelled to engage, even though every word he spoke felt like splinters of shattered glass — death by a million cuts, his every word laced with barbs that poked, pricked and tormented her to varying degrees. She could never tell if he was ever genuine, viewing any potentially honest exchange with suspicion. The very air they shared scented with aversion and distrust. It was exhausting and she could never truly relax. She knew the games he played, his traps laid out in front of her like a deck of cards. A tarot reading of swords, towers and fools. Tension trolled her veins.

Cressida pleaded for sleep to come to her rescue. It was late and she always felt more vulnerable when she was tired. He prowled in shadows, dominating her headspace and she needed to be on her guard to keep him at bay. She did not know how to be free of him, how to rid her thoughts of him. He was dead. He was gone. Yet he remained larger than life.

She rolled over. The stuff she had discovered since the cave, about Pythia and how the women lived as a collective, about how they were one with the Goddess, the whole idea of sharing a divine spark, was proving too difficult to concede any ground to forgive him. Really? Like fuck! She recalled Harrownight. Those women had been like her mother, but stronger. Her mother was a sad excuse for a woman.

Revulsion sat heavy as the image of her mother slunk in. Her mother had made her choices. Unfortunately, those choices were purely selfish. Surely if you had children, you would have loved them enough to leave, or at the very least stand up for them against his violent outbursts. She sighed into the darkness. She would never seduce sleep while these thoughts remained rampant.

CHAPTER SEVENTEEN

They met a few days later at Angela's house. Angela had popped into the Taverna to tell Cressida she had received a response from her colleague. When Cressida arrived, Angela was sitting at the table with the email in front of her. Angela dispensed with the niceties and read sections from the main body of text.

"There have been fragments of somewhat similar cave paintings found in Mycenaean palaces such as Pylos, Mycenae and Tiryns. These were influenced by the Minoans with similar themes and motifs represented as hunting, bull leaping, and goddess worship ... your photographs ... the paintings ... we have nothing of this integrity, nothing to compare with ... The narratives appear very dense ... Intriguing ... I am afraid their meaning eludes me ... blah blah, nice hearing from you, send me more details blah blah."

Silence settled as each woman sat engrossed in her own thoughts. Angela shifted in her chair. Cressida scratched her head. The silence grew louder. Angela was the first to break from its hold and voice her frustration.

"Nothing. He tells us nothing. I can't read them. I don't know how."

Cressida did not reply. She watched the older woman grow

more flustered.

"I know this one," Angela's voice tapered off, couched in uncertainty. She pointed to what they each thought was a boat. "It, um, suggests a priestess, one child and an oarsman left many nights to an island, or part of an island, or part of land on the same island perhaps. All this correlates with your story."

Cressida sat impassively, not quite engaged. Angela's words seemed to waft. They hovered on the periphery, not quite finding passage to her ears. She could hear words spoken, but without meaning attached. Nothing could infiltrate a growing vagueness. She sensed a spreading numbness through her body and her mind wandered away from Angela's commentary in search of its source. She was vaguely aware she remained seated, calmly watching as Angela became engrossed again in the photographs.

Angela laid the images in front of Cressida on the table. She shifted a stack of papers onto the floor to make more room. Like a jigsaw, she placed them in the order she had numbered them. They totalled fifty images.

Cressida began to speak.

Angela looked up.

"*Synchórisi mou parakaló?*" she asked. "I'm sorry?" she repeated in English. She straightened up to look squarely at Cressida. Cressida's voice had an indiscernible ambience she did not recognise.

The faintest suggestion of soft muted pinks and beige coloured the room. Angela blinked, hoping to regain focus, and laid her hands flat on the table for support. The air seemed indistinct and blurred. Time slowed. To offset her growing confusion, Angela began to re-arrange the photographs. An unknown voice flowed from Cressida's lips.

We lived in the village for 14 generations, our ancestral bones connecting us to this place. The originals have long crossed over, their contribution seen in the eyes, blood and familial lines carried in our wombs.

Our foremothers prepared well. Our village prospered, sustained through trade, livestock and agriculture. Our oil was the finest in the land, traded far over the seas. We established alliances to raise daughters and sons. We have nourished strength and respect and integrity. We have bred children to provide balance to humanity in futures to come.

Cressida watched as Angela re-sorted the images. She felt no impulse to speak. A shawl of calmness hung loosely from her shoulders. She sat motionless, unaware of the conversation in the room.

"There," Cressida's mouth voiced, indicating the photo in Angela's hand. "You see those vessels?"

Angela nodded, though not sure who it was she was answering.

"Caskets for our crossing. To return to the Mother's embrace."

Angela sucked in air. The room danced in front of her.

"They are for the journey. My crossing will be soon."

There was a quiver and the room straightened, righting itself, cleared now of its muted tones. Angela saw a light flicker in Cressida's eyes.

"Cressida?"

Cressida blinked and nodded. Angela sucked in a deep breath and shook her head, unsure of what had just transpired. The photo in her hand offered something solid. She waved it in front of Cressida.

"I think you were inside a tomb, perhaps a communal tomb, given so many jars." Angela started to count the earthen vessels in the photograph.

"Seven," Cressida confirmed, yawning. "I'm so sorry but I just feel really tired now. I need to get a drink of water and I think I need a nap. Sorry, do you mind if I go now?"

Angela nodded, watching her leave, deep in thought.

The following day, Angela met Cressida at her work, and they sat over a coffee during her break.

"I can't be too long," Cressida said, "but I do need this."

She looked at Angela, waiting to learn what the source of her agitation was. Angela coughed and cleared her throat.

"Last night I read about this professor of cognitive science from the University of California. He studied perception and wrote that the world presented is nothing like reality. He described his work as straddling the boundaries of neuroscience and physics. And he wrote, well he wrote that it is all a magnificent illusion."

Angela paused, taking time to gather the words she needed to explain. "It is not my field, just something I have been looking into."

She cleared her throat again.

"There is a classic Darwinism argument, that it was our ancestors who 'saw' things accurately and were therefore the ones to survive natural selection. Hoffman, this professor, he said if you saw a tiger but thought it was a palm tree, then you were in trouble. And so, while that may sound plausible, he argued it was false. That it misunderstands a fundamental fact about evolution. He described how a given strategy achieved the goals of survival and reproduction... but..."

She stopped and eyed Cressida. "Are you following any of this?"

Cressida frowned. She was trying to stay on track but it was difficult.

"Keep going," she encouraged, hoping Angela would get to the point sooner rather than later.

Angela nodded. "Evolution has shaped us with perceptions that have allowed us to survive."

Cressida tilted her head as if to help her see from another angle as Angela continued.

"These perceptions guide adaptive behaviours, but part of that also involves hiding stuff from us that we don't need to know. If you had to figure out what was a palm tree, the tiger would have already eaten you. We have all been shaped by perceptions to stay alive. If I see something that I think is a snake, I do not pick it up. I do not step in front of a bus. But Hoffman said that it was an illogical flaw, to think, if we take something seriously, we should also take it literally."

She looked at Cressida. "You saw that woman. She was there for you. You survived your panic attack in the cave."

Cressida wondered where this was leading. "Bottom line please, Angela," she asked.

"Of course, let me try again," Angela replied. "I'm paraphrasing here." She took a breath. "We have conscious experiences; pain, tastes, moods, smells, emotions, *nai*? Yes? Part of this, called conscious structure, is a set of all possible experiences. When we have an experience, well, based on that experience, we might want to change what we are doing. So, we need to have a collection of possible actions we can take, so we can change how we act. That's the basic idea." She grinned.

"I can talk to you about my headache and believe I am communicating with you because you've had your own headache. Same thing as," Angela searched for some random examples, "apples, the moon, or the sun. Just as you have your own headache, you have your own moon. I assume it is like mine. However, that is an assumption that could be false, but that is the source of my communication and it is the best I can do. Hoffman concluded that the experiences of everyday life — my real feelings of a headache, my real taste of chocolate — are really the ultimate nature of reality."

She sat back and breathed in deeply. She looked at Cressida expectantly.

Mud, Cressida concluded. Angela was talking clear as mud. Then it dawned.

"You saw the woman?"

"I saw the woman. Well not, 'saw her'. She spoke. Yesterday. Through you."

"Through me?"

"Yes."

"While I was there?"

"Yes."

"Yesterday?"

A very pregnant pause settled on the table, interrupted only by overly cautious sips of now-cold coffee. Angela watched as Cressida consumed this information.

Cressida scowled. "That is so weird. I don't know how I feel about this. Like, am I like, you know — The Exorcist? Am I possessed?" She looked to the older woman for reassurance.

"I've been thinking about your panic attacks," Angela said. "With panic attacks, we stop all mental activity and slip into a simpler state of trance in which our sense of self, our boundary between our internal and external worlds becomes greatly diminished. We literally enter a state in which we and the universe are basically one — sort of regressive really, returning to a primitive state of being by shutting down individual awareness. There is no 'I', no other, no environment, no reflection — only experience and instinct."

Cressida nodded. Maybe.

"In this state, you were open to changing your perception, and subsequently, your reality."

Another thought crossed Cressida's mind. She looked into those big kind brown eyes. Angela believed her. She let the thought settle. She swallowed. Angela hardly knew her, but believed her. He never had. Punishment meted out on the premise of her lies. Hit for making trouble with her so-called stories. She swallowed away the growing lump in her throat and rubbed her eyes.

"I want to change my reality," she said getting up, "I don't want to cry." She hugged her new friend tightly. "Thank you," she whispered coarsely.

CHAPTER EIGHTEEN

Cressida looked forward to the times she worked on the images with Angela. She felt, dare she say, happy. It was in the smallest of things that Angela would say, spontaneous comments she made, and that, now and again, Angela would touch her. And it didn't hurt. Ever.

They met whenever they were not working. Usually at Angela's stone house, which although small — having just one compact living space and a single bedroom — was a place of refuge and comfort. They would select a group of photographs and spread them out on the table and floor, talking freely and easily about the stories they inspired. Aside from the initial emails that Angela had sent, they kept Cressida's discovery secret.

"You know I don't care about anyone else knowing. I only wish I knew what it means. I am just happy you want to help," Cressida said.

Two timeframes began to emerge, distinguished by slight differences between similar images and the style of the paintings. Angela and Cressida agreed the first timeframe portrayed the history of the first village that Pythia had left. A small pile of photographs was marked accordingly. The second they reasoned, represented the women's village.

Cressida's recollections helped to develop a pictorial glossary and the two women became adept at allocating the images to either period.

Cressida held up an image. "Do you think this looks like a ceremony, like an earlier image? Like that one. Over there."

She leaned across the table to pick up the photo. She held them together to compare.

"Both are pretty erotic, really. Do you think this one is also of Sacred Union? It looks a bit different."

"Do you know anything about Sacred Union, other than what the woman in the cave told you?" asked Angela.

Cressida shook her head. "Not really, only that Sacred Union sounds pretty raunchy."

Angela picked up a small book. "There is a definition in here," she said, thumbing her way through the pages. "Ah *nai*, here it is. *Hieros gamos* or *Hierogamy*. In Greek, it means holy marriage."

She traced the words with her finger as she translated. "It refers to a sexual ritual that plays out a marriage between a god and a goddess. The couple incarnate as deities." She looked up to explain. "In ancient times, a priestess performed sexual purification rituals. Remember that term you used — Negation. Was that it? Remember, with Vrados?"

Cressida nodded, recalling the story.

"In some cultures, all women were required to serve in the Temple at some time. The men made offerings to the Goddess to participate in sacred ritual."

Angela put down the book. "This may explain why the Bible refers to women of pagan cults as prostitutes. There was a transaction. Men made an offering, which I guess was interpreted as payment for sex. Idiots. Sex was perceived differently then."

She put a loose strand of her long dark hair behind her ear as she continued.

"In ancient cultures, especially within matriarchal societies, sex was considered ennobling and uplifting. Sex was a pathway to the Divine. It could bring you closer to the Gods, or Goddess in our case. I remember an archaeological dig in India that had come across goddess figurines. The ancient transcript referred to the Goddess as an 'independent woman,' when translated in Sanskrit, was synonymous with the word harlot. Harlots, prostitutes, do you see a theme here? Words that have now been desecrated. Like the word virgin. Did you know these priestesses were called virgins?" Angela asked. "That sex had nothing to do with being called a virgin?"

"Well, I do know if you have sex, you are not a virgin," said Cressida.

"Oh," laughed Angela, "you misunderstand me. On the contrary, the Goddess and her Priestesses were Virgins and as these images show, they definitely had sex. I know you are familiar with Artemis who was called the Virgin Huntress. Same thing. It did not mean these women never had sex. It meant they were independent of any man. The fertility goddess was always a virgin. She belonged to no man but gave herself to any man. Hers was a service of fertility, after all. And the man serves the Goddess."

Angela spun another thread. "I think, and correct me if

I am wrong," as if Cressida ever would, "that the meaning of virgin changed alongside a growing concept of paternity. In some cultures, this correlated with private ownership of livestock. With the introduction of ownership came the desire for men to bequeath these herds to their children. For a man to identify his children, women had to stop having sex with other men. So, 'belonging to no man', soon became synonymous with not having sex with a man, equated to being a virgin. Control over women in the earliest patriarchal family structures."

Cressida sat quietly taking in this information. Angela knew so much. She always seemed to see things differently than other people she knew. She liked this.

Angela was on a roll, immersed in her topic. "Women and sex have always been a difficult combination for patriarchy. Language is such a powerful tool. Nowadays virgin and harlot are on opposite ends of the women's sexual spectrum. We either do not want it or want it too much. It is another example of dualism, opposite extremes."

Angela jumped out of her chair and ran into her room. She called out to Cressida.

"Have you heard of the Malleus Maleficarum? The Hammer of Evil-Doing Women? Apparently, it was a bestseller, second only to the Bible in terms of sales, for almost 200 years."

"No," grinned Cressida, "but I wish I had. Sounds gruesome."

Angela returned waving a book in the air. "I have to read it to you. Greek," she explained. She sat down and flicked through the pages. Finding what she sought, she placed the book in her lap to enable her to demonstrate air-quotation marks. She read, "All witchcraft stems from carnal lust which in women is insatiable."

Cressida interrupted, "Insatiable? Like all we crave for is sex. Now this is an argument for projection if ever I heard one. You don't think this guy is blaming women for his inadequacies?"

Her question hung in the air as Angela continued to read. "While Eve is viewed as a sexual temptress, the epitome of women's carnal nature, the Virgin Mary is revered because she transcends sexuality — she remains the perpetual virgin."

"Aah," nodded Cressida, "I was once told by an amazing expert on this stuff, something about the word virgin meaning 'remaining true to oneself.' It has nothing to do with sex at all."

They both laughed.

"Patriarchy has so much to answer for." Angela sighed.

Cressida tried to fit her modern-day understanding of naming women sluts or whores into the evening's discussion. It surprised her that priestesses had been called both prostitutes and virgins. But then again, she reasoned, since the cave, and since she had met Angela, she was learning so many new things that appeared right off any scale. She couldn't understand how women like Pythia and Ashtar, who were so strong and clever, could be dismissed through history based on whether they did or didn't have sex.

A phrase, *know thyself,* flashed though her mind. It did not make any sense so she didn't ask Angela what it might mean. She was content to sit and acknowledge that what she thought she knew yesterday and what she had learnt today were so different from what she thought she knew or what she learnt in school. It was like calling the colour yellow a cow. It just didn't fit.

Cressida looked up. Angela had asked her something.

"Sorry, what?"

Angela held up the two photographs Cressida had been comparing.

"If we take it that this first one is Sacred Union, then I think this other one is also some sort of ritual associated with sex, perhaps fertility, but I'm not sure, it has things that are different. Good pick-up Cressida," she praised. "Do you have any ideas? Have you had any vision about this? It seems integral to something. Otherwise, why would it be here?"

"I can't recall anything," said Cressida. However, the question stirred something faint. A faint what?

"This is something like, like what has evolved and whatever this means is what has changed. All conjecture of course, but I think…" Angela paused, pondering the point.

"Well, it does look different, somehow." Cressida tried to be offhand after Angela's compliment. "There doesn't seem to be one particular man, like with Pythia, you know, the Consort, not that I can see, anyway. I don't know what these other women mean either. What do you reckon?"

She looked away, feeling uncomfortable. The differences she could see were puzzling. Something just did not seem right, did not make sense. She looked at Angela from the corner of her eye. Angela always seemed able to laugh at herself. She easily claimed ignorance. She was laughing now even while trying to recall what she knew to fill in some of the gaps.

"Well, it's pretty clear women from both communities copulated in ritual. This one suggests sex, which of course happened in the Sacred Union, as we know. But you are right, Cressida, it does looks different. Perhaps it's—"

Cressida interrupted in an attempt to deflect her feelings of incompetence. "Perhaps? This is all Perhaps. It must drive you mad there is not some formulated equation to solve this. All we know is what we don't know."

"*Nai*, of course, you are correct," grinned Angela.

They looked again at the photos, half hoping the more they looked, the more they would see. Surely, by becoming more familiar, what may or may not have happened might bring truth to light? Cressida was right; Angela was frustrated it was all speculative. But that was the nature of the territory. With the photo in front of them yet to be deciphered, part of their pleasure lay in discussing the possibilities.

Angela broke the silence with a hypothesis. "A purification ceremony is my guess. If we look at the first one there are, see this, these bracelets. Do you think they look like snakes? You remember the Minoan goddess sculpture I showed you earlier from the book, where the priestess has them wrapped around her arms?"

Cressida nodded.

"Remember when you first asked about Pythia?" said Angela. "Remember the Delphi Oracle was described as Python, as Pythia, and that Pythia was slayed by Apollo. Now there is a classic example of patriarchy vanquishing Goddess worship: the priests of Apollo took possession of the Oracle by destroying the Python. Snakes were sacred, a sign of the Priestess. Oh, remember Ashtar. You told me about Ashtar being kissed by the serpent."

Hearing Ashtar's name spoken aloud brought a flush of joy to Cressida. She realised she had not had her recurring dream since the cave.

"The snake as wisdom indicates learning," said Angela. "Yet in this image, these women don't have snakes, and they appear older. I do not think they represent priestesses. I am not sure of the connection to the youths they are coupling with, but I agree there is some sort of connection. Except for this image."

Angela held a photograph depicting an image of an older woman with many young men. Cressida stifled an urge to make a joke about cougars and toy boys but held her tongue. Somehow, it did not seem appropriate to denigrate these women. Angela was too engrossed to notice Cressida's restraint. She leaned in to examine it closer.

"Have we seen that woman before?" asked Cressida. "Or maybe I am seeing these photos over and over and over, and I am losing track."

She looked at the image again. "Are all these lines snakes? They are everywhere."

"Some of them are. There is a lot I agree. Perhaps this one here may refer to travel over the waves. I am not certain."

Cressida rubbed her head. It was starting to hurt.

"So, you think a purification ritual then, eh?" asked Cressida, hoping to distract the gnawing fuzzy cloudy sensation, which was creeping into the back of her mind. It was like a well; dank, dark, moist and full of unknown shadows, but knowing that deep, deep down, there would be water.

"*Nai*, some sort of an elaborate ceremony. These usually represent the passage from innocent and pure child to the duty-bound adult. These are really different."

'Focus,' Cressida instructed herself. She widened her eyes to help her concentrate on what Angela was saying. The darkness at the back of her head was distracting. She absently clapped her hands hoping to squash a mosquito buzzing around her.

Angela was absorbed in trekking a path through a jungle of information and did not notice Cressida fidgeting.

"There were seasonal rites as well as personal rites. Rites of passage are initiations coinciding with birth, cutting of teeth, puberty, menstruation and death. These naked female images represent more than just fertility; they represent procreation, nurturing, death and regeneration. That is why I think this image is important. I just can't work out why."

Angela paused to draw breath. Her cheeks glowed. In silence, she followed a tangent of thought into a dead end and returned empty handed. She looked at Cressida and apologised.

"*Lipame*. All I have done is collate the research with what I know about some basic rituals. I am superimposing this on the paintings. Cressida, I am laying on a slab of my baggage so please don't take it as gospel."

Cressida giggled. Angela's use of the English language was at times so funny.

"*Lipame*? Excuse me?" Angela looked confused.

Cressida shook her head, trying to maintain her composure. Angela looked back at the photograph. Cressida beamed. Angela was wearing, her 'logical, rational, attention to detail' cap. Slightly hunched over as if her head weighed her down, drawn into focus with a knitting of her dark thick eyebrows. Her eyes were so dark you could not discern the outline of her pupils as she peered into some abstract chasm of explanation, thought or rationale.

"Rites of passage seek to increase a person's inventory of spiritual energy, but here, what is this?" Angela dived deeper. "The image suggests a process of a rite, I can see this, but, but, what is the meaning of this?"

Silence became a third person in the room and took a seat, settling in, making itself comfortable. Angela remained absorbed in the photo. Cressida watched the mosquito fly away.

Finally, Angela spoke. "This one here, see this? This is an uroboric symbol, see?"

"The snake eating itself?"

"Yes."

"I see the snake eating itself, but I don't know what uroboric means."

"This image, see?" Angela sorted through the pile of photos "This is an ancient symbol depicting a serpent swallowing its own tail and forming a circle. It is self-devouring in the sense of constantly re-creating itself. It represents the infinite cycle of nature's endless creation and destruction, life and death. It is uroboros. In Greek literature, Plato described the uroboros as the first living thing created in the universe which became the earth itself."

"Another snake?" Cressida shuddered.

Angela found the photo she had been searching for.

"Most ceremonies in tribal communities have a similar set of stages." She listed them, counting down on her fingers. "Offerings, purification, cleansing and prayers. What we see here, I think, is that there was purification through water, possibly just sprinkling. Given they were seafaring folk, as we know from the first village, perhaps this ritual continued."

"And why is this circular, this bit? It doesn't have a snake?" Cressida pointed to some lines and images that seemed to spiral around other images.

Angela looked carefully. "Time moves in cycles, not a terminating line. Regeneration follows death. The proportions of the womb on these female images promise regeneration from the body of the Goddess — re-entering the goddess body to be reborn."

Cressida sat back. "You are aware I am finding this incredibly difficult?" she said. Her head was starting to spin.

"I should hope so," said Angela. "This has taken me years of study."

Laughing comfortably, Angela continued in jest. "Okay, now for Lesson number 537: Primitive Ritual Ceremonies. Context, of course, and I will try to be succinct."

"Will it help me understand?" asked Cressida.

"I hope so," Angela said. "Okay, the first stage is usually Purification, the objective is to clean away all sins and stains of the body. Many ceremonies used Holy water sprinkled over offerings as well as over their body. In some societies, the cutting of hair was important but I am not seeing that here. Cleansing and Purification often went together, and in our case, were administered by a High Priestess, the Pythia. Cleansing is not just with water, sometimes it can be done by wafting smoke."

"The blackened walls in the cave?" suggested Cressida.

"*Nai*. Exactly. The walls and ceilings of caves have retained this evidence of ritual performed in caves."

Cressida shifted unconsciously at the mention of the cave. Angela continued to explain.

"And the last stage, well almost, are prayers, which most likely were chanting and dancing. Along with music, they could bring on altered states, trances and the like, through sound or frequencies."

"Then the grand finale of fucking?" Cressida was too tired to mind her language around the older woman. Moreover, she reasoned, they had been talking about sex all evening. That was her excuse, anyway.

"*Nai*, you are right, the final stage is copulation. Professionally, we refer to it as an orgiastic ritual where the men plant the seed in the Mother. But this," she said, retrieving the photo they had initially been discussing, and placed it on top of the splayed images, "you are correct, it is different. Look here, these images denote grain, suggesting seed. See it is a woman who carries it."

Cressida was becoming too sleepy to look closer. She leaned back instead.

"Hah," she replied, "so instead of the snake tempting Eve

with wisdom, it is our Eve who is carrying the seed tempting the young men."

Angela looked at her. "What? I never thought of that. *Nai*, seeds of wisdom. Oh well done Cressida. Very astute!"

Cressida turned away, not quite knowing how to respond. In the cloudy recess of her mind, she had some vague murky thought about men fucking their mothers. But ewww, too gross to contemplate and she was too embarrassed to ask. She yawned to distract her thoughts.

"I'll do some further research on this one and call you if I find something. And you, are you still practising your meditation? No, seriously. We need your visions and dreams, and the connection you have. They are really helpful."

Cressida stiffened. It was scary to think about seeing spirits.

"I am free next Tuesday ok? Also," Angela said, "if you have any time off, you should go to some ruins on the island. I remember you said something about the rock holding the story, well go and touch some rocks." She smiled, but Cressida could see she was serious.

The two women quietly packed up the photos and tidied the books, lost in their private thoughts about the evening's discoveries. Cressida exhaled loudly, her head dense and bleary.

"I need a glass of wine, or five," she joked.

"Should you?"

Cressida froze. The growing blob inside had lost its demanding crawl inside her skin and had become like a hermit, reclusive, hidden and unobtrusive, as if its survival depended upon not being felt or remembered. Cressida had not thought of her condition in the last few days.

"You know?"

"I am familiar with the signs. I am sorry if I have intruded." Angela turned to re-straighten the neat pile of papers.

"Aright, then, a cup of hot chocolate," said Cressida surprising herself with a light-hearted response. "Come for some hot chocolate with me?" she asked. Angela nodded and turned off the light as they left the house to head down to the taverna.

CHAPTER NINETEEN

Cressida had not intended to return to the north coast on her day off, but Angela's suggestion to go and visit sites felt like the right thing to do. She found herself sitting on a worn cold stone in a slightly excavated, slightly restored ancient theatre. The birds around her twittered excitedly and, like the villagers back on the south coast, already knew too much about her, more than she would ever guess, more than she would ever tell. They flittered in, out, and around her as she had walked along the timeworn pathway of uncovered paved stones.

Back at the information centre, she would have learnt about the site's initial discovery and excavation, but she had arrived early and there was no one to take her entrance money, nor give her a brochure to explain the many mounds of piled rocks. There was no sign to tell her whether the ruins were Minoan, Hellenic or Roman, but she guessed, that as a once bustling town, it would have been etched on some Linear B tablets now kept safe under glass in a more austere and controlled environment. Not like here where she walked freely on and over the site and could sit at leisure on an aged stone. There were cyclone wire fences on the site, designating areas waiting patiently for exploration. Anticipation not yet paying the cost required for deeper probing.

The site was reminiscent of many sites in Crete: destroyed by earthquakes, ransacked by pirates, appropriated by following civilisations. Fields strewn with rocks, each with a story to tell. This site was inhabited by pesky birds who shared her story without permission, and flies that swilled around the sweaty troughs of her underarm pits, buzzing around her face in the hope of less rancid moisture. Other visitors to the site had followed a somewhat gleeful cry "I found the Roman cisterns," leaving her to sit quietly on the aged stones of an amphitheatre, taking in sights, sounds, images and feelings, all vying for attention.

'What would they have performed here?' she wondered.

A breeze meandered through surrounding olive groves and she sank into a deep calm, enjoying the peace emanating from within. Happy was a place she rarely visited, so she lingered awhile. Too short a time before tourists disturbed her solitude. She left them to photograph the many angles of rock on rock. She strolled back to her car concluding she would take another, longer road trip to harvest more of this contentment. Happy was not to be underestimated. Within such a landscape she might find resolution.

She sat in her car. 'What next?' she wondered. Across the bay, the peninsula summoned. Close to Artemis' cave.

Cressida walked into a small stone church. She was not sure

what she was looking for, but felt perhaps some of the stories held in the 13th century walls might confide past truths. The icons with their lowered heads, gazed at her. Byzantine lives in a palette of reds and golds; haloed, embracing babes in arms, killing dragons and much to her surprise many with fingers raised in a mudra reminiscent of Hindu statues of Shiva or Buddha. Listening into the shadows, she could almost hear echoes of past incantations of deep timbre masculine voices. Deep, smooth velvet, a caressing soundscape accompanied by a residue scent of incense permeating the walls from centuries of ceremonies and — the thought struck her — of rituals.

The Church has appropriated everything.

Was this something Angela had said? She paused. She felt the frays of a faraway dreamy fog expanding from minuscule droplets into oceanic depths of her mind. It brought with it a gift of sleepiness without fear or fright. Her head warned of an approaching headache, she closed her eyes.

Within a gentle darkness, Cressida observed from a faraway place, a man in black, wearing a black jacket. Coat? No, a black frock. His beard was as black as his eyes and he wore a black hat over black curls stroking his neck. Man in black reading from a large book held lovingly in large hands. Large hands with black hair on the back with black tendrils curling up his fingers. She watched, entranced.

The man in black finished his incantation and bells tolled. Cressida held her breath, eyes closed, no interruption from anything as noisy as inhalation or exhalation. Her eyes opened to her mind's abyss. The man in black was no longer there. A woman, not in black but with long black hair, black eyes, eyebrows defined by their blackness, but with too much skin tanned the colour of earth to ever be described as a woman in black, stood in his stead. Skin shining through purple robes tied at her waist but long and open. Her breasts are revealed; normal bosoms except they are not covered. Her legs long, strident. Pythia? She stands strong and defiant. Her incantation fills the man in black's pause. Bells no longer toll. Drums beat. Her song accompanied by hand-drums drumming.

The woman's voice textures the air with melodic, rhythmic chanting. Her song laced with a power, coming from beyond the body vessel that gives it shape and resonance. She sings in ceremony, in reverence, in honour. She sings her song of truth and beauty, of life and death, hunger and pain. She sings her song of rain and ocean, of rivers and springs, of heat and wind, and harvests of fruits and grains. She sings of sacrifice and offerings. Of the moon and the sun and the stars that guide to faraway places and glitter in reverence to ancestors' glory. Of mothers and babies; love in its most powerful form. Of earth and soil and homes and hearth. Singing of blood like water, streaming from stone, weeping of long ago times, bleeding the anguish and pain of forgotten rituals, unkempt altars. Of faith and compassion and forgiveness. Her song swirls in the whirlpool of the mind's evolution from magical and mystical to logical and cerebral. Explanations and phenomena, that which is and always will be, the unknown, the unexplained, the unspoken. Where knowledge and outcomes and realisation are reduced to apples in the garden and a snake in a tree. The tall, strident, strong woman looks at Cressida, her gaze piercing into the core of her being.

Cressida swayed gently. A wave gushes up from the foundation of all humanity and she trembled, feeling as if the earth's water — the earth's blood, washes through her. It is a tsunami of tears, her tears, and melts her from inside to out. She dissolves into the stony floor, slipping through the cracks into the trodden ground to find herself within the earth's beating heart. It is as if she is a whirlwind of light and dark, energy and entropy, action and reaction, movement and rest. Tiny molecules beat as one, pulsating with the undulating breath and heartbeat of the earth, until slowly, ever so slowly, Cressida exhales. The noise reverberates from cell to cell, and she awakens in the small stony 13th Century church, having only momentarily closed her eyes.

Serendipity prevailed and Cressida's visit to the north coast coincided with the rising of a super moon. It must have been Angela who told her this was special. No one else she knew would know something like that. Cressida searched her memory. Angela had said something about spirituality and the ego contesting. She had compared it to Pythia and Vrados. Cressida had been unable to shake their story from her thoughts. It felt like a part of her, and that somehow the island had colluded. In some vague way, Cressida felt connected through a sense of place. The land felt powerful underfoot. It was as if invisible tentacles had emerged from the soil, winding up her ankles from the sand, wrapping around her legs, upwards towards her heart. She felt enmeshed in a delicate web of translucent filigree.

This feeling was a constant companion. She couldn't say how, or even what she really meant, but she had learnt enough Greek to say, *"Ti na kano,"* what can I do? As the land took hold, she learnt to follow its flow. All of which had led her to this hillside overlooking the bay to watch a full moon rise.

Cressida considered Angela's remark about spirituality and ego contesting. The comment poked her insecurity. She knew nothing about spirituality except what she had learnt at Sunday School. She pulled her hoodie over her head and hugged herself, the evening carrying a slight chill on a lazy breeze.

Touching her body served as a reminder. Her morning sickness had receded, the embryo hiding behind an obsession conceived in the cave. She sought answers outside not inside. That seemed okay, there was still time to decide. The noise in her head had abated, drawn into conversation with the images from the cave. Everything else seemed less important. For now, she was on a peninsula, on a rock, facing northeast and waiting for the sun to set behind her and for the moon to rise. She had navigated tiny narrow maze-like streets that twisted and turned through isolated timeless villages carved from stone for this privilege.

Clouds, larger than puff, positioned themselves a fingertip above the horizon, spreading along its axis. Above these clouds, pink and baby blue pastels hoarded up the remaining sunlight to orchestrate a scenic serenity; sky and water immersed in softness.

Other people arrived, and Cressida relaxed. Her choice of where to be and when to be there, affirmed. Not knowing what time the moon was to rise, she was anxious she might have had to wait awhile. The newcomers conveniently heralded a soon-to-be timeframe. United they witnessed the ocean stealing the pink from the sky and transforming itself into a pink-grey smoothness, flat as an iron-starched tablecloth spreading towards eternity. As the pink leached down to sea level, the clouds remained staunch, their white fluffiness sitting abreast deeper shades of blue, almost grey, slowly darkening in unison with the swallowing of light from the west.

The clouds conspired to disguise the moon's entry into the world and tricked Cressida into thinking the moon would alight from the horizontal line separating water and air. Instead, it burst through the clouds, already high in the night sky. Framing the moon, the clouds haloed its entry as an ethereal godly-like being — the light reminiscent of a Joseph Turner painting, captured in oils to be held in perpetuity. Cressida was glad her moment was ephemeral. It felt too special to remain permanent.

That night Cressida dreamt of the tall black-haired woman. In her dream, she heard a whisper. Something... something about knowing stories, and she experienced a sense of rejoicing flood her body as she drifted in timelessness, recalling the magic held in the cave. The scent of flowers was strong, and Cressida breathed in deeply, stirring in her sleep. She observed the tall woman awakening, rising from a bed of flower petals.

The celebrations and festivities of Sacred Union had finished in the early hours. Upon awakening in the Temple, Pythia walked down to the village to ensure that the women who did not reside in the Temple had returned safely from their trance and were in their compounds. She sprinkled holy water through the narrow pathways for this final blessing, her feet skimming softly over the cobbled stones. Her silence juxtaposed to the cacophony of snores, grunts, farts and belches. Pythia laughed quietly. She felt light-hearted amid this base humanity that was unfiltered in sleep. She was distracted from sensing shadowed figures at the crossroads until the moment of touch.

Cressida watched on, unable to call out a warning.

Strong hands grasped Pythia. A cloth forced into her mouth. Her gasp stifled, she bristled at the indignity of male hands accosting her on this very night of the Mother's Sacred Union. Enraged, she sought to identify her attackers, but was prevented by a clenched fist. The force spat her to the ground.

Cressida slept on, horrified, unable to wake, unable to help.

Pythia rolled inward, protecting her stomach. This provoked a change in the men's attack and strong calloused hands lifted her. Pythia could smell their fear, their anger, their brutality. Okri could not disguise the violence of their souls.

The onslaught of punches focused on her belly; her sacred space filled with the night's offering. She vaguely realised they were not intent on killing her. Of course, they were too cowardly to face the repercussions of the Mother's revenge, but she was stunned to think they would seek to kill Her child! Had they no idea of a Mother's wrath? Incredulity succumbed to unconsciousness.

The men, feeling the fight leave her crumpled body, dropped her: a dishevelled mess of body, blood and bone. They grunted, acknowledging their deed and then fled.

Cressida woke with a start, holding onto her belly, distraught and fuelled with anger.

Angela looked up from a reference book. "Are you aware of the theory of parallel worlds?" She had brought out more books from her small bedroom that were now stacked in assorted piles in and around the table. Cressida accused Angela of having a secret library hidden in an underground cellar.

"Mmm," replied Cressida, her head buried in Angela's laptop. She knew Angela was trying to find something logical to put the recent events into a context of scientific enquiry or at least, rational thought. 'And she thought quantum physics might do it?' Cressida smirked.

"Parallel worlds are a speculative theory of bizarre consequences inherent to quantum mechanics. But hey, we are swimming in bizarre at the moment, don't you think?"

Cressida was too absorbed in her own reading and grunted. Angela continued reading aloud. "All possible alternative histories are real, representing an actual, though parallel world. It is believed parallel worlds can and do interact."

"Ahah." Cressida nodded. She looked up from her reading, inspired.

"I have to go there."

Angela put down her book. "And where is there?"

Cressida spoke too rapidly to pretend any semblance of coherent speech. "Yes. I am getting these dreams and visions, which is helping to unfold the story. Then, well, I should then, don't you think? I should visit. Yes. Oh, where? Delphi. I think I should go to Delphi. Have you been? Ashtar, yes Ashtar went there. Perhaps going will help me understand more. Maybe not, but maybe. And Pythia, remember what you said, she was the Oracle of Delphi? Something like that. I have to go."

Her enthusiasm radiated.

"Can't argue with that." Angela grinned.

The thoughts multiplied in Cressida's mind.

"I remember something, well I think I remember, who the fuck knows, well, the woman had said something like 'I know your story by knowing my own; I know my story by knowing yours.' Hey, did you say that too?"

She tried to recollect the conversation, before continuing her line of thought.

"Well I think this will help. The Oracle was in Delphi, if it is our Oracle and by knowing her story I will know mine, and ipso fatso, I will know the woman's story too. Yes?"

"Ipso fatso." Angela grinned and raised her eyebrows.

Cressida lifted her coffee cup, her eyes alight.

"To Delphi," she toasted.

"To Delphi," Angela replied.

It was the cats who welcomed her; three of them mewing in greeting. The two males rubbed against each other lovingly. The smaller black female joined them, though maintained some distance. Cressida tossed her bag over the small gate, padlocked to keep out intruders. She hesitated and then stepped on a small bar of the gate, laid her stomach on the top bar and heaved herself over. Once on the other side any caution she may have felt dissolved, and she strode resolutely down to the site. She was halfway down the path when the cats joined her. Delighted, she took photographs. The three felines accompanied her to the ruins.

"Where shall I sit?" she asked them, but they just ran alongside playfully, offering only companionship. She walked to the central ruin, the main Tholos, now a crumpled form of dislodged boulders. Ignorant of details but from somewhere deep inside her, Cressida was aware the space held more power than she could imagine. She set her things on a fallen stone and quickly, and mind you, very guiltily, stepped over the wire barricade into the centre of the great monument. Impulsively she opened her arms to the sky, her heart to the earth, and turned around 360 degrees. Without thinking, she held hands over her head with palms together, and then touched her eyes and mouth. She quickly stepped back over the wire to return to the side of tourist, not priestess, and sat to collect her thoughts.

Her attention diverted to the cats. Their mood had changed and the larger cat now stalked the smaller black one. Again, and again, tail twitching, pausing and holding still, then lunging. He chased her over rocks and ruins, stalking and chasing. The female responded with hisses. They ran off, away from Cressida.

'Corny as all fuck and sure as hell, I will not be telling anyone, but I know this place. I have been here before.'

Pressure welled behind her eyes. Impulsively she kissed a stone. Perhaps a mistake, as feelings she could not identify flooded her. Around her, she saw a collection of fallen marble laid along the path awaiting a reconstruction that would possibly never happen.

Ashtar watched her. She felt the young woman's desire to walk amongst the stones, to touch them, lay upon them, embrace them. Ashtar knew these rocks would gladly hold her, to help her to find the space within all that is.

'That's apt,' thought Cressida, looking around at the rocks. They were symbolic of past belief and rituals that lay idle, patiently waiting for another day. The celebration of the Great Mother and the worship of all goddesses had long passed their due-by date. Cressida sat quietly, content with her exploration of the site and feeling that as much as it was an external, physical discovery, it was internal. Warmth flowed through time immemorial.

A heavy accented voice interrupted her thoughts. "You know it is not allowed you be here?"

"Yes," she answered, truthfully.

He turned and walked away. She wondered if the guard would use his walkie-talkie for re-enforcements to evict her. But perhaps, since he had already opened the gate for other tourists, it was no longer an issue. She had no idea how long she had been sitting there. Voices, footsteps crunching the gravel path, the presence of people now intruding. Feeling conspicuous, she mourned the loss of solitude. Her feline companions were gone. She listened as the guard spoke to a tourist, all the while cameras clicked to capture a memento, a memory, an inspiration. The guard seemed uneasy and returned to question Cressida about some oil he found on the Temple step. His discomfort disturbed her, so she gathered her things. As she walked up the hill, she felt a profound sadness descend. Perhaps she did not achieve what she thought she would — whatever that was. She ambled slowly back to the main Delphi ruins further up the main road, the ones belonging to Apollo.

The two sites sat either side of the hill, within easy walking distance. Cressida breathed in the scenery. It was so pretty, with a panoramic view that encompassed sheer grey-green mountains, a gorge laden with olive groves that wound up from the sea of ancient Kirraba and beyond to the gulf towards Corinth. Cressida had read it was at an altitude of around 500 metres and was glad she was there in summer rather than the snow whipped winter.

'*Ormorfo topio?*' she thought, wondering if this was correct Greek for beautiful scenery. She wished she had remembered to bring her book or could ask Angela.

She paid her money and walked through the gate, entering

properly this time into Apollo's den. She was hot and there were people everywhere. Sweat trickled down her back. She felt she was carrying the weight of the torturous sun, its heat threatening to consume her. She sat in the shade on an ancient rock of no apparent significance to knit her thoughts together, oblivious to various languages wafting around her. She looked up the pathway, up the hill, waiting for the tour group to move on. It was the path to the Omphalos stone. She knew the marble monument marked the centre of the world, its navel. She had read it was a copy.

'How ridiculous to have a fake one, here in this place of all places,' she had thought. Apparently, it was one of many.

This site did not feel the same as the other. This was a surprise. It was not as intense. Hot yes, but not intense. There were no cats here either. She stood up and walked up the old stone steps, preferring them to the newly constructed concrete path. The marble underfoot was smooth. She walked the path of antiquity.

Ashtar watched her, noting the shadow of disappointment that flavoured the scene. She smiled. Truth was glorious in all its secrets.

Cressida stopped at the Rock of the Sibyl.

'Sibyl? Why not Pythia? Is this where she spoke?' It was a

rock, not sculptured as she had anticipated. This surprised, yet pleased, her. Beside the rock was a small bush. Not very old, although admittedly she could only see shoots from a sunken trunk.

'Perhaps an ancestor of the Oracle's laurel tree,' she hoped.

Cressida looked around at the people on the path and again at the bush. She was tempted. Just one leaf... but her desperation was not committed enough and she failed to overcome her hesitation and lost courage. The moment passed. She faced her cowardice with moral platitudes about doing the right thing. Angela might be proud of her, but she tasted disappointment.

Her head throbbed; a headache loomed. She walked up the path and then decided on a photo, a selfie to capture the memory. She held her phone up and looked into a grinning reflection that belied a descending fog of weighted pain. She did not even look like herself. She blinked as Ashtar beckoned.

Refreshing spring waters purified and washed away the dirt, soil, trials and tribulations of human existence. It was here Ashtar first bathed her naked body, washing off the long and weary travel from the island. The gracious hospitality bestowed by the Great Mother; ripe cicadas singing to ethereal spirits, entreating all to listen into the moment; lush undergrowth offering cool respite, serenaded by water tinkling down the slight decline of a hill slope; breezes soft, pleasant to the pilgrim. The dignitaries made the long journey, as did the women. Coming to celebrate the Great Mother's power, grace and prophesy. Their pilgrimage consists of a well-trodden path from coast to mountain. Destiny calling too loudly to ignore.

Cressida emits a small spontaneous sound, a little throaty moan. Euphoria floats within her cells and she feels light and flimsy as she looks out from Ashtar's eyes in a faraway time, a faraway place. White oleander spotted through the glade. Ants scurrying, carrying messages as required.

She hears the bizarre language of foreign tongue rolling in her mouth producing sounds and phonetics unfamiliar. She recognises Kleodora and Daphnis from Pythia's stories. They stand beside her. She watches from deep within as this vibrant life extols itself. She watches the flow of past and present as it mingles, connecting rock, air, sun and human matter. She doesn't understand the words she speaks but knows the voice is from further on, further back. Time, space, earth held in one breath. A shared thought flickers. A name forms in her mind. Ashtar. Is the thought hers? Cressida wonders if it is simultaneous, sharing both feeling and hearing, speaking words of alien dialect. The doorway may be open but who peeks in while the Oracle sits and translates all that comes from this crack in the world?

Insight is her map. New knowledge becomes her truth. At first, the Shrine was not here on the hill but on the coast. She can see it. The Temple built in a wooden grove beside a spring. Pillaged by pirates, the Oracle moved up the hill to where the spring and cave offered safe and sacred shelter. The first Shrine made of beeswax and feathers. The cave remains a whirling centre of ceremony. The air smells heavy of sex, the preparation rituals leaving their weighty scent drenched in the morning dew.

She wears a purple veil and a short plain white dress. It is stained red from her moon bleeding. Her body is the direct incarnation of waxing and waning, life and death cycles. She is at her most powerful. Future Pythias will also sit on this rock overlooking the valley and the sea beyond, watching pilgrims as they travel up the gorge from the port. Just like she is doing.

Kleodora places a live kid goat in front of the altar and sprinkles it with holy water. Trembling reveals favourable omens, and the goat is slaughtered. Upon sacrifice, Kleodora examines its organs, particularly its liver, to ensure the signs remain agreeable. She burns this outside the altar. The rising smoke indicates the Oracle will receive pilgrims.

She descends into a cave, to bathe in the spring and anoint herself with oil. Returning to the Omphalos, Cressida mounts the tripod seat, holding laurel leaves. She feels her skin as it stretches and her figure enlarges, her hair on end, her heart panting, her bosom swelling and her voice becomes guttural. She begins her song in lyric poem expressing thanks to the Great Mother.

The beauty of their shared connection; of soul, timeless and eternal, overwhelms Cressida, and Ashtar feels the trickle of a gentle tear. She sends a silent blessing. Cressida emits another small moan in the colours of a Picasso painting, expressing earth, body, air, soul, heart; an ethereal well of pure emotion.

A thought crystalizes, 'I am spread over the landscape. I am inside things, in the clouds, the rocks, in the animals that come and go, in the splashing of the waves, and in the procession of the seasons. There is nothing with which I am not connected, not a part of. I am the space for the spaceless, the history of what will come and go.'

The camera clicked. Time cleared all images except for the selfie captured in frame.

A whisper from the past floated by: *every revelation of the sacred needs to be modified by a new spirit that speaks from a different position.*

CHAPTER TWENTY-ONE

"I need you to play with me on this one. Can you see this?" Angela placed a photo in front of Cressida. It was late afternoon and Angela had a slow cooking casserole seeping temptation through the kitchen. The two women had finished work for the day and were pleased to spend the time together after Cressida's return from Delphi. Her tourist photos appropriately scrolled through and commented on, they now returned their focus to the work at hand.

"See this early bit? It reads like some sort of transition, not quite a transition but indicating some sort of change."

Angela laughed before embarking on another theory.

"These are opposites, not opposites that are contrary but that lie together. Here and this one, here," she said pointing. "It is difficult to explain, for me to find the words but it speaks to me of breath and body; two parts of the one whole. Like air and matter. *Katolaveno* — understand? If you think about this on a continuum, well then, this image, it suggests the time was the time of body. This is sensible, *nai*? Of course." She slapped her forehead. "It is the time of earth, *nai* of body."

She looked closely again at the image.

"I wonder?" she said quietly, shaking her head.

Both women stared at the photo, one waiting while the other scratched her head.

"Wondering... yes?" prompted Cressida, too impatient to wait out Angela's long pause.

The older woman absently twirled her hair and placed a wayward strand behind her ear.

"I believe they knew they were going to die well before they set the cave up as a tomb."

Cressida did not disguise her frustration.

"Like we all do. What do you mean? I don't get it? What can you see?"

"This." Angela whispered, as if uttering her words might scare away the picture that was starting to emerge. "See this? This alludes to planet alignment. It indicates they possessed a deep understanding of astrology. See this? It reminds me of Stonehenge."

Cressida looked closer and nodded hesitantly. "See what?"

"Those images represent planets and they are aligned to the time of the body moving on, transitioning to the time of, um breath. Um, maybe."

She stopped to think of the words she needed.

"*En daxi*, okay, it is like air, like thought, thinking, um spirit, not ghostly spirit, or even religious as in Holy Spirit. Or maybe? *Isos*, like *pneuma, nai*. In ancient Greek, *pneumais* means the form of circulating air that sustains consciousness in a body. It is air in motion, like breath or wind. It is the element from which all else originated, encompassing the whole world."

In exasperation, she reverted to Greek and a flood of words

bounced out of her mouth, rejected. Angela faltered and groaned. Even her mother tongue could not help her with words that either did not exist or had long been forgotten.

Cressida watched her friend struggle. She could see how frustrated Angela was and grinned. She always reverted to Greek when she was trying to articulate difficult ideas. She loved how her mind worked, picking and selecting from a palette of information and research amassed over a life of study. Even from this position of knowledge, Angela always listened to Cressida's uneducated input. She never put her down or ridiculed her. She never rolled her eyes. Instead, Angela listened and took her dumb thoughts seriously. Watching her now brought a wave of emotion. Cressida waved away the prickly feeling.

"What?" Cressida pulled away from her tangent thoughts to concentrate on what Angela was saying, hoping she had returned to English.

"It was a time of transition, from the body and into the — I don't know, breath? spirit? light? A way of thinking? Like consciousness, a shift in consciousness?"

Angela bent down from her chair to restack the stacked books still under the table. She emerged and faced Cressida.

"We have no word for it. But Cressida, they knew. Pythia leaving the village and setting up the community, she knew. She knew the energy of the planets was shifting."

Cressida felt goose bumps prickling her arms. She did not understand any of it, in Greek or English.

'Not for the first time,' she thought, grinning.

They sat. Both women constrained, one by language and

the other, confusion. Both focused on the image. Neither knew what to do with this perspective. Angela broke the silence. Again. She always did. Was this a Greek thing?

"Of course, this analysis could be disputed." She laughed away her unease.

Cressida sought to untangle her thoughts. "I am not following. Sorry." She screwed up her nose. "You are talking opposites, death and transition. So, the body — you said matter, do you mean like earth? Like the worship of the Goddess — who was earth, this time was ending? That Pythia knew this. But she also knew the women of the community were coming to an end? Is that it? Is that what you mean?"

"I think what we have here," said Angela cautiously, "is a line in the sand. It is the threshold of transition. Like it was, I think, prophesised. *Isos*. I mean Goddess worship for this community, was maybe, shifting into early patriarchy. Your story of the first village, suggested this. Children becoming the property of men, remember? Well, these cave paintings suggest they may have been aware of the greater meaning of these changes, of a transition. And that it was, this suggests, an energetic-planetary thing."

Angela paused, her train of thought leading into murky territory.

"They seem to be preparing. It is weird because contemporary data suggests Goddess worship continued for centuries. We know the Mycenaean brought their Olympian gods to the island and that was at least a thousand years before Christianity. What were they were preparing for, I wonder?"

She looked at Cressida. Cressida looked back blankly. No

answers here. Angela inhaled deeply then breathed out slowly. She retraced her steps.

"We tend to think of opposites as being poles apart, diametrically opposed but this is not necessarily true. They are connected, each opposite existing side by side; pleasure, pain; love, hate; sorrow, joy. If you watch children, they will often laugh and cry at the same time. Look here."

Angela pointed at an image of a bull with a serpent and lion below it. "The bull for the Goddess and this below, we know symbolises day and night, heaven and earth. Do you see? They are next to each other but opposite; female alongside male. Opposites but not necessarily dualism. You know what I think."

It was not a question.

"I think it was the beginning of a transition, the beginning of an end, and the women knew it. It was in the stars. I think they were setting up a new community to manage the transition. Guide through it without the violence they had experienced. I wonder if they had prophesied the onslaught of patriarchal aggression. Like, you know, what we have lived through in these last couple of thousand years? If so, were they seeking a way to retain the worship of the Mother Goddess? Like early day, very early, Puritans or Quakers. Funny this has come to light now." She stopped. "Serendipity rather than coincidence? Jung would think so."

"Jung? I have heard of Jung. Who is Jung?" Cressida asked.

Angela was too absorbed in her thoughts to respond.

"Don't you ever question why it was you who discovered this cave? Like why you? With your panic attacks, and your visions."

CHAPTER TWENTY-ONE

"I was the idiot out walking during a storm, remember." Cressida said.

"And now perhaps we are living in a new transition. You know that 2012 was the end of the Mayan calendar. Some people wrote about it as a planetary shift, the end of what they called Draconian energy, which coincidently has been with us for the last 2000 years."

Revelation dawned. "Maybe, the two opposites are finding balance?"

Cressida was desperate to piece together the conversation. "Like, body then breath, or thought, whatever. First as opposites and now, not separate but one, together, whole?" She shook her head, frowning. She still did not get it.

"You catch on quick, my friend," Angela replied, then giggled.

Cressida was about to explain that she did not get it at all but saw Angela's face and her frown melted as she giggled. The absurdity of Angela's comment was funny. Cressida knew she was anything but quick. Angela was pulling faces trying to regain her poise, pursing her lips, scrunching her nose, failing miserably. Cressida laughed at her friend without restraint. Angela's shoulders jiggled, her body shook. She looked away, then back at Cressida. The more they looked at each other and tried to stop laughing, the more impossible it became. Both tried, really tried. When Cressida simultaneously guffawed and farted, both women cracked up and fell about, shrieking out hard and loud — at themselves, at each other, at their findings, projections, at their intensity. They laughed full bellied, open mouthed, snorting and whooping.

They laughed themselves into convulsions. Hysteria turned to tears, proving their now called 'opposite theory,' as pleasure turned to pain and they held their sides, pounded the table and begged each other to stop.

It took a toilet break to settle. It was clear the mood for scholarly exploration had retired early. Cressida sat comfortably in her chair watching her friend. Gorgeous with long, black, thick, heavy hair. What was she? Around forty, fifty? Not married. Why not? Why wasn't she married? She spouted some strong views about the Church and patriarchy. Did these scare men off? Was she a lesbian? She was Greek and everyone knew what a strong male culture the Greeks had. Could she not find a husband?

Cressida was reluctant to ask, for fear of saying something that might offend. Sometimes tact was a good ally. Sometimes, but not tonight. It was no good; the question entered the room almost of its own accord. Fortunately blunted and somewhat disguised by what Cressida had considered a careful broach of the subject.

"Are you a feminist?" she asked. Not the question she had in mind, but she knew some questions have consequences.

Angela shrugged. "I guess. *Exartarté*, it depends. It depends on how you define feminism. If, say from the perspective of the work we are doing around Goddess worship, I would have to say the devaluation of women's power, the denigration of women's bodies, the distrust of women's will, and the denial of women's connections have all been instigated by patriarchal religion. I guess accepting that perspective might just make me a feminist. What about you? How do you see yourself?"

Cressida frowned and thought for a moment before laughing. "That moment, just then, well that was about the extent I have ever thought about it. I don't know. I sleep with men. Like I really like sex, but I don't know if I particularly like them. Well, I don't like some of them." She paused, and then stopped. Enough said, about herself and about trying to find out more about Angela. None of her business.

However, Angela having spied a crack dived in.

"Do you like the father of your baby? Will he support you?"

Cressida swallowed, metaphorically kicking herself. 'Idiot,' she silently berated. 'See what happens when you ask questions.'

Her heart beat fast as she searched for a safe answer. There was none. The word 'father' screamed at her. She looked up at Angela, tried to think of an excuse to leave, to run, but all she saw were those big kind brown eyes. There may not be a safe answer but here, possibly here, was a safe place. She exhaled, not even realising she had been holding her breath.

"He was just a one-night stand. He's gone. Knows nothing." She paused then added jokingly, "I was doing my service for the Goddess." Cressida relaxed slightly. "Hey, I'm a Sacred Prostitute." And then felt the hard slap of recrimination from her father hitting her, calling her a tramp. Yep, he was right. Again.

Cressida looked up to see those big kind brown eyes watching her. The love they exuded softened her internal turmoil, the see-saw of light and dark that made her giddy, off-balance. She heard a gentle question, probing her pain.

"Perhaps we need our own Harrownight?"

"Oh, god no," said Cressida, "I would never collect any wood."

Cressida felt feeble, but was okay. It was still a safe place. Her father's voice receded.

"And the baby?"

Cressida looked away. "I don't know. I really don't. That's how I got stuck in the cave. I was walking, trying to think what I should do. I didn't know there was going to be a storm."

Angela nodded.

"Hot chocolate time," Angela said, getting up. Cressida almost swooned as a warm flow of relief melted her tensed muscles. She got up to help.

CHAPTER TWENTY-TWO

Angela was waiting in the Kafenion for Cressida.
"I have something for you," she said as Cressida pulled
a chair from another table to sit across from her.

"For me?"

Cressida's heart pulled a string.

"A poem. I really like it and I think it is perfect for you."

Angela handed her a piece of paper. Cressida looked at the
hand-written script.

"It's in Greek."

"*Nai*, I will tell you so you can remember."

Angela quoted:

She walketh veiled and sleeping
For she knoweth not her power;
She obeyeth but the pleading
Of her heart, and the high leading
Of her soul, unto this hour.
Slow advancing, halting, creeping,
Comes the Woman to the hour!–
She walketh veiled and sleeping,
For she knoweth not her power.

Cressida sat quietly allowing the words to settle.

"It is by Charlotte Perkins Gillman," said Angela.

"Thank you," whispered Cressida. "It is the best gift. Ever."

Overcome, Cressida sat back and crossed her arms to hold herself. Silence became a sister and she sat content amidst the hub of the Kafenion.

CHAPTER TWENTY-THREE

Cressida sat up. It was the woman from the cave. In her room. Cressida's heart danced steps of surprise, fear, exhilaration, back to fear. Bom, bombom, bom. She swallowed down her panic and summoned her courage that had fled to her bowels. In a soft whisper, she sought permission.

"Can I talk? To you?"

The woman's eyes twinkled and the whole room became lighter in density. Clear, shimmering. 'I'll take that as a yes' and she swallowed again, this time to clear her throat.

"What Angela was saying, it umm, seems wrong."

The woman's smile remained, as did Cressida's feeling of airiness.

"In your room? Oh my God. Not in a dream but you saw her. You talked to her? This is amazing. Did you ask her about the section we were looking at yesterday? About transitions? What about the Tribal Women, were they Amazons? Were we right? Are we on the right track? And what about... Oh God, did you ask her where the cave is?"

Cressida stared at her friend in dismay. What an idiot, how

dumb could she be? Of all the things she could have, should have asked. She swallowed back her shame.

"I only asked one thing, well two, actually. I asked if it was okay to speak," she admitted, "and I asked her about the, that ritual, you know? It seemed wrong. I mean if I hadn't been an only child and my mother had to, you know? It's not right. It's incest. It's really been bothering me. You know? I must be a prude or something, but really."

She tapered off.

"And?" asked Angela, "What did she say?"

"She said," Cressida closed her eyes trying to recall the feeling of floating before pulling out a piece of paper from her pocket. The paper she had scrawled on in the morning when she woke up, not knowing she had fallen asleep. But she knew it hadn't been a dream. She had sat up, she had spoken to the woman and then she woke up.

"She said," Cressida repeated, then read, "Woman gives birth just as the earth gives birth: woman magic and earth magic are the same. The per-son-i-fi-cation of the energy that gives birth to form and nourishes form is properly female. In your now, she meant our time here," Cressida clarified, "your goal is to detach and become independent in the world. To break away from your origins to be reborn into the world. Desire to be dissolved and absorbed. It is all the same. The relationship of the son to the mother is of the personal to community and decides the fate not only of the one but of the many. Great Mother takes the child back into herself to be reawakened after being immersed in death."

"Can I read it?" asked Angela. Cressida passed her note over and watched Angela devour it.

Angela looked up smiling. "You wrote this from hearing it once? When you woke up in the morning? Well done."

Cressida's discomfort grew from a different source. Praise was harder to accept than self-criticism. Angela re-read it then looked up again at Cressida.

"Uroboric incest is a form of entry into the mother of union, of union with Her. Oh Cressida, this is so Jungian."

Cressida shook her head. "I still don't understand. You said earlier that uroboric was something about cyclical nature, eating itself and rebirth, something like that."

"Absolutely. Okay, look at it this way. In ancient times, identity belongs to a group, not the individual. As we have seen from the images, the community engages in various rituals to ensure the basics of survival, like good harvests, safe sea voyages, birthing, but also, they are a community of knowing and feeling through their religious gatherings. They participate in rituals that allow them to re-live, create and sustain identity."

Cressida said nothing, but really, *re-live, create and sustain identity*? What the fuck?

"In this ritual, what is being suggested, well at least in Jungian terms, oh," Angela paused, hearing Cressida's question from the other day, "Carl Jung was a psychologist, a student of Freud. He said, 'That which we do not bring to consciousness appears in our lives as fate.'" Angela looked puzzled for a moment before explaining. "He has done a lot of work on archetypes and myths."

Satisfied by Cressida's somewhat vague acknowledgement,

she continued. "Anyway, that's not important, but he would say that the embryonic ego, umm the developing ego, is annihilated. This, oh my god, this is exciting. Truly it is."

Angela's passion danced the salsa. "This ritual symbolises the creative element not the personal, not the young men themselves. It is concrete evidence of worship through coitus."

'Paper actually,' thought Cressida, watching Angela wave the sheet about.

"The mothers don't just represent the Mother Goddess, they become her. It is sexual union in a ritual context like Sacred Union. With spiritual transformation, the act is Divine. It is just that it is the mothers incarnating as the Goddess, not priestesses. Therefore, it is not about planting the seed. In this case, it returns to the very foundations."

She paused and thought for a moment. "For everyone, and I mean even us, there is a time when the mother's body is the whole universe. Oh, Cressida, there are so many examples we can draw on. There are so many myths of the Mother Goddess and her son-lover. Have you read The Golden Bough? Doesn't matter. *Nai*, let me think. There was Attis, Adonis and Osiris. They were their mother's lovers. They too were slain, buried, grieved then reborn. The Mother becomes the Death Goddess. I cannot believe I did not think of this before. It's not incest, it is Divine embodiment."

She raised her eyebrows at Cressida questioningly. Cressida could see she was excited, but she was struggling to keep up.

"Talk to me Cressida," said Angela, "tell me what you think I am talking about. What does this mean to you?"

Cressida nodded. Familiar terrain. This is what they did to understand the story. Together. There was never any threat of aggression or blame.

"So, the mothers fuck their sons, like you thought, but it is not the mothers, but the Goddess, through them. Not to impregnate but to — annihilate? Kill the sons?" she replied tentatively.

"This ritual is an initiation ritual, a sacred ritual — I think you were right, I think this is how mothers may have taught their sons."

"But Lydia seemed different," said Cressida.

"Lydia?" asked Angela, switching her conversation immediately to face Cressida. "Who is Lydia? Is she the woman in the cave?"

Cressida shrugged. She felt exposed, silly. She didn't know why she said this or where it had come from. "I don't know," she replied quietly. "I don't know. It just came out."

Angela got up to make some coffee. She returned with two cups.

Cressida took her cup without looking up. She felt small, vulnerable, scared. Like she had made a mistake and now Angela would ask her to leave.

"A dream, perhaps?" asked Angela gently.

"I don't know, I really don't, but..." Cressida hesitated.

"Go on," encouraged Angela, gently. She placed her hand lightly on Cressida's leg. "You are here with me now. This is our story. Your story is my story and we are okay. We are okay?" she asked.

Cressida didn't hear her, the numbness spreading too fast,

weighing down her tongue. The fog seeped in quickly from behind her eyes.

"Oh no... no nononoooo."

She whimpered pitifully as if she were a tiny kitten flung against a stone-wall. Her breath jerked on impact.

She gulped for air and swallowed rain. Tension flooded her body and Cressida found herself gripped by a storm. Was she in the Gorge? She looked around. No. Confused, overwhelmed and tossed about by a buffeting wind and onslaught of rain. Breathe in, air sloshing around in water but finally filtering into her lungs. Taking in as much as she could in one big breath, she gave voice through a long deep wrenching howl that swallowed up her air and surged up and out and choked and gagged her.

Enraged at the rain, then consumed by fury birthed from her depths of being. She spiralled down out of control. Nausea became an interloper as Cressida gasped for more air, which when achieved, fed more howling, intermingled with fast, desperate gulps. Her anger became despair became sobbing, still gasping for breath, all together in an orchestration of a manic storm. Shrill winds from every direction, swept her aside in a channel of frenzy. The clamour of emotions; anger, guilt, pain, frustration and fear, all echoed through each minute capillary in accord with a deep growling of thunder and pounding waves banging in her head.

She convulsed for breath, for her very survival. Each intake seeking to drag up some solid base of gravity, and from the back corners of her mind, she prayed to regain control. No chance for composure. She wiped her nose; water, snot, tears.

She thrashed around, desperate for control. Please. To little affect. The wind ignored her. Overcome with its own sense of majestic grandeur, it whipped through her tiny frail battered sodden fear-struck heart. She stood, no, she cowered, alone. Option? Flight or fight? Not a happening thing. Rooted to the spot as the menace of the storm struck out again. Fuck. Fuck .... Cressida was smacked into action by stinging sand biting from inside her skin. A partnership of wind, rain and sand lashed at her with whipping grains of dark matter, drawing her out from a blithering trance. She looked around into the blackness before curling up into a ball. Into herself.

When she woke, it was dark. Her head pounded. A light beamed dimly from another room. Where was she? She felt safe. That was good. She was in a bed; warm and cosy. Okay. She closed her eyes and slept some more.

Angela brought some tea in the morning. Cressida watched her put the tray on the bedside table. She was too embarrassed to speak, so she kept her eyes closed until Angela left. Left the room, left the house, left her.

She drank the tea, her hands shaking. She wanted to get back to her flat before Angela returned, but as she opened the front door, there was Angela, about to come in. Plan aborted. She looked into those familiar eyes to apologise.

"I..." she started to say but stopped as Angela pulled her in close and held her tight. Cressida sank into her arms for what seemed forever. It was unknown territory to be hugged. Simply hugged. She was too weak to protest. She didn't want to protest, so she stayed in the arms of her friend, content to say nothing, do nothing, just to be there. Being held.

Finally, Angela gently released her and said, "Go home. Take a nice warm shower and relax. I have spoken to your boss and you have the day off. I will come around this afternoon with some lunch. I have a story to tell you."

CHAPTER TWENTY-FOUR

"You became her. *Oxi*. No, but you became, ummm not yourself. Yet you were."

Angela was desperately trying to find the words, any words, in Greek, in English, to describe her experience. She paused and then tried again.

"*Milises. Oxi. Den milises.* It was more like you channelled. *Nai*, that is the closest I can get. It wasn't like before, when she spoke to me through you."

She took a deep breath.

"The story came from inside you, but you didn't speak. You put the story inside me. Not in my ears, or my mind. *Oxi*. In my heart. Lydia, the woman you mentioned, the woman from the cave, she put the story into my heart. I understood it. I did not hear it. Aaargh. How am I ever going to find the words to tell you it? Oh Lydia, help me. Please. Oh, forgive me."

"I know this place. Oh, this is just fabulous. After all your crummy explanations and examples, finally you are making sense."

They burst out laughing, speaking simultaneously. "This makes it real!"

Cressida felt her shame from last night dissolve and looked warmly at her friend. She had never felt so close to someone.

It felt good — more than good.

Angela was still searching for words.

"Her story told through you wasn't with words, or even pictures. Imagine getting the imprint or impression of the paintings, but in thought form, not literally Cressida, not visually. I did not hear or see anything, but I felt it. Really clearly. It was like I just knew it. It was deep inside me, not from the outside. No, I mean it was, but..."

In her weakened state, Cressida snuggled happily into her blanket. She watched Angela spoon out the soup she had brought for lunch. The concentration doing this simple task seemed to give Angela time to organise her thoughts. She turned to Cressida.

"Lydia rarely spoke, in her village, that is. Not many had heard her voice. She communicated though, through her weaving, but also, I guess through what we would call telepathy."

Angela nodded, content with her definition. As Cressida settled deeper into the couch, Angela sat in her reading chair.

"The stories were shared through ceremonies where they sowed the seeds of purpose and responsibility. From the first landing of twenty-eight women and some children, a bustling village developed. The village was administered through the Temple and involved all sorts of trade. The women strengthened their alliance with the Tribal Women. Together they established rituals that flourished with each generation. Their shared practice of child rearing ensured the mix of blood and propagation of seed continued. For many years of settlement, they experienced peace. The brutality experienced by their foremothers never reared its ugly head. Rites and ceremonies for the Goddess were woven into the fabric of daily life."

"They were an agricultural as well as a fishing community. In the village, there were three main divisions of labour, each respected for their contribution to the whole community. There were administrators and business operators who were responsible for economy and trade. This included importing and exporting raw materials and produce. Then there were the craftswomen, farmers, workers of the fields and seas. They farmed sea snails, would you believe? Women, as well as men farmed sea snails which provided dyes used for cloth as well as paintings and decorations."

In her chair, Angela looked like a grand matriarch sharing ancestral secrets.

"It was your Pythia who discovered that sea-snails projected a secretion when attacked. She taught the farmers to poke them, so they could milk the juice without having to crush them. It was highly valued because the colour did not fade easily but became brighter with weathering. No surprise, the most prized colour was of clotted blood."

Cressida tried to imagine the colour of clotted blood and thought that perhaps it was like a dark burgundy or purple.

"The last group were the Temple women. These included a Pythia and Select, who as we thought were priestesses or those in training. There were also weavers, beekeepers and artists. Lydia was part of this group. They were all, to varying degrees, responsible for rites, offerings and spiritual connection. Everyone followed their calling or as Lydia described star-path or destiny. Many daughters remained at the Temple while some returned to the Tribal Women to be warriors. But all women participated in Temple ceremonies and overall, the village thrived."

Angela looked at Cressida, engrossed.

"Lydia lived at the Temple. She was not a priestess but worked on the looms, weaving cloth for ritual skirts as well as blankets and items for trade."

Angela closed her eyes. "Lydia described several of the dress combinations. Some were designed for bare breasted ceremonies, other were fully clad. Some priestesses chose to wear only a hip belt made of string or leather or used their hip belt to support either an apron or an entire fringed skirt. The skirts began below the waist hugging the hips, with many decorative white incisions of dots, zig zags, net patterns or checkerboards. Lydia wore a skirt that narrowed below the knee with a slit in front. How lovely they must have looked in their reds, purples and gold. They also adorned themselves with gold medallions that clinked when they swayed or walked. Do you know I could actually hear it as she described them?"

Angela looked pleased. Her words had flowed easily, describing an ancient past neither could have imagined. Angela's passion for this history glowed. Cressida beamed at her friend, who needed no words of encouragement to continue.

"The Temple was the centre of all life where worship and ceremonies and daily life merged. The Temple realm belonged to the women and all daily chores were sacred. There were areas for looms, spinning wheels, kilns, bread ovens and grinding stones. The ground floor housed ceramic workshops. It had a large oven for firing pottery on one side, while the other side had a work surface for decorating and polishing pottery. There was a bench in the middle to hold and store flint blades as well as delicate deer and bird bone implements. Flat stones lay ready to crush ochre into decorative pigments."

"The ground floor had round windows and a huge wide entrance. Images of the Mother Goddess decorated walls, either in three-dimensional wall-reliefs or frescoes. Your Pythia had painted the first section of images in the cave, as well as the Temple frescoes. Many were in honour of Ashtar, who had left the village in the first season to establish a Temple at Delphi. Upstairs, the second floor contained several altars, offering places, figurines, pottery offerings and a variety of *pithoi*, you know, those big jars."

Angela drew a long breath. The image was strong.

"The Temple was like an energy vortex; vibrating and humming. The vibration sang of the past, the vision, endurance and passion of the women who had established the village. Whenever spinning, Lydia told me, she would lose herself to the rhythm of the wooden wheel and would often move through dimensions of space and time. She said she could free herself from physical constraints and reach the depths of the Goddess. She had never spoken of this in the village. She had not understood its significance until now. She was never one for idle chatter. She was teased for her dreaminess, all in jest and good fun, she assured me."

"Lydia also spoke prophesy. She told me, well not told me,

but, well you know, she let me know she had prophesised her task of painting in the cave. It was she who had prophesised the destruction of the village."

CHAPTER TWENTY-FIVE

Lydia

When the Great Mother first awoke, Lydia sat quietly in the cave between the veils of time. She watched Cressida nuzzle into the Mother's rocking, like a pre-born babe, ignoring contractions that would ultimately expel her back out into the cold, bright world. Cressida had slept, gathering strength until full dilation. Then, as the Mother contracted for the second time and roared, Cressida's hiatus from the outside world abruptly ended.

Lydia saw the terror in her eyes, wide with fear, running aimlessly around the cave. Panic throbbing from each movement escalating towards escape. She watched as Cressida scrambled up and out through the crack in the side of the cliff back into her own world.

She sat quietly as the Great Mother sealed up the crack, closing the tomb from intrusion. Closing it forever from discovery. She had completed most of her task, but remained silhouetted at the juncture in time. It was not yet time for her to surrender into the Mother's embrace.

She looked at the walls of the cave, reached out and

caressed it lightly with her fingertips. There were fourteen generations of stories, each laden with hope. She had painted herself surrounded by animals and plants. Surrounded by flowers and dressed like a Pythia with a necklace of dragon-flies and ducks.

Lydia awoke at the roosters' calling. She got out of her cot quickly and headed to the Temple. She had work to do and her time, she had learnt, was limited. She had received instructions that night: she was to weave.

In threads of red, gold, blue and black, with purple and yellow, she wove through several suns and moons. Some Select spun the colours and threads she sought, others provided food and sustenance and left rugs at the Temple so she could take rest as required. Her work was under guidance from the Divine Mother so everyone in the compound was available to help her to complete the task.

Tying the last knot and cutting the thread, she picked up the cloth with bloodied and blistered hands and offered it to the Pythia. The Pythia bowed and kissed Lydia's palms before unravelling it for all the women of the Temple to see.

Within a border of spirals and serpents, the images portrayed her prophesy.

After the Olive Harvest but before Sacred Union, ten suns of the Great Mother's turbulence would prevail. Her pulse would arrive from the north. She would swallow the sun and blow its unsurpassed bloom of heat across the land. It would take less time than to milk a goat.

Lydia wove a layer of darkness growing on the horizon. The vision unfolded.

Explosions would mark the journey with everything in its path of destruction flung aside by tremendous forces of wind and engulfing heat. The last breath of the living would scorch lungs, set afire hair, skin, and robes. Bodies would peel as the consuming heat cooked flesh. The land would blaze furiously. The great forests of cypress and oak would burn with vengeance, leaving charred destruction, wreckage and death in its wake. The sky would alight as ear-shattering thunderous booms echoed, reverberating death throes. As the vibration travelled south, the Great Mother would summon the tide to cleanse her battered and blistered body, washing debris into the sea.

Lydia's work was powerful and stunningly beautiful. Her prophesy gave the women time to prepare. Lydia returned to her compound to sleep off her endeavours.

The Olive Harvest

Lydia scooped the olives into sewn bags of goat hide. Her work in the olive grove was finally finished. She had worked the last seven suns, helping to lay out woven netting under the olive trees. The netting caught the olives as the women stripped the fruit from the branches. Once netted, they sifted out the twigs and leaves to ensure a clean press. It was gruelling work but everyone from the smallest child to the eldest crone contributed to the task.

She heaved the sack across her shoulders and carried it to the pressing room. There it would be pressed between two huge stones and stored in pithio jars. The jars were to be loaded onto caïques for those departing. In past seasons, the men would be busy cutting branches, stacking the larger limbs for firewood in preparation for the cold winter days. The smaller branches and twigs fed to livestock. There was no pruning this season.

She was tired and glad to make her way back to the compound. Wiping the sweat from her brow, she stepped nimbly over a tumbled wall. Since the Mother's last surge, fallen rocks littered the fields. Constructing stone-walls and buildings with different size rocks and stones allowed for movement without total destruction, but there was still a lot of damage. Boulders from the cliffs had dislodged and the plaintive bleating of goats and sheep, told stories of those pinned under rocks, others distressed and calling for their kids. There was much slaughter to accept the sacrifices made. Arriving at the Temple, she stood, taking in the pleasure it bestowed. It stood radiant, facing north with proud strength and reverence. Tonight, the offering would take place at the altar. Their last Olive Harvest received with gratitude.

The Rites of Preparation followed the Olive Harvest festivities. While there would be no Sacred Union this season, the young men of the community still required initiation. After this ceremony, they would leave the island to travel afield to propagate their seed. Most women and children would have left by then.

⁂

On the morning of the Rites of Preparation, Lydia sat in the sacred olive grove with the small group of initiates. Some were eager, others hesitant, unsure of what the initiation would entail. Lydia smiled wistfully. She had been serving the Mother for a long time now and she took satisfaction in this last Ritual. The young Select beside her was in training to take her place on foreign shores.

The Select was playing a melody on shell pipes. It was pleasurable to sit and listen to the ancient tune that told of the first meeting between the ancestors and the Tribal Women. Many of these young men had mixed blood between the two communities. It shone through their eyes and clear skin. The music finished and they looked to her. She looked at them tenderly, and began. In the ensuing silence, they opened their hearts to receive her story.

"The plague spread from the north causing chaos and mayhem, sickness and death. It was slow in movement and not easily detectable. It came and corrupted patterns that would have kept us thriving, replacing harmonies with horror and suffering. Pythia had watched its seed find fertile ground, spreading its roots deeper each trade season, but she did not know what she was looking at.

Her courage to disconnect from sacred connection of

body and earth in the old village flows through our blood. Of twenty-eight women, some carried patterns of the disease requiring cleansing through Harrownight. But the disease is insidious and we watch for it carefully should it filter through the generations.

It is a disease of domination and segregation causing severance from earth. One becomes lost from language, frequency and vibration. Such is the story of Vrados: his disconnect fuelling patterns of vanity and entitlement.

The seeds of the past birthed contaminated children. As the patterns of disease became imprinted in the psyche, people repeated and replayed the same ugly rhetoric, and so, generation after generation it spread. Many lost their original template of humanity, betraying the Great Mother.

Through our alliances, we have remained aware of this disconnect, of the killing and evil abroad. Such was foreseen by the Great Mother and spoken in the oracles of our ancestry. Birthed and raised in a loving and caring community keeps us balanced in harmony. We are not crippled by fear or hatred. We are not born that way, nor are we taught. But we too, once carried the imprint of dysfunction, so we continually seek to weed out this aberration.

Your time is ripe to consummate with the Great Mother. We celebrate your Rites of Preparation as the final stage of your childhood, moving now to enlightenment. Hold true your life. The disease has eons left to play its ugly hand and what we do now is for the truth of the child and for the Great Mother in a future that will be. Embrace the teaching from the Great Mother, rebirth to know thyself."

The Select put aside the shell. The small group sat in silence as the essence of Lydia's teaching found its place within each heart.

When the young men stood up to leave, each respectfully kissed Lydia's palm. One young man remained hesitantly. He approached Lydia and as he kissed her palms, spoke softly to his mentor.

"I am afraid, Lydia. I am afraid I am corrupted. My blood contaminated. What if I am of no service for the Mother?"

Lydia looked into his clear eyes of blue, eyes of the north, and nodded. She had known him as a young pup, coming directly from the Tribal Women. His eyes spoke of blood flowing from cool mountain waters. They were eyes you could fall into and never reach the depths. From a whelp, he had grown, full, bronzed with the sun, kind and helpful. Lydia did not know his path for she had not received any vision concerning him, but she had witnessed his virtues as he grew into a young man and believed he would do well. He had spent his youth learning the trades of the sea. The salt encrusted his soul. Soon he would leave and live the life he was destined but first he must be deemed worthy.

Lydia remembered the song-lines of the Tribequeen and Pythia, sharing blood in their practice of raising sons worthy of their daughters. The Tribal Woman had spoken words of beauty and strength, bestowed with pride and grace. She shared these now, hoping the words of his linage offered some comfort.

"Our divine souls take on the patterns left for us by our ancestors, and we add to those tapestries, threads of creativity and expression with each breath. An apple tree is planted, tended and cared for, grafted, and nourished. Many creatures benefit; from the apples, branches, shade and orchards. But we, the Mother's children can take these apples and continue creating. Pie, cider, butter, jam, sauce ... this is the gift of creation we share with Mother Earth. We add to the garden of diversity."

This young man was one apple of many raised in their village. Over generations, their orchard had produced a healthy abundant crop. Lydia words of reassurance pulsed through his chest.

The Divine is here, in the heart of surrender.

Lydia watched as he left to join the other young men at the Temple. Their hair would be cut, as their cord had been at birth, and placed in a woven bag. After initiation, a cloth with wiped semen and the Great Mother's juice would be added, and the bag thrown into sea. Lydia loved this simple ritual, connecting earth, air, water and fire.

The rites would take place in the sacred olive grove when the sun retired from its peak. In the new dawn, the exodus would be over. These men were to be the last to leave.

The Rites of Preparation

The Rites of Preparation were well underway by the time Lydia arrived at the Sacred Olive Grove. She could hear the Pythia welcoming the young men, her voice reverberating through the stillness of the evening.

"Your body of earth connects to creation. Listen. Observe. Nurture Breath. Walk alongside love and beauty, drawing upon the healthy patterns of Divine Mother. Learn to discern truth, health from sickness, and trust the knowledge that comes from the body. Love what is healthy and whole. Feed not that which is not. Practice great generosity and take only what you need. Walk the path of truth and connection to know thyself."

The drumming started and the young men passed around a bronzed cup, sharing an herb concoction. Lydia watched Pythia address the mothers.

"The sleeping serpent lies coiled. It is the Divine Mother within that we awaken and release. Given the danger of our sons being contaminated, watch carefully to ensure they express Her light. Our Service is to identify any deviant cells, those out of harmony with health and the source code of love, and to dismantle the patterns that have consumed the cells, leading the body towards death. It is only by identifying corrupted cells that we can begin to heal them. Mother-born, be aware of your ties and dependence upon which you sprang, now is the time for them to learn to stand alone."

The young men stepped up to the fire and threw in offerings of wild boar, pinecones and herbs. They chanted invocations, a melody of words and prayer overlapping and harmonising.

Born and birthed. Brought forth now.

To complete the passage from youth.

She receives me.

Re-entering, I complete Her.

Relinquish the cord to re-enter the world.

I give back my seed to nourish and replenish all I have taken, all that I owe.

Moving from boy to man. I remain of Her and from Her.

Mother Divine receive me. Atone my misspent youth. Cleanse my ignorance.

I seek rebirth. I am whole. I am sorry. I forgive you. I thank you. I love you.

In tempo with the drumbeat, the young men, their arms outstretched and holding onto each other's shoulders, started to circle the fire pit. It was a dance learnt as young boys. Tonight, however would be different. They circled the large pit, which bellowed out embers and smoke flavoured with their offerings, as well as laurel leaves, thyme, snake-skins and the decapitated head and organs of a sacrificed bull. Around the fire, were hundreds of small clay and earthen figurines of the Divine Mother and the Sacred Bull.

As the energy started to build, the Pythia intoned a deep earthy chant beginning from the earth's core that echoed through her body and released into the night. The youths continued to dance and chant around the fire. Pythia, eyes closed, swayed and rocked her body, linking her breath with the young men. Their breathing became heavier. Suddenly, the young men felt a great impact of a rising force within them. The intensity was so tremendous it lifted their bodies off the ground. As they landed, they set off in an exultant pace of leaping and jumping, whooping and howling. Their sweat flickered into the night, into the fire, and onto the women who had formed a circle around them.

As she watched, Lydia felt a cool breeze on her fingertips. The base of her spine tingled. She relaxed into it. It intensified then surged up her back as a wave of euphoria and happiness permeated her being. Entranced by sensation she floated in bliss. Around her, a continuous fountain of dazzling white lights erupted through space. The brilliance of these lights shone brighter than the sun but possessed no heat. She opened her eyes to the swirl of energy and emotion.

Some of the young men had dropped to the ground with involuntary jerks, tremors, shaking, itching, tingling, and crawling sensations in their arms and legs. Others moaned as waves of extreme sexual desire lead them into a state of whole-body orgasm. Lydia knew in their altered states, they would become sensitive to light, sound, and touch. Most would succumb to feelings of bliss, infinite love, connectivity and transcendent awareness.

She watched carefully for those young men who wandered vaguely, out of sync and discordant with their peers. She knew this rite was not necessarily good for all. She watched for patterns of any emotional upheavals or surfacing of feelings or thoughts held captive within their spirits. For these boys, this was a time laced with numbness often followed by pressure inside the skull making them vomit. She knew the power of this ritual could have an adverse effect, with difficulty for some to come back to the fold of the community. She had seen times where young men lost their hunger, suffered extreme gaiety followed by blackness, complained of recurring pain and either loss of sleep or oversleeping. These young men were sent to the Tribal Women for their workforce or Sacred Rites. Their mothers watched as carefully as she did.

At the height of their immersion, the Pythia sent an

unspoken vibration to each of the young men who received her message beyond body or mind constraints.

"The sacred impulse, the desire to unite with Mother Divine, is no longer distinguished from the desires of the flesh. Feel the desires of spirit flooding your body. Feel your longings that will never be realised on this physical plane. The sacred becomes profound as the body thrashes, and releases those desires that belong to the realm of Spirit."

The women gently touched their sons' shoulders and the young men turned. Together they swayed as one, enthralled with the fire of spirit and passion. The young men knelt as the women placed decorative bull masks over their heads before leading them into the olive groves. The words of the Pythia wafted through the evening air.

"As you immerse in the body of the Great Mother learn the knowledge of worshipping every woman as Divine. Born to die, dying to be born, yours is a season of all that grows."

The drumming pulsated, reverberating through the grove. Pythia chanted the ancient words, blessing all.

"Woman first exists as Mother as man first exists as son

The youth is killed as the sun sets, every night in sleep

Dying with the Sun

Sinking back into the depths of darkness to be reborn in the morning

To begin the day anew."

Lydia felt the heat of the fire receding. Her elation remained and she felt drenched in bliss. In past ceremonies, she had been called upon as Mother incarnate to teach those sons whose own mothers had been unable to participate. Tonight, all was well with the world. It was a good omen. Soon she would join in the chanting and dancing procession to the ocean where the precious woven cloth bags offerings were to be thrown into its depths. Then there would be feasting.

Angela paused. It had been a big story and she looked tired. She looked at Cressida snuggled down on the couch. Cressida remained mesmerised, but met her eyes and nodded, encouraging her on.

"Lydia told me their rites enabled their sons to break away from their origins to be reborn into the world. Only the Great Mother can guide them in this. Lydia had said, 'Our daughters bleed their death and celebrate the blood of promise, of life. Our young men need to return to the Mother to be reborn. The mother is before the son. Woman comes first, but man becomes. He is only what has come out of her."

Angela focused on Cressida. "What do you think? What are you thinking?"

Cressida sat up. "This is huge," she said. "Fricken huge. I mean, fuck." She dismissed the image of her mother and sought to distract the unsettling intrusion. "Our daughters bleed? Does this mean our periods? We pay homage through our periods? I like that."

CHAPTER TWENTY-SIX

It was a couple of days before Cressida was able to pop around to Angela's house. She found her sitting at her table absorbed in reading her laptop.

"*Kalispera* Cressida. Good timing. I have discovered something interesting. Listen."

She started to read.

"The earth shook nonstop for two days. Residents fled the city. Some managed to leave the Island."

Angela looked up.

"This is Akrotiri, on Santorini. It was, and I quote, 'a sophisticated society with an advanced civil protection mechanism to respond to earthquakes and possible volcanic eruption.' Cressida, they could monitor a big explosion building up. I will tell you what I believe. I believe the volcanic eruption that Lydia wove in her tapestry was this one. It was the biggest the earth has ever experienced. Ever!"

"Listen to this." She read from her screen. "For six days, more than 90 billion tons of molten rock ejected into the air. Volcanoes swallowed into the sea forming a caldera and creating a massive tsunami that swept across the Aegean to slam the northern and eastern coasts of Crete, destroying the Minoan fleet and vast tracts of crops. Acid rain fell over the next few years decimating flora and fauna. Volcanic ash covered the entire island in a 10-metre-thick blanket. Devastation was total."

The women looked at each. Cressida shook her head slightly as she tried to absorb this information. After a moment Angela said, "It was Spring, around 1450 BC."

CHAPTER TWENTY-SEVEN

A familiar sound entered her dreamless state.
Memory produces hope. Birthed from recollections of the past Hope is born for the future. Like a sacred flower, it blossoms in the shadows, nourished by our stories. Never forget the power of story and its potential for change.

Cressida woke suddenly, wrenched into alertness. She was not ready for this. She had not dreamt lately, and had indeed been, at long last, able to sleep. This came without warning. It was unnerving. She was not prepared. She turned on the light to chase away the shadows. Her breasts were tender as she rolled onto her tummy to bury her head into her pillow.

On her journey back to slumber, she got lost in that place between time and consciousness. Was she asleep? She must be.

Two women sat together, sharing wine and conversation. Cressida recognised Pythia. In her dream-state, she felt like a voyeur. The other woman was talking, conferring rumours that had washed up from other shores. The Tribequeen spoke plainly.

"The stories from the north speak of Great Mother as mother and sister to a god they call Cronos. They say Mother's union with Chaos birthed Uranus, and from his Sacred Union came those they call Titans. Cronus was one of these and castrated his Father to control the skies. The Great Mother is revered as Mother of all gods, people and beasts, but reverence has been split and aspects of Her are worshipped separately, not as a whole. Divided one falls. We know that from battle."

The Tribequeen's voice quivered, her cheeks flushed. She sipped her wine before continuing, "The people, Pythia, live now to a different order, a different rhythm and there is much violence, many battles are waged, much hate and rage contaminate Her landscape. The people compete where before they shared. Things are to be bigger, better, but not for all, only for those who are strong and powerful. We Tribal Women still fight but now our fighting has shifted and we fight to protect our own. They steal, rape and enslave our daughters. They have no respect, no courage to fight us directly. They no longer walk the path of the Mother."

Grief rode the waves of her breath. Pythia knew the Tribequeen liked order in her world and these changes would sit heavy in her heart. The changes divined were coming faster than she had expected. There was still so much work to complete.

"Are the people content?" she asked the Tribequeen. "Do they prosper in their hearts and minds as much as their bellies?"

"I do not believe this to be so."

Pythia sat quietly reflecting on the implications. "Do we

need to prepare ourselves? Do they look to expand their villages?" she asked.

The Tribequeen thought for a moment. "We fight them to preserve our right to our rituals. Perhaps one day you may need to do so as well. A Tribal Woman is always prepared, my sister."

"Do we need to learn their stories?"

"No."

The Tribal Woman's answer was swift and adamant. "Their stories demean the Mother. As if any woman, let alone the Divine, would be consort to a man."

Though the Tribequeen scoffed, Pythia had already seen this. Her concern was the plethora of gods. The Great Mother now perceived to be one of many. How could that be? They had even given the Great Mother a name. She who was all and everything Divine. Once named, once someone has your name, you can lose power.

"These heathens call Her Tahrra, Ariadne or Gaea," the Tribequeen added. "In your home village She is named Rhea."

"Tell me," Pythia began, motioning a young Select to refill her guest's cup.

"Ahh," interrupted the Tribequeen, raising her cup. "Your wine, sister, is worth the journey over many seas. You honour me."

The Tribequeen took a long drink. Wiping her mouth with her hand, she continued with the heavy news she had carried over the oceans.

"They say the Great Mother birthed four gods whom Cronos, fearing he would be usurped by a young buck, swallowed whole. She birthed a fifth and hid him in one of Her Sacred Wombs high in Her mountain. The story claims that this youth, so called god of thunderbolts, killed his father and released his siblings thereby birthing them. Him! The people call him the King of Gods. Homage now goes to the young buck, and the Mother's gifts dispersed. These are the stories flooding our towns from west and north."

She scowled, suppressing the rage that had quickened her breath.

"Her Temples are desecrated, stolen to worship usurpers. We maintain what rituals we can and still govern Her Wombs. But it is a different tribe born today and their worship is divided. Those of the seas honour new named gods for the very milk bestowed from the Mother. Those of the mountains speak of the Mother as one of many. You do well to keep yourself as you do — retain the purity of the Mother. For this will we protect you, as we did yesterday, so too tomorrow."

Pythia nodded. Retaining the purity was a good metaphor.

"Dear sister," she said, taking the Tribequeen's hand and kissing her palm. "Your insight and wisdom honours me, though your stories disturb my heart. I give thanks for your sharing and acknowledge the pain this has brought to you in the telling."

The two women stood and clasped hands. As they embraced, an image flickered behind Pythia's eyes and she saw her dear friend in battle take a sword through her shoulder and a spear through her hip. Her blood would flow on foreign soil.

"Goodbye dearest one," she whispered. "The Great Mother lives through you and your sacrifice. You are loved and honoured, admired and feared. Your daughters are strong and brave, and clever. Your story will continue around many fires. A life well lived."

She kissed her, and the Tribequeen, having felt the shift of oracle through Pythia, stood tall and proud.

"Our work together will continue," she said as she left.

Darkness descended with a peaceful interlude and the remainder of Cressida's night was uneventful. No residue of the dream entered her waking state.

The overcast morning slouched like a bored teenager. Uninspired and tired from a disrupted night's sleep, Cressida was in no hurry to get up. She lay looking up at the ceiling, allowing her thoughts to wander in and out at whim. Had it only been just over three weeks since the night of the storm? It felt like a lifetime ago. So much had happened. Trying to decipher the photos with Angela had kept her happily busy and preoccupied. Distraction, diversion, same same but different, she conceded. She knew she should not hold off any longer. There was a decision to be made. Sooner rather than later.

The weather had been unseasonably inclement. Rain on the north coast had closed the Gorge entrance for a few days. Buffeting winds and high seas on the south coast meant the ferries would not leave their docks. The tourists were cautious and sought other holiday locations. Without customers in the

Taverna, Cressida's offer to take a few days off without pay met with enthusiasm.

"Perfect timing," she announced to Angela, "for that long-awaited road trip."

The east of the island was particularly alluring. Target a place far enough away from everything where she could think. Yep. Faraway was where she needed to be. Perhaps there she might find her answer. She hired a car and drove to destination: the end of the world.

On the way, she stopped to pay a visit to Zeus. The God of Gods, God of Thunderbolts, had some explaining to do. She felt traitorous but colluded with the tourist App, which acknowledged the site as sacred before the time he was there.

'Time of the Mother Goddess,' she thought, cementing her loyalty.

She wanted to feel something but wasn't sure what. What a sacred site felt like perhaps? Or perhaps to feel the Goddess? Answers were not forthcoming. Not knowing the question didn't help. She had heard that places like this cave were special, that they had a magnetic energy. So perhaps just to feel.

She had also heard that people connected with such places, which was why churches were often built on top of older temples and in sacred caves. Cressida thought it was more about practicalities, given there were stones and foundations already in place. As she now knew, this was an island prone to earthquakes. It must have been convenient to have a few stones lying around for a re-build. Angela had suggested it was easier to assimilate a new religion in existing places of worship; first Zeus, the sky god marrying the earth goddess, then later with Christianity.

These thoughts kept her fear at bay. Cressida was amazed that she was walking up a stony path to yet another cave. Mount Ida watched from dizzy heights. An awesome, magnificent, brutal rockface guarding ancient secrets behind a sheer veil of delicate droplets, disguised as low cloud. Or was it fog, sweeping over the plateau below and snaking its way upwards to her peak.

After a shortish uphill hike and, of course, having forgotten it was a Monday so the ticket office was closed, Cressida ignored the locked gates and jumped the fence. This was becoming a bit of a habit. At the mouth of the cave, green tinged walls snatched her breath. She stopped. There were paved steps leading down into its gaping crevice.

'This is different,' she reassured herself. 'This is different,' she whispered repeatedly, a mantra spoon-feeding courage as she descended into the large cavern.

To distract the gnawing blackness appearing somewhere around her kidneys, Cressida got out her phone to take a photo. She was shaking so hard she couldn't hold it. It dropped.

'For fuck's sake pull yourself together, girl.'

She picked it up and focused outside of the cave, into the bright light. It was reminiscent of a huge peephole of brilliant blue surrounded by black. The fog from the valley was not high enough to cover it with any grey heaviness. Turning back to face inside the cave, she took another photo, this time looking into the cave's yawning crease.

'Like a vulva,' she laughed, wishing she could tell Angela. 'I love it! Rhea or Gaea: it is Mother Earth giving birth to Zeus. The God beyond God is God's Mother. Of course.'

Happiness eradicated the grimy edges of a distant clawing fear. Relaxed, Cressida took several photos, simply playing tourist. As she climbed the steps to leave, she stopped to consider how she felt. Nothing came to mind. There was nothing to feel, no images, or thoughts. She sat by the mouth of the cave, on what she later learnt was an altar for sacrificing animals, to try harder.

Despite her disappointment, she persisted to find the words to describe the nothingness she felt. There was something. It was small, but she noted it anyway. Even though it did not really register as something, not really, it was too small, almost inconsequential, she took out her notebook and wrote, 'The cave is awesome, but it hurts my head.'

Committing her thoughts in ink, she continued. 'I feel this tightening in my head and as I try to explain and write it, the wind keeps pushing over my page and my scrawl is too hard to read. I am glad I am here. I just wish I could hear the voices from the stone, or had the imagination to feel the throng of pilgrims giving offerings, embracing the Goddess or the gods.'

She was aware however, that if she had heard voices, she most likely would have panicked; anxiety attack take three, waiting in the wings.

She kept writing. 'What do I get? A fricken pain in the head.'

She tried to summon up the exactness of the feeling. Maybe focusing on it would intensify it so she could describe it properly.

'My head hurts, inside expanding, growing bigger and bigger, filling and consuming the air and space. The ballooning of my brain makes my skull feel small and tight. I'm not sure how to interpret this. Perhaps the Goddess speaks on a different frequency?'

She put down her pen, "Hahaha, that's it. Ow my head hurts."

Walking back down the hill, she tempted fate.

'Maybe a dream tonight? Or maybe not,' she silently pleaded.

The following day, Cressida woke, not having any dream she could remember, and in fact had forgotten she even wished for one. While sitting quietly over a coffee and texting Angela, she thought about her headache. Had her head hurt in the cave? She could not remember. However, it was the same feeling she had at Delphi and some of the other ruins. She was sure of that, now she had thought about it. So, OK, she did feel something. There was something she was aware of on some level. Just because she could not interpret it, did not mean it was not real. 'After all what is reality if it isn't how we feel about things?' she mused.

Back on the road heading east, she thought back to the conversation she had with Angela after telling her she was going. Angela accused her, admittedly very gently, of running away. They had been in the middle of discussing an image that could have represented human sacrifice.

"Barbaric," Cressida had judged.

"Blood plays a leading role in fertility rituals. Blood and fertility," Angela had explained. "If the woman does not bleed, she produces life. The shedding of blood is death. Remember, you called it 'homage through our periods?' Sacrifice was a sacred act. Ancient tribes often believed the earth must drink blood to be fertile. We can see this in the paintings."

It made her think that the earth was demanding blood sacrifices, with corpses the preferred choice on the menu. She drew a comparison.

"Do you think," She had ventured, "that our wars, with all that blood and dead bodies, is sort of like our modern-day sacrifice?"

She had been joking. She should have known that Angela would consider her question more seriously than she intended.

"On the premise the female earth needs the fertilising blood-seed of the male, it is an interesting analogy. Do you think there is a connection?" Angela asked her.

Before she could answer, Angela reached her own conclusion.

"Woman is connected to blood, with her blood, she makes life. It is of no surprise that often a Goddess of fertility was also a Goddess of War in some cultures. Look at Artemis."

"No wonder men think women are dangerous," Cressida laughed, before tripping blindly into regret.

Her voice had trilled, raised loudly as if to fill the space with her rant. Echoes remained etched in her mind. "You know, this whole God thing, or Goddess, they are supposed to be so fricken supreme or benevolent, or whatever, well perhaps if She existed, She should care more about those who worshipped her. Sacrifice, death, pain, suffering; how could this happen, if your Mother loved you? Truly loved you.

Where the fuck was the Goddess when Pythia needed her? These women believed in this Goddess. But really? Where was she? Why did she leave them to die in the cave? Why didn't She just send a lightning bolt and strike down Vrados in the first place. It's just bullshit. If She existed then, where is She now? I mean, She hasn't been around in my life? If She is real, then why didn't She help me? And since when were mothers the answer to everything? Motherly love? Hah! All these mothers just didn't care? Didn't give a fuck."

Angela gently interrupted. Cressida could still feel the heat of shame returning, even now so many kilometres away. Her tantrum had been stupid. Her tears more so.

"Why are you thinking in terms of human judgement? Why do you attribute these to the Mother Goddess, to Divinity?" Angela had quietly asked.

Cressida slid back into herself, wishing she could just suck it all back. Angela shook her head.

"Your honesty with yourself is needed. Here. *Tora.* Now. You need to view your life with dry eyes. Not through tear-stained despair or blame. The Goddess, or God for that matter, does not care how you got where you are, what you did to whom, where you went wrong or were misled. Recrimination and blame have no place. You need to see without clouding it with emotion, where you are now and what you can do about it. You need to shift yourself perhaps onto a different track. If you are looking for a sympathetic hearing and a space to 'feel your feelings' you won't get it by running away. But if you want a cold hard appraisal of the next step, try listening to the voice of the Goddess within you."

She seemed so stern. Cressida had never seen Angela like this. She was not angry, but she certainly was not happy either.

"What do you think has been happening here?" Angela had asked as she swung her arm over the table indicating the photographs. She asked again. "What do you really think this is? Have you not been paying attention?"

Her outburst surprised both of them.

"*Lipame*. I am sorry. Forgive me. *En daxi* Cressida," Angela said. "Okay, Go. Go on your road trip but please, use this time to listen, to hear that voice of truth, which speaks the words you have denied. Drop your resistance. Listen to what is being said for you really need to hear it, to resolve it, no matter how it feels. Truth is important."

Fuck. Cressida swerved the car away from the tree that had jumped out at her. It was a tricky drive. First she was on the wrong side of the road — the right, not the left — like she was used to. She was driving a manual, the gear stick requiring operation with her right hand, not her left, like she was used to. And then, the roads were engineered to climb mountains and weave around precipices in a series of switchbacks, hairpins and all manner of swerves, curves and inclines. All this manoeuvring before the scenery — the utterly, gobsmacking, jaw-dropping scenery — seduced and enticed her. Landscape siren calling her name. Every corner held a new delight. It was so hard to concentrate when all the mountains, rocks, boulders, valleys, eagles, vultures and contours of the land herself, all connived to distract her through sheer splendour. Not to forget the goats and weird looking sheep either; those white ones with splashes of black, those of stocky frame on spindly legs. Cressida exhaled and shifted down into second to navigate around another hairpin bend, unprotected by any guardrail.

CHAPTER TWENTY-EIGHT

Cressida sat patiently. She was not alone. All those sleepy mosquitoes, tired from a night's exertion of blood sucking, or loitering perhaps, still seeking one last piercing for liquid gold from some unsuspecting warm-blooded fool before returning to some cool damp respite in more watery location. She covered her legs to thwart their mission. Later she discovered, to no avail. The birds had awakened at the same time and were testing out their chirrups, chirps, tweets and twitters before going full throat to herald the sun's arrival. The cats -- again cats, everywhere the cats — also joined her and contributed with velvet purrs of contentment. These were fat cats, which was a bit of an anomaly for the island. The dogs from up the hill were most rambunctious but forgiven for perhaps mistaking the sneaking shadows as sheep rustlers. The flies and insects clicked, buzzed and hummed loudly around Cressida. Impatient at the sun's dawdle they paced the air as if sound vibration alone would get the day moving forward, faster to full heat.

Cressida sat at the lower level of the villa complex to catch the first glimpse of the morning reunion between sun and sea. Already the cliffs were awash with pink gold hues. She watched as a radiant glow expanded across the world touting its majestic entrance. The sun rose gloriously, reflecting its celestial glamour on the mirrored slick sea, suspended in awe. Helios at his majestic best.

A growing momentum of sound accompanied sunrise. Bleating sheep joined other land-locked creatures chorusing the sun's sojourn from night-time depths. There was even the familiar clunk of goat bells in the distance.

'The irony,' she thought. 'Despite all this noise, it is so peaceful.'

Within this sensory vibrancy, a calm stillness settled in her soul. She felt safe, safe to think about what she should do next. As she sipped her green tea, the cat left to find a sunny spot for its morning wash.

It was a day for meandering. Before visiting the much-anticipated archaeological site, Cressida explored a little way up the Gorge. Valley of the Dead, the sign read.

'Were these caves tombs as well?' she wondered. She could see a few small caves high up and marvelled at the commitment to carry — maybe drag? — a body of dead weight up for... not burial? Entombment? Maybe. She watched enthralled as sixteen, yes she counted them, crows or ravens danced on air drafts in the gorge. Time lingered patiently.

Arriving at the archaeological site, she paid her money at the entrance gate. She could have viewed the site from outside the cyclone wire fence but she wanted to walk the cobbled paths and immerse herself. A vague memory teased the edges of her mind. Pythia had described her village from a cave. Up through terraced rows of olive groves Cressida could see a cave, watching over the village. Was it from this place, or another? Cressida shrugged. It did not matter. Whether it was here, or any other ancient site, it made no difference to her.

She walked around following outlines of stones indicating ancient, narrow, paved paths that wove in and around, different areas of the site. The open central space had a sign that advised a shrine had once been there. Turning to her right, another sign told her this area had been administrative buildings. And over there were the remains of a threshing circle.

No one else was around. Cressida relished the luxury to amble at ease, directed by whim and fancy. She looked at stones set out in distinct square patterns.

"I read about this," she said to no one in particular, "a storeroom."

Yes, the sign confirmed. Large earthen pottery jars had revealed fossilised grains and some sort of forensic discovery of honey, oil, perfumes. Gold had been found here as well. Gold as brilliant as the first pure glint that demolishes dawn on a cloudless morning. Bright and illuminating, used, she learnt, for jewellery and trade. It was at some museum, safely away from plundering hands.

Cressida looked around her. Ruins now, but once a community lived here. It was so many years ago, thousands in fact. So long ago it hurt her head trying to imagine it. She ventured deeper into the site, led indiscriminately by signs posting details about specific areas; this and that, here and there.

She remembered Knossos where large earthen jugs remained in situ. She had liked that. It helped her limited imagination. Here, there were just rocks, and more rocks. And turtles. The turtles surprised her. No one had mentioned turtles.

Cressida sat down on the old stones, feeling their smooth coolness. This one was circa 1700 — 1500 BC. She felt a bit naughty; she would never have sat on a stone like this back home. This rock would have been enclosed in glass. Without warning, tears welled. Her vision became muddy. She absently rubbed her forehead, her head hurting. A breath-less state imposed itself without exertion. She sat quietly. 'Fuck,' she whispered.

With some effort, she got up. She photographed this rock, and that, this paved path, those steps. A queen's bath. Another palace? 'Doesn't fit the story,' Cressida thought abstractly. Sometimes this stuff was confusing.

After her experience at Knossos, Cressida had decided she would rather remain ignorant than trust what someone else had written. She liked her own story and it really did not matter if her truth varied from world truth. She had never been truly at one with the world anyhow. These ruins however, were different. Aside from literally being at the farthest end tip of the island and off any well-trodden tourist path, there was little restoration, or tampering. Cressida looked around. Boulders and rocks strewn, created from an enormous shattering earthquake, possibly a tsunami. A gap of wondering yawned wide and Cressida peered into the abyss hoping something might connect the stories from the cave with the destruction around her.

CHAPTER TWENTY-NINE

After losing the battle with a mosquito, Cressida woke grumpy. Sleeplessness was not a happy state. A morning swim before another visit to the ruins offered the best option. Perhaps being surrounded by death and destruction might lighten her mood.

She swam without bothering to count her strokes over gentle rock formations laced with purple sea grasses inhabited by small, speckled fish levitating in weightlessness. Everything around her seemed surreal. She couldn't see straight. She floated and closed her eyes, heavy with a dull and arduous tiredness.

Night. Middle of the night. Sometime dark. Her sweat-soaked sheet clung possessively. Each joint birthed pain delivered in agony. Eyes leaking, mouth drooling. Cressida could not move, only groan. Rolling over was too painful, so she lay still, her body alternating between cold, hot, sweats and chills, all competing for victory over her shell of flesh.

Later. Probably afternoon. It was at this point that complacency reigned and the sun was no longer adored or worshipped. The owner, coming to clean Cressida's room, knocked on her door and entered.

"*En dakxi,* are you OK?"

Her faltering English lisped. Bespectacled eyes took in the scene of sprawled body, rampaged sheets and she returned somewhat later with a bowl of pilaf rice in broth.

Consciousness persisted, and Cressida awoke to semi-darkness. She spied the soup, sipped her spoon out of polite habit. The wrenching in her stomach lay close, anticipating the slightest encouragement. Cautiously, she stood and stripped off her bedclothes. She took herself to the bathroom, which had become far too intimate a space from her earlier visitations, and stood under a stream of warm water. The horror of the last day, or was that plural — days, had spiralled away. Tender pat-drying, new t-shirt and another sip of soup. Enough for now.

Next morning, she felt strong enough to make a cup of tea and sat warming herself in the morning sun on the veranda. She sipped tentatively. 'Weak, pathetic,' she berated herself.

Another bowl of soup appeared in kindly hands. The woman explained in more broken than faltering school-taught English. "To love *Kriti* you wash everything out. To make room. Feels like catastroph. It is the..." She paused to search for the long forgotten disused words that slurred against the roof of her mouth. "Seasons. Changing storms. But *Kriti*," she said, "she has you now."

She placed the soup on the table next to Cressida and entered the small room to strip the bed and clean the room.

Cressida nodded in agreement and building up her strength quietly replied, "*Nai.*"

She woke after the riot had started, fleeing an aggressive downpour of glass. Running away, hanging on tight to some unknown person also caught up in the unexpected violence. Running together united in fear, confusion, seeking escape. Glass slithers falling from the sky. Desperately hoping the glass would not transform into shards that would pierce. Her nightmare terror permeated reality and Cressida woke and lay clutching the sides of her bed. She took stock of her surroundings: bed, room, here, not there.

She collated pieces from the dream puzzle. It had started as a celebration for someone she did not know very well, and she felt like the outsider she lived in her waking life. There was a young woman who lay in the arms of a hippy boy lover and pronounced, "The new age is born through us, we do not enter it."

Why was this familiar?

She saw the bus she needed to catch. It was the last bus. Oh no. She ran but missed it, so decided to go another route to catch it at a different stop. She ran to the harbour then turned up the main road to head back towards the bus stop.

Were these directions significant? She did not know. In her dream, it was late, around midnight and everyone was heading home. All the buses and cars were full and travelling in the opposite direction. She hurried on, only to see her bus — the last bus — turn a corner.

She was alone.

She walked back to the party to seek a lift, but the celebration had finished and a protest rally had started in its stead. A mob raged around her as the glass began to shower down.

Someone called out to run. She turned. There was someone next to her. She could not see who it was, but they clung to each other as they ran. She, into wakefulness.

Cressida checked the time. Sunrise. There was no point going back to sleep. The dream left a disturbing imprint she was unable to shake off. Trapped in its residue, she padded forlornly to the window. She opened it, hoping the familiar sounds of morning would help. She heard the dogs first, yelping at the break of light. Barking and whining, reminiscent of the cries of protest heard from most dog kennels. Like her, they too were trapped, and perhaps, aware of their plight, greeted each day in protest. As Helios climbed higher, the pack quietened except for one maverick who howled the many verses of a domestic prison medley. Roosters joined in, though not as convincing, nor as committed.

As the light surpassed dawn, the stench of loneliness filled her senses. She was alone because she deserved to be alone. She was the outsider, always going in the wrong direction. She couldn't hide this, even in her dreams. Even there she stunk of wretchedness. Realisation made her misery acute. She was a waste. A waste of space, a waste of time. Self-hate tasted sour and she gagged. He was right, as always. How often had he needed to belt this into her? She was a slow learner. Even Angela … the thought of her friend made her cry.

"Well done Daddy — you broke me. Yep, good job." Her tears streamed. "I give up, you win. I can't do this any longer. You have stripped away everything."

She curled up and as she closed her eyes an image of big brown eyes, smiling brown eyes offered comfort.

Daylight kicked in more earnestly.

She awoke. Was it because of a noise from outside? She listened carefully. It seemed to come from the trees outside her window. She concentrated. The breeze whispered:

One cannot travel on the Path before one has become that Path itself.

Confusion twisted the moment.

'What?' She asked the wind.

Every thought will tear open wounds. Eyes of the flesh rendered blind to illusion. Ears deafened by the cries of roaring untruths. Sooner or later you must pass through the agonies of emergent wakefulness. It is the unwary Soul, that failing to grapple with the mocking demon of illusion, falters.

Delirious, was her resolution. Contemplation offered to pop in for a visit, but she refused and chased it away.

'Why must it be so hard?'

She was weary; she had a gutful of herself, and her harsh, bullying self-talk with its critical and dismissive reprimands only made things worse. A lifetime of emotional self-flagellations had left unseen welts and invisible scars. She faced her father. Why did she keep his words alive, as if he was still there? Why did she let him control her from the grave?

"No," she said. "You are fricken dead. You can't hurt me, not anymore. You hear me. You hear me. You cannot hurt me."

She began to crumble, but rather than run away, she swallowed and, with the flimsiest scrap of audacity, decided to sink into herself to look at what was there.

A memory stirred and she recalled what Angela had told her when they first met and talked about the labrys and initiation. In the labyrinth, the individual would face her deepest fear — that which prevented her from moving forward in life. Cressida nodded. This was her labyrinth.

She took a breath, hoping to breathe in courage, and as she opened her eyes, was surprised to see that her tightly woven threads of shame and denial were just flaws and simple failings. She was more than this. Shame and denial did not define her.

Gentle wisdom opened her sleepy eyes and began the task of cleaning out the stockpile of harsh unyielding rocks of abuse and loathing with a warm and caressing flush. In doing so, a timid but resolute compassionate grace emerged from the shattered debris of her past.

CHAPTER THIRTY

"Was it Tinkerbell, who said every time you didn't believe, you killed a fairy? I wonder if that was what happened to the Goddess? People just stopped believing in her."

Cressida returned from her road trip without resolution, but with the excuse of being sick. She and Angela met at a dockside taverna and she sat, or rather, sprawled out, in a large beanbag. The taverna was somewhat retro. It reminded her of the hippies who had been drawn to the island in the 1960s during the dawn of Aquarius, or something like that. Her body was splayed across a sheath of velveteen containing three billion polystyrene balls, each colluding to ensnare an unsuspecting body, her unsuspecting body, in one massive trap. Once in, escape was impossible. She cursed her choice. Fortunately, her frappe had a bendy straw so at least she could sip without spilling. Angela had wisely opted for the two-seater love couch.

Cressida looked around, drawn by the sound of knives being sharpened behind the counter. In the corner sat a priest. Padre? *Pappas.* She had not noticed him coming in. Dressed in black, a large shape holding human form by a grey belt tightened around his midriff. His beard speckled grey, betraying his age in a way his clipped dark hair refused to do. Sunglasses hid his eyes and he sat quietly sipping his espresso. Cressida had one of those 'walk over your grave' shudders. The power of the Church was palpable, and she was uncomfortable thinking that their conversation about the Goddess might be overheard. She lowered her voice.

"Why don't we still worship the Goddess? I mean if she is the Earth, Gaea or whatever, you know? Do you think she will be resurrected, have a second coming?"

Cressida giggled at her little joke.

"Do you mean, like an awakening of a feminine conscious-ness?" Angela answered.

Cressida thought Angela looked like she was on the verge of a tangent. She waited expectantly but Angela chose instead to answer her question.

"I think there could be several reasons, politics and religion for a start. I think, from a scientific perspective, that how we think, how our minds have evolved, has played a large part. In one way, Cressida, the Goddess has survived. We may not worship her, but knowledge of her exists. Actually, this was something I wanted to talk to you about."

Angela looked somewhat earnest. "I love your synchronic-ity," she said.

Cressida sipped thoughtfully from her straw. Perhaps a tangent may have been a good distraction. She was amused at Angela's enthusiasm manifesting through big bright eyes, and watched as she placed a wayward strand of hair behind her ear. Always her right ear. Always just before she would embark on some theory or logical explanation.

"In mythology throughout the world, the original Creator was feminine. It was only with the coming of the patriarchy she was replaced by a male god. Sometimes she was conquered; sometimes killed by the new god. Either way, once patriarchy became the model of governance, it served well to reduce the Goddess's credibility. Over centuries she was diminished, her name sullied, you know, portrayed as a whore, a prostitute, as we talked about. Those who worshipped her were persecuted, butchered, raped, massacred, driven into the ocean, burnt, and generally killed off. A slight disincentive, don't you think?"

They shared a frown.

"I believe it was Friedrich Nietzsche who said the Christian Church was an encyclopaedia of pre-historic cults." Angela said. "And language, oh, *nai*, language. Worship of the Goddess was a cult, pagan, or a sect. It was never a religion in its own right."

"Poor Tinkerbell," said Cressida.

"Language is such a powerful tool, and as it developed, our thinking processes evolved. Do you remember when Vrados said he was thinking differently? Pythia had said he had disconnected from the Mother. Do you remember? I have often wondered if that was an early indication of our consciousness changing. We experience too much rationality, too much cerebral control of our feelings and intuition. Before rational thought, our minds worked through emotion and did not need words. Before that, the mind functioned through image. Like the way Lydia communicated with us. No wonder I had trouble trying to put her story into words."

Angela paused, reflecting her experience.

"We have lost the capacity to communicate through our body sense and emotion. Although, you know," she looked kindly at Cressida, "our work together, on the photographs..."

Cressida nodded. She understood their sense of togetherness. It was pleasing.

"We have been using the intuitive part of our brain. We have tapped into this felt sense to help us articulate meaning from the images. You have taught me this, Cressida. Not so long ago I was part of the rational scientific culture, ignoring the phenomenon of felt sense, trying to find an explanation within a paradigm of conventional communication." Angela beamed. "*Efharisto poli*. Thank you so much."

Cressida felt the strong need to check out how much coffee she had remaining. Slurping noisily, she distracted herself, trying to suck up the froth clinging to the sides of her plastic cup. The taverna was filling up with patrons and it had become tricky to speak as quietly as she would have liked. She stole a furtive glance at the *Pappas*.

Angela didn't seem concerned and ploughed on.

"The development of consciousness, the way we think and articulate, is potentially a death sentence for the Goddess. Belief in the Mother Goddess thrives within the intuitive part of our brain. She will die if we become dead to that non-rational part of our life."

"Well," said Cressida, "what a bundle of fun this chat is."

"On the upside, if we can transcend the bastions of old science with its logical and rational approach, then quantum physics, string-field theories, advanced molecular biology and psychology may open up to a new way of thinking possibly aligned to new pathways of consciousness. Like your feminine awakening. Like my theory. Maybe, in this scenario the Goddess may have a chance."

Angela drained her cup.

"Theory?" asked Cressida. "We have a Tinkerbell Theory?"

"Yes," confirmed Angela, and bent down to retrieve some images she had brought in her bag.

"I want to talk with you about something that has been bothering me. This image, can you remember this?"

The image conjured another in Cressida's mind. She could still feel the coolness of the cave, its stillness. Traces remained embedded in her skin. The hard, earthen ground, some bits slippery and that greenish tinge highlighted by her mobile phone's torch. Even the tiny glitter on hard rock. She sighed. The memory of the cave held none of the terror she had felt at the time and in some bizarre way, she almost missed it. She was disappointed she could not revisit it after learning so much more about what she had seen. Or perhaps more accurately, what she had not seen.

The photo Angela held was an image they had previously agreed was a boat; oars and sails indicated by wavy lines. They had joked, agreeing that it looked more like a marketing logo. 'Brand Caïque', they had called it.

"This was from the beginning section," Angela said.

"Yes, I remember," agreed Cressida. "Is there a problem?"

"It was easy at the start to identify this as a boat of some sort, but now, well, what seems to be coming to light, the research and what I have been reading, well," Angela took a deep breath, "it is a somewhat unconventional theory that somehow seems, *nai*, seems connected. This image is in other photos. In a lot of them almost hidden in the background. Like a watermark."

Cressida tried to take a better look but her wriggling only sunk her deeper into the beanbag.

"I think now, well, perhaps it is not a boat. Given its presence, here, here, here and here," and with each example she produced a new set of photos.

"I believe it is something more integral to why the women left the village in the first place. I think it is like..."

She swallowed. "Consider if these lines were not water but blood," she said.

Cressida wished she was not stuck in the beanbag like some upturned turtle and that she could take a serious look at the photos. There was something being said, something between the lines, but she couldn't achieve anything from where she sat. From the depths of her incarceration, she tried to dignify her position.

"Ok," replied Cressida, "if it is blood, then what do the lines mean? What are they?"

"DNA. Well, genes, genetic material."

Cressida blinked. Well, that was certainly left of field. She had not seen that one coming. She laughed at the absurdity of it. What was Angela suggesting? That these women, who mind you, did not have a microscope, living around 1500 BC and sacrificed humans to a Goddess who may or may not have existed, knew about DNA? Fuck, even she did not know about it.

"Oh Angela," she blurted, "Did they even know the world was round?"

"I'm serious Cressida. This image is from the very beginning section of the cave paintings and it is like a motif carried through the various paintings of rituals, rites, ceremonies, right up to the end."

She brought out the photo of the huge jars where the image decorated the rims.

"I think we, um, I was blinded by my initial perception. Think about it. What if the women knew there was a connection to blood and their environment, in some capacity? And so, they made sure their blood, and the blood of their children and children's children, that their whole ancestral lineage carried the gifts of the Mother Goddess. Gifts like love, hope, strength, integrity, valour. Definitely not violence or aggression."

Cressida was speechless. She started to laugh but stopped when she saw Angela's face. Angela was serious, really serious, like she had never seen her. Stunned, Cressida sat and stared at her friend. She ignored the goose-bumps up her arm. She assessed the situation. Here was Angela, her friend, whom she had not known for long, but knew better than anyone else in her life, whom she knew well enough to describe as clever, rational, and logical, even if somewhat anal-retentive, scientific Angela who was always saying 'where's the evidence? Show me the proof.' She believed this? Cressida shook her head in disbelief.

Angela tried to explain. "The common idea that DNA determines so much of who we are — you know, eye or hair colour,

our addictions, disorders, is a misconception. We are not necessarily victims of our heredity. It may be that a person's perception, not just genetic programming, spurs action in the body. That our beliefs can affect our genes, affect our behaviour."

"No," Cressida interrupted her. "That just wouldn't pass the pub test."

"I don't know what that means."

"Try, it's off the fricken planet. I don't get it. I don't understand. I am trying, but..." Her sentence trailed off. Angela's idea challenged everything she had been taught. She was not used to questioning the status quo. She could feel herself getting angry and was not sure if she was angry with herself or Angela. Neither was a good option.

"*En daxi, nai,* I agree. This is somewhat radical." Angela answered with quiet determination.

"Somewhat radical?" Cressida was incredulous.

"The book I am reading is by an international authority on emerging biology into cellular activity. His name is Dr Lipton and he was a researcher at Stanford University School of Medicine, a renowned cell biologist and internationally respected. His book is about uniting mind-body and cellular science with spirituality. It incorporates theories of molecular biology with quantum physics. I believe his theory should be part of our considerations. He says the brain's biochemical functions are affected by thought. I am basing my interpretation on his research. You know I read somewhere that the brain cannot recognise the difference between fantasy and reality."

Cressida jumped into the lull of her pause.

"This is bullshit. How could these women know anything about DNA? It is a scientific term created — when — when was this word made up? Certainly, not BC thousands of fricken years ago. How could they know anything about DNA? Just bullshit."

"You take this too literally," replied Angela. "I am not saying these women knew about DNA per se. Not the language of DNA, but I am saying they knew the power of blood. Their whole existence focused around blood: birth, death, nourishment, sacrifice. You are correct; they would not have called it DNA, but just because the language is not the same doesn't mean we disregard the concept."

She spoke quickly so Cressida was unable to interrupt.

"I don't think they escaped from the violence of their village for their immediate survival, I believe they left with a mission for the future. This is as much as you have said from your visions and dreams, and now the images I see tell me that too. They do. Of this, I am certain. I would even go so far to say the painting is the story of their future not their past. Of bloodlines and teachings that carry the messages of love, respect and integrity. The foundations for a humanity that..."

She stopped and looked at Cressida.

"I think these women were breeding out violence."

Cressida chewed her straw to give some time for the words settle around her. God, she wished she were in a better position to debate this.

Angela watched her for a moment then continued, "They created a new community to keep the bloodline clean. I believe they may have also established Delphi partly for this reason. They reared the children of the Amazons, and they raised sons and daughters to nourish and nurture the earth. The Goddess has not been completely eradicated, despite everything."

"But they all died," cried Cressida. "Circa 1450 BC — you said — biggest earthquake, volcanic eruption. Tsunami, you named it. You called it. Their civilisation was wiped out. You said the cavern was a tomb. If what you are saying has any truth, and don't take me wrong for I am not in any way agreeing with you, but if there was any skerrick of truth in what you say, then they lived for nothing. All gone." Cressida felt like weeping. This was awful.

"Only those left remaining in the village, but even then, they may have resettled, off the island, or perhaps more inland," Angela said quietly.

The *Pappas* stood up, put on his black pillbox shaped hat and picked up his two black bags in either hand. He did not need to pay for his coffee; it was a gift from the establishment for gracing the taverna with his presence. He ambled slowly down to the jetty as the ferry docked. Other tourists had gathered to leave. Now suntanned and relaxed from their seaside bliss, they were ready to swap places with new arrivals; a boatload of fresh faces who would replenish the village with their language, their delight, and their money.

'And seed', thought Cressida wryly, having watched the *Pappas* leave, and holding her lower belly where she was just starting to thicken.

She turned back to face Angela.

"Well, I truly want to believe in Tinkerbell, but I just don't know," she said.

With a huge effort, she finally managed to roll over and struggle onto her feet.

"Leave this with me," she said waving the small white slip of paper, and unlike the *Pappas,* paid the bill before she left.

Angela sat for a while thinking, before she too, stood up to go.

CHAPTER THIRTY-ONE

Cressida lay comfortably on the warm, dark sand. Her ears filled with the sound of tide in, tide out, tide in, tide out. So much seemed to have changed but so much remained the same. The story she was living: the cave — her worst nightmare — was now something extraordinary, so alive in the light of day. The women from the past; Pythia, Ashtar, Lydia, they were amazing. She felt like one of them. Connected. Strong. Brave. She closed her eyes. Not looking to meditate, not looking for resolution, not looking for answers. Simply closing her eyes on a warm afternoon lying on a beach she loved. It felt good to be here. She had changed. Right in this moment, she felt happy. She recognised its glow and liked it. She breathed in and out, synchronising with the waves. She lay listening: to the sea, to the birds, to her heart.

She opened her eyes and gazed over the crystal waters. Each individual water droplet shimmered within a sequined ocean gown. Looking up, there was some sort of sea eagle, soaring, floating, dipping, or perhaps it was a buzzard. Cressida wasn't sure. She never could tell the difference.

A boat hummed into the shore. Close despite the shadow of a reef. Close despite the buoy indicating a boundary. Engine off to drift. The waves gently slapped against the boat, and the boat subtly reprimanded, manoeuvred away. At the jetty, someone was reversing to extract a craft from the water. Birds fluttered around; checking for fish, then soared away.

'Summer swallows,' Cressida thought lazily.

Her world had holiday feet, sand between her toes and kissed by salty sea. Everything seemed a bit easier. She was not sure of the turning point, only that each day seemed less painful than the last.

Serenity permeated the air. The sun witnessed all comings and goings with an intense passion and as the heat penetrated her skin, Cressida sunk into its radiance with pleasure. Life at this moment existed as a tapestry of sounds and silences. She listened as one entered her sphere, and then another; each sound overlapping in a cacophony of natural and unnatural audio frequencies. There was rarely silence, but there were lulls. Within the lulls, her own white noise inside her head still testified to an ongoing presence. It seemed less persistent perhaps, but it remained. Everything was all a bit hazy, a nonchalant serenade of noise and rhythms of machine, waves, breezes, birds, and far off laughter.

It was not father, but mother.

The thought screamed at her. Cressida jolted upright.

'Mother?'

She screwed up her nose. Her mother? Her mother had no power. Her mother was pathetic. She had failed her. It was good she was dead.

Realisation struck without mercy.

I don't want this child, not because it is a boy and could grow up like my father, but that I could grow up and be like my mother.

She sat, stunned.

Cressida got up. She knew what she needed to do. She ran to Angela's house. Angela was not there so she opened the door, the door to many days and evenings of companionship, laughter, trust. The door that was never locked. She put on some coffee and sat at the table to wait. Her patience was never great at the best of times and after about an hour, she could feel her strength dissolving. Perhaps she should leave. No, she thought, and then spoke sternly to herself aloud to commit herself to staying.

"I need to talk with my friend."

"About what?" came the soft voice she revelled in. As Cressida turned she looked, as she had done many times in the last weeks, into those wonderful eyes where she felt safe. She was safe. She could be brave.

"Will you raise this baby?" she blurted. "I would not be a good mother. I could never be. But you, you would be fantastic."

Angela put her bags down slowly.

"Oh Cressida," she said reaching for the young woman's hands, "I am honoured you would think so, but apart from being too old, apart from our friendship just growing and still quite new, apart from even just the logistics of what you ask, this baby isn't about me. It is about you."

CHAPTER THIRTY-TWO

Boom. Cressida was surprised the explosion had not knocked her down. She was not sure what the sound meant until she spun around to see a gigantic grey column of rock, ash and gas shooting out of a volcano. She started to run but her legs became rubbery, reduced to heavy running-through-treacle steps. Her footing was terrible — worse than scree — and she had to watch carefully where she placed her feet while boulders and large smouldering rocks fell from great heights. She kept falling and scrambling to get up. Sounds of bubbles bursting amid loud explosions and the rumbling, hissing, roaring of a jet engine breaking the sound barrier filled the space in her head. Coarse particles of ash felt like whipping grains of sand. Every breath stung her lungs with tiny glass-like particles, until finally, rescue came, ablaze and dazzling, an illuminated whiteness which swallowed everything and she woke.

There had been no respite since her realisation on the beach. Dreams plagued her sleep, her nights becoming busier than her days.

In the dark of pre-morning, she woke with a jolt. She lay catching her breath. Her hands throbbed from a heavier slumber she envied.

Angela had told her to write everything down if she woke during the night. Easier said than done. She would lie half-asleep, half-awake, desperately wanting to sleep. Her mind, held captive by obligation, argued mutiny.

Upon waking, an inner pleading grew louder. Do it in the morning. No, she would forget by morning, it had to be now. Obediently she would clutch at the last image she could remember. Sometimes, despite her best intentions she would lose it anyway. She ignored her own cajoling pleas to roll over and snuggle into the blankets. She dragged herself out of bed. Turning on the lamp, she grabbed her writing materials, wrapped herself in a shawl and headed into the kitchen.

Already much of the night's entertainment had receded into a foggy bog of distant past. Cressida pulled some loose threads from the residue bits of dream remaining. Her hands, the blood needing to flow, tingled with anticipation of regaining feeling.

She remembered waking after the volcano. But she must have slept again. Then she had fallen. Two images lingered in the shadowy twilight between wakefulness and sleep, just beyond her grasp. She squinted into recall. She had been on a mountain path. She could not remember if she was walking or driving, but she was travelling up a hill. She was greeted by Angela's aunt, whose small bent frame was, like most of the *yiayias* of the village, shrouded in black. Looking up from the obligatory dowager's hump, were familiar eyes, a maternal inheritance framed by silver white hair. She spoke in an overdose of excited Greek exclamations, which like in real life, she shouted louder and louder when Cressida shrugged, *"Den kataleveno.* I don't understand."

Cressida tried to summon her dream. The track had been prominent. There had been a series of treacherous switch-backs on a steep mountain. Any other images faded away.

Well, she was awake now. Might as well soak the lentils she had forgotten to do before going to bed. She got herself a cup of tea and sat there in semi-darkness. Time to think. Well, not quite thinking, just letting her thoughts roam over terrain mingling past and future. Rocks featured everywhere.

A comment from Angela floated past and she latched onto it for closer inspection. They had been discussing the tremor, Cressida sharing how small and feeble she felt. Cressida sipped her tea. Angela had said something strange.

"What is up for examination is your beliefs, don't you think? All the undercurrent ideologies you've been carrying, your very belief system of being on this planet."

At the time, Cressida had taken it at face value, to be about the impact of the ground shaking. Angela always spoke big. 'All your beliefs' she had said. All of them.

What are my beliefs? Cressida thought. Her head was fuzzy and an image of an uroboric snake swallowing its tail flashed to mind. She grinned. She tried to remember their conver-sation, but like her dreams, any thoughts or pictures that seemed reachable were like decoys and allowed other, more important images to vanish into oblivion. The word 'denial' loomed in the shadows. It was not a good word. Angela had said something about denial. About her? Angela would never be so direct, well maybe never. No, she had introduced the idea as a bigger denial of seemingly unrelated things that Cressida knew, would eventually include her. Angela thought like that, big contextual stuff then narrowed it down to focus on the smaller detail. Smaller detail — like herself and her story.

Cressida took another sip. Mmm, it was something about what was happening now, some sort of planet stuff that Angela had a habit of including when she explained things. She liked to connect those bits with the cave stuff. Cressida paused to let the warmth of friendship express itself in a broad smile.

She pulled her shawl in a bit tighter and re-focused. Angela had said something about this being a time when you could see denial in everything that was happening on the world stage. Things that had been denied were rising to the surface and demanding attention, or as Angela suggested, to be healed. Angela had said planetary energy indicated it was time to look at our denials. Her attitude had been, 'your problem, you created it, deal with it, fix it; time to clean your mess.'

Angela talked big picture stuff; things were coming out in the open. According to Angela, this was a good thing. Cressida was not so sure. But then they played their game of 'adding to the picture', the way they did with the images, where nothing suggested was wrong, just part of the process of sifting out the most plausible explanation from all possibilities. Some of the world's current denials preoccupied them for a while.

The bigger the denial, it seemed the bigger the problem.

Angela used the UK as an example. England had colonised other countries and now those countries were returning to inhabit the motherland, as it were, saying the same thing generations later: 'we're going to control your resources and you will be our citizens and we will look after you in exchange.' Their denial resulted in Brexit. Germany having been responsible for refugees fleeing during WW2 was opening their borders to receive refugees from other wars. Cressida thought that denial seemed to be like karma. Angela considered it as coming to terms with the consequences of past actions and dealing with the resulting shit.

Suck it up, Cressida had laughed. Only Cressida did not want to look at her mess, did not want to 'suck it up,' so instead, she had detoured from this path and asked Angela about her denials. She knew this was dangerous territory, this personal stuff, but she asked regardless.

Angela had paused. In that pause, a sweet half smile surfaced from somewhere so deeply sad that Cressida wanted to stop her from saying anything. Only yet again, she was too late.

"*En daxi,*" Angela had replied. "Fair question. My mess is my grief. Only I do not want to fix it. I can't. Some things can never be fixed, you never get over them. Some things can only be carried. I carry this, always. We Greeks know this. When you are in pain, we will sit with you in your pain. We are with you. We are not there for you. It is yours to carry. But we will acknowledge the weight you bear. It is in those places, when the world around you has shattered and you cannot fix it. Losing my child cannot be fixed. It will never be healed.

Grief is not an obstacle to be climbed over or get through. But you need support to carry it. My husband couldn't be there with me. He carried his own grief and then chose to heal it by having another child. With another woman."

There was nothing Cressida could say or do. Nothing. So, she had just sat there.

Cressida took another sip of tea, revisiting her horror at her clumsy stupid offer to give Angela her baby. What an idiot. She gathered her shame up in her shawl and plodded back to bed. Perhaps she could steal a bit more sleep before the sun came up. As she lay down, she felt the heaviness of slumber sneak up. Her last thought rode upon starlight taking her to a place of ease and beauty. Words she would never remember in morning light were mellifluous in her ear:

You reside in a beam of pure reflection. Look to the flower
and smile, embrace the rain and weep, for all is but a glimpse.
Rejoice. The path is yours to dance. You are, because.

CHAPTER THIRTY-THREE

Dinner was at Angela's. It was the end of October and the season had officially closed. The taverna owners had packed away their outside tables, stacked their chairs, and Cressida could see some had even dismantled their latticed roofs from outdoor seating areas. Heavy thick wire fences now graced the front of the tavernas. There was never any threat of theft, only potential damage from wayward goats. Predominantly black or red utility trucks lined up at the docks. All trays stacked with bags and boxes ready for departure. Some were stacked with locked beehives, heading for sheltered locations and perhaps winter blooms. A few tavernas with rooms would remain open during the colder months but generally, the south was closed for business. Cressida was taking the ferry the following morning. Angela still had work to complete for the Parks Management, so this was their final dinner together before meeting up again in the city, as planned.

It was still light and quite balmy as Cressida made her way to her friend's small house. She had cleaned her flat and packed her bags. Everything finalised and ready to go, except for a resolution. She had kept herself too busy to think about anything more than leaving. She spied a cat wandering through the narrow street. She had heard the season's kittens would not be there when she returned next May. She had not wanted to think about the implications of that either.

"I was thinking some more about those blood lines," Angela said as she pushed her plate aside, finishing her meal. "There is a whole field of science called Epigenetics. In a nutshell, it is a view which encompasses all the possible developing factors on a person, and how these factors not only influence the person, but how the person also influences their own development. It's the relationship between heritance and environment."

Angela hung her head in mock shame, "I could be shot for a definition like that."

Cressida laughed, "I agree. That was a shocking attempt at simplicity. You are going to have to try again."

Angela groaned and reconsidered her options.

"Okay. Epigenetics is the study of heritable changes in gene function that cannot be explained by changes in DNA sequence. Which means," she said holding up her hand to stop Cressida protesting, "that the environment interacts with DNA to influence change. And," she continued quickly, "these changes may be reflected at various stages throughout a person's life, even in later generations. There are studies. I have proof." She smirked. "I have proof that provides evidence that environmental factors influence the risk of developing behavioural disorders."

She focused squarely on Cressida. "You know what I am talking about, *nai*? Both the perinatal period and childhood years are regarded as sensitive periods for the developing brain. You know this, you have stopped drinking. The child is particularly susceptible to epigenetic changes that can influence development. But Cressida, some parts of the brain keep developing at least until early adulthood."

Angela was smiling broadly. "These women were watching for signs of the stressors which would reveal the young men as aggressive or violent. They were literally weeding out the strain. It is, as you would say, fricken unbelievable."

Angela placed her hand over her mouth in mock horror at quoting such a phrase. Cressida could see she was proud of herself. With that definition? She despaired. She toyed with her fork and waited for Angela's encore. She knew this was just the intro to something more pertinent. She was not disappointed. It just took a little while to reveal itself.

"We are the sum of what has happened to us. We are our cells, our biology. We are the sum of our experiences. What we do, what happens to us; we are the product of our experiences."

Cressida sat quietly letting Angela's words sink in.

"So, our cognitive framing, that is, our interpretation, or our choice of language, these frame our experiences. We talked about the importance of language, remember? Well, the story you tell, the story you choose to tell, can change your physiological — your body's chemical response. Our body responds and continues to respond within this physiological framework. Change the story, and you change the chemical reaction. Fundamentally we can change the past as it is recorded in our cells, in our body memory."

"Whoa, hang on, this is a big jump, let me repeat it so I

have the words in my head," said Cressida. "You are saying, because of this epigen-whatever, the story we choose to tell about what has happened, can change what has happened. So, I can change my story and not be pregnant?"

"*Oxi*. No. This is not what I mean. It is the story we give to experiences that can change our physiological response. For example, the experience of trauma seen through a particular lens creates a physiological stress response."

"Like anxiety?"

"*Nai*, yes, like anxiety. But, in changed or altered states, like hypnotherapy or even meditation, we can change the story and therefore our chemical or biological response to the story. We literally re-contextualise it, thereby we change our past."

"Altered states, like a trance?"

"*Nai*."

"Is this what was happening in Harrownight?"

"I hadn't thought of that, but *nai*, more than likely."

"Fuck."

"With the capacity to change the past, we can, in effect change our future. I think, *oxi*, I believe, this is what the women knew. This was why Pythia left the first village. This is the story Lydia was telling you. Telling you, Cressida — you with a baby in your belly."

Cressida felt the slap. From Angela? No surely not. Impulse kicked in. Run. Run away. She started to get up from the table. 'Baby' was not a word she wanted in her head, bad enough in her ballooning body. She shuddered. Tears welled. Angela put her hand on Cressida's arm.

"Don't run. Please. Don't."

Angela looked shattered. Her hand trembled on Cressida's arm.

"Please."

Cressida relented and sat back slowly, remaining perched on the edge of her chair. Angela spoke quickly, not allowing any hint of a pause to give Cressida an opportunity to flee.

"It's this fantastic paradox, a contradiction where you can change something that has already happened. Think about what it is that you keep from the past?"

Cressida said nothing. Both women locked in eye contact, connected by intangible bonds of trust, kindness, friendship and love that anchored them to the moment — to each other.

"Memory," Angela answered for her. "You keep memory. It is the story that runs on loop in our mind, of what has happened and somehow, we allow this to shape us, shape our future. We feel we must be a certain way because of what has happened. But memory and experiences are transformational, they allow us to change the framing of who we are. We can literally change who we are, reconceptualise who we are, and what we are doing and everything that happens. We are not choked by our story but strengthened by it. My story is your story is our story. Remember?"

She moved her hand down Cressida's arm to take hold of her hand, cupping it in both her hands. She leaned forward, closer to Cressida.

"You are more than you think you are, Cressida. You can decide to interpret, change your perception, re-explain the things you have lived through. Everything — time and space and mind and future and present and past, all the things from the cave, from Delphi, everything you grappled with before. All of it, and all of this. You can choose the story you tell. You can choose your story."

Cressida smiled, and in that smile, hope was born.

LYDIA

Bleakness hung heavy in the air. Everyone moved in earnest as the village mobilized towards completion. The children had gone, sent to distant lands. The echoes of their chatter retreated into memory. Greyness seeped into the spaces left behind.

She would enter the cave today. This was her destiny, woven many suns ago.

Her monthly offering to the Mother had dried but she remained strong. While her body never bore children, she had birthed creativity. She took a final look around her. It had been a happy hearth of stone providing shelter and protection. She wondered if it would remain standing. Most likely it would fall, scattering stones through the fields, dispersed amongst flowers and horta, to lie in perpetuity, nimbly leapt upon by wild goats who may survive the havoc.

The cave seemed gracious in greeting, complicit to her task: to serve the Divine Mother until her blood was spent, her flesh dissolved and her bones lay brittle. Her final offering so she may be reborn.

The effort to climb into the pithio stole the rest of her strength.

Are you afraid? Are you afraid of death?

Death is not the end, but a crossing over. It is a fallow period, a refuge in the Mother. What is there to be afraid of?

When grace came upon her it brought an unutterable bliss she had never known. She wept with happiness and gratitude.

ACKNOWLEDGEMENTS

I was fourteen when I read George Johnston's *My Brother Jack*. It opened my eyes to the possibility of living on a Greek Island. Many years later I did just that in Crete. For one glorious year I walked and danced and wined and dined on this amazing Island. I fell in love with its rocks, trails, beaches and of course its people. Thank you to the Viglis and Marinakis families of Agia Roumeli and Skordolou for welcoming me into your home and your hearts.

Thank you to those talented writers who contributed to this book via thoughts, feedback and support: Iosif Alygizakis, Christos Tsantis, Jane Ormond, Julie Szego, Bec Colless, Matt Cram and Kathryn Gauci.

Grateful thanks to George Papadantonakis and Markella Semkoglou, John and Susie Rerakis, and Bruce Mildenhall, who waited patiently in the middle of hiking some gorge or atop some mountain while I answered the muses' call.

A big shout out to Susan Fawcett who read the first draft with such enthusiasm and love.

And thanks to my children Dominique, Stefania and Louis, who make the world a better place.

Karen has worked as an independent writer and director in Australian theatre for over thirty years. She has written and produced play scripts including physical narratives for circus performance, and has successfully toured nationally and internationally with her work. Karen has contributed to several non-fiction anthologies and produced two booklets about the history and performance making process of her award-winning production, *The Women's Jail Project*.

Dancing the Labyrinth is Karen's debut novel.

KazJoyPress

How to reach the author:

https://www.kazjoypress.com

kazjoypress@gmail.com

- I am happy to come and chat at your book club or event either in person or via ZOOM
- Please sign up to my mailing list via my website

By the author

the Bringer of Happiness

"I should have assumed with parents known
to the world as Mary Magdalene and Jesus Christ,
I would be different."

The Bringer of Happiness is the second book in the thematic series *Women Unveiled*. Each novel can be read separately but are united by a distinctive feminine narrative exploring societal boundaries and transitions. The series blends Greek mythology, history and imagination in the telling of (almost true) stories.

Work in progress

Delphi — Sequel to Dancing the Labyrinth

Printed in Great Britain
by Amazon